Freya

C^{The}olour
^{of} Red

Enjoy

July 2017

The Colour of Red

Tales from the Cultural Revolution

Nima Lee

Matador
9 Priory Business Park,
Wistow Road, Kibworth Beauchamp,
Leicestershire. LE8 0RX
Tel: 0116 279 2299
Email: books@troubador.co.uk
Web: www.troubador.co.uk/matador
Twitter: @matadorbooks

ISBN 9781785898655

Credit to Graphic Designer Freya Thomas

British Library Cataloguing in Publication Data.
A catalogue record for this book is available from the British Library.

Typeset in 11pt Aldine by Troubador Publishing Ltd, Leicester, UK
Printed in the UK by TJ International, Padstow, Cornwall

Matador is an imprint of Troubador Publishing Ltd

For my mother, in memory of the handful who refused to follow and paid the price, and to all those currently striving for freedom of speech.

Preface

The stories in this collection cover the period from 1966 to 1976 starting at the outbreak of the Cultural Revolution and ending with Mao's death. When it was all over, the Gang of Four (officially the Central Cultural Revolution Group) were blamed, and almost everything else swept as much from official memory as possible; this lost decade became euphemistically known in official parlance as 'The Ten Year Upheaval Period'. It was a time of collective madness that gripped the world's most populous country. I am often asked if these stories are true. In short, yes, however bizarre and surreal they look, although this is historical fiction. Literary licence is used wherever it is required to create the true feeling of that time, yet many of the events and details are precisely what happened, albeit perhaps compressed together, and elaborated beyond what is available as written historical text. My aim is to describe in a way that would be impossible in a single narrative, the scale, chaos and sheer implausibility of the time. I have avoided writing about the extremes of violence. The stories are normal; the experiences of the majority.

I have used the standard system of romanisation, Pinyin, throughout. Wikipedia has a good guide for those wishing to correctly pronounce names. Some readers may be more familiar with other forms of historically important names, most notably the Nationalist Army, Guomindang (Kuomintang), and its leader Jiang Jieshi (Chiang Kai-shek).

Most people will have heard of the Red Guards, the early evangelists of the Cultural Revolution. Red Guards were young people, from secondary schools (age fourteen upwards) and universities. As the movement gathered pace, units supporting the Cultural Revolution were formed at institutions such as factories, communes and offices; open to people of all ages working at the institution they included many older people, and come under the broader term of Rebels. While Red Guards were also Rebels, they remained a very distinct subset.

Nima Lee

Contents

Sugar and Spice

…And all things nice
That's what little girls are made of
(Trad)

It had not been such a beautiful morning for a long time in Beijing. Spring sand storms were over, the dust had settled and been washed away by May showers. The sky was cerulean blue, deep and tranquil, not a wisp of cloud. The sun had just touched the tips of the boulevard trees. The streets were bustling like an orchestra, bus horns, bicycle chimes, a sweeping truck's bell. On the pavement, passers-by exchanged greetings, wearing smiles on their faces.

In the Year 3 classroom at Beijing Shida Middle School for Girls, the last revision lesson had started for the final year exam of Proletarian Morality. Teacher Liu, a plump middle-aged lady, delivered her homily on obedience and sacrifice, and went through the key points that the exam would cover. She asked if there were any questions, but the class was quiet, tame, in perfect order, and the girls had already buried their faces in the piles of paper and books, chewing their pencils or knitting their brows. The classroom, in a brand new building, was spacious and comfortable, glimmering with soothing early summer sunlight through the large window panes. Teacher Liu sat down by the dais and began browsing through student workbooks languorously, then she stood up and went out.

Instantly Li Xiaohua slouched in her chair, opened her desk drawer quietly and got out an envelope. The letter from home brightened her face, and she was engrossed at once, her free hand absently twisting her long black hair into a rope. Father said this year's crop was looking very healthy, thanks to the plentiful rain and the tractor they had bought with the proceeds from last year's harvest. They had bought a set of furniture for home and a new bed for her. Her sister was going to a local secondary school after summer and she was so looking forward to it. Her little brother was now in the middle year of his primary school and was doing well, inspired by her. Reading that, she smiled. The letter also reported that they now kept three pigs and twenty chickens, food was plentiful and they even ate meat twice a week. Her forehead puckered slightly into a frown as she read: 'Everyone is so glad there are no more political movements to bother them.' She couldn't quite grasp the meaning of it.

Whispering and tittering from behind broke her concentration; she turned around curiously, only to be rebuked by two pairs of rolled eyes from the girls Yang Lian and Ma Huifang. She turned away quickly and looked down, but it didn't stop her ears standing up, antennae on full power. While listening, she scribbled a cartoon of the two girls, average height, average looks and average intelligence; they didn't belong to any cliques, but they had the sharpest tongues and an aptitude for tormenting.

"We shouldn't be here, my cousin's school doesn't do exams any more."

"Really? How come?"

"Revolution is coming."

"What revolution? Haven't we had it already?"

"Don't be daft – after all those class struggles we've been learning about?"

"Oh?"

"The Politburo meeting said. And a big poster in Peking University, rebelling against the authorities."

"Why?"

"It's called the Cultural Revolution."

"Cultural Revolution? So it's peaceful then, not a guns and battles kind of revolution? How do you know this?"

"News from the back door. I heard it from my father. Something is going to happen. No more lessons or exams. Believe me."

Li Xiaohua could feel an incipient excitement building up. All these years in school she had been ensnared in perpetual failure, smothered in a dense atmosphere of feminine subtlety. She often dreamed she was like a character in a novel, fighting like a boy, side by side with boys who were free from the restraints of trivial power struggles and gossip. She longed to be a boy. They had more freedom than girls. They were expected to be naughty, boisterous, and allowed to speak plainly without a tactical subtext. She felt herself too coarse to fit into this refined setup, the first born of a three-generation, poor peasant family, who were profoundly grateful to the communists and devoted to Chairman Mao. Her family had scrimped and saved to give her a good education and enrol her into this ivory-tower school. She felt she had let them down.

A sudden clunk of chairs from behind catching her attention, Li Xiaohua turned around again. Fan Ping, the form prefect, tall and slim, propelled herself down the aisle to Yang Lian and Ma Huifang and rapped their desks gently. The whispering halted. As Fan Ping turned back, Li Xiaohua caught a faint scent of bitterness: "teacher's pet".

The Beijing Shida Middle School for Girls was one of the top ten middle schools in Beijing. The six hundred girls boarding here were predominantly from elite backgrounds, though a large minority were commoners like Li Xiaohua, winning their places solely through the intensive entrance exams and their pure red backgrounds. It was considered a 'royal school' as Mao's daughter had graduated from here. The school had a reputation of high standards and a glittering track record for sending girls to Peking or Qinghua universities. The teachers were the best of the best, heavily scrutinised and vetted. The girls, many daughters or nieces of members of the Standing Committee of the Chinese Communist Party, boarded here with the astonishing sense that they were being groomed to become the leaders of the future, and would one day run the country.

The revolution did arrive. First it was just disrupted lessons, cancelled exams; then all the accessible walls on the campus began to disappear behind layers of posters that reviled and vilified the school authorities and teachers. Party Secretary Hu, a successful early communist and an outstanding history teacher, became a particularly conspicuous target. Within a month classes had completely stopped, the teachers were sidelined and subdued. Girls roamed around the school campus without parental or tutorial supervision. Some were lost; some were in heaven. Then the Work Group turned up, sent there by the Central Party to take back control of the school, bringing an end to their limbo, or perhaps fetching them down to earth.

Stepping out of the office building after chairing a teachers' Mao's Book study session, Li Xiaohua was exhausted and frustrated. It was obvious to her that the teachers were all evil revisionists, but they were as stubborn as mules and refused to admit their wrongs. She smeared her sweaty forehead with her palm and looked up at the dense, low sky. A distant rumbling obtruded into her thoughts, the sky darkened, followed by a crash of thunder.

"War? Is it war?" a lower year girl ran screaming out of the building, then went back when the rain came, pouring down in vertical streaks. A crowd sheltered with Li Xiaohua at the building entrance, watching the rain wash off the ink, and strip the posters from the walls. No one actually cared. The posters had served their purpose, allowing the creators to rant on and demonstrate a rabid revolutionary aspiration. Suddenly, Li Xiaohua sprang out of the shelter, reached out her arms, face turned skywards, twirling.

"Come on! It's so cool!"

A few of the girls joined in, splashing water at each other with their feet, screaming and laughing. Their thin summer clothing stuck to their young bodies and hair plastered their faces. One moment Li Xiaohua was hooting with laugher, the next moment she was roaring with rage and anger into the gloom of the storm as if she had just broken out of a cage.

"Be careful, lightning!" a teacher shouted from an upstairs window, but was warned off by his colleagues that it wasn't the time to give children advice.

Under the Work Group's leadership, and adhering closely to the lead provided by front page articles in the *People's Daily*, school lessons had been replaced by Mao's Book study periods and struggle sessions targeting teachers and the school authorities.

"Why are we sitting here idle?" Yang Lian intruded into Fan Ping's reading. "Other schools are out demonstrating in the street and revolting against the teachers. They even beat teachers."

"Beating teachers is just wrong," said Fan Ping.

"Beating is the only way to help teachers to accept thought reform, like parents disciplining their children, right?" Ma Huifang said.

The other girls laughed.

"We've never been disciplined by physical violence here though, so why should we do it to them?"

"Because we are revolutionary. We are good and they are the baddies. It's obvious," said Li Xiaohua. A smattering of polite applause provided faint encouragement.

A sudden burst of tumultuous noise breaking in from the street outside roused the girls from their torpor. They looked at each other as if they had forgotten that their actions no longer needed approval. Li Xiaohua made the first move, but the classroom was soon cleared out leaving only Fan Ping and Han Mei behind.

The girls rushed out of the school gate, following the source of the noise around the corner. The road in front was blocked by hundreds of students, led by a lanky boy in a vest brandishing a red flag, marching behind their teachers. Every now and then, teachers were jolted and thrust forward from behind. Li Xiaohua grabbed the sleeve of a girl who was chanting slogans and asked: "What is going on?"

"Chairman Mao wrote a letter and endorsed us, the Red Guard. We are revolting! Down with teachers and the authorities!"

"Us? Red Guards?"

"We are Chairman Mao's Red Guard from Qinghua Affiliated Middle School. You'll read about us in the newspapers, you will!" The girl rushed to rejoin her troop and left Li Xiaohua standing on the sidelines, flabbergasted.

When the news that the Year 6 girls had officially formed the Red Guard of Beijing Shida Middle School for Girls echoed around campus, the Year 3 girls went wild. They had watched with adoration the inception of the Red Guards at Qinghua Affiliated Middle School and their subsequent support from Mao, though there had been indignation that this revolutionary trophy had been taken by the rival school; the girls believed that they could do better. Everyone yearned to join.

The Year 3 classroom was on the boil, as hot as the August heat, the girls were in high spirits, scurrying around, printing leaflets and making flags, and preparing the black ink posters that demonstrated their staunch support for the Cultural Revolution and Chairman Mao. Fan Ping came in, shoulders straight and chin high, an astonishing appearance that instantly drew a circle of girls around her.

"Where did you get that?" Yang Lian pointed at her brand new army uniform and red armband printed 'Red Guard'.

"I just joined the Red Guard."

"That looks so cool." A ring of admiring eyes were glittering.

"Can I join?" several girls asked at the same time.

"What did you have to do to join?"

Fan Ping delighted in the attention and quickly asserted her control: "Quiet! Let me speak," she said. "It's so cool, isn't it? It's the current fashion and only the top schools have it. You can have one too, but only if you join early. They are being given out by the army."

"What did you do there?"

"Well, they asked my name, my year and my family background. Then I swore loyalty to Chairman Mao, which of course I'll do anyway, and committed myself to the Cultural Revolution …" She suddenly stopped and said: "Do you know what Chairman Mao said? 'Teachers have treated students as the enemy and have used examinations as weapons to attack students', and also, 'The days of bourgeois control of our schools is over'."

"It's like Chairman Mao spoke from our hearts," Yang Lian said.

"Down with teachers!"

"Join the Red Guard!"

Half of the girls flew out of the classroom, leaving the other half to continue.

"Do you think I could join the Red Guard?" Han Mei asked cautiously.

"Probably not. Your father is a rightist, isn't he?"

"He wasn't to start with. He volunteered because he was the leader. You don't believe me, do you?"

Fan Ping didn't reply.

"Because Chairman Mao said '95% of people are good people', at that time, so 5% had to be rightists. Do you know 5% is equivalent to the entire French population? All of them had to be rightists. There were not enough actual rightist lecturers to meet the quota, so my father put his own name down. He said there were still not enough rightists, so they had to vote. They voted against a quiet lecturer, 'Like throwing the weakest into the lion's mouth,' my father said."

Fan Ping was shocked, and nodded sympathetically.

"What about a peasant-worker-soldier's children?" Li Xiaohua interposed.

"Not at the moment."

Li Xiaohua rolled her eyes and grunted with indignation.

Unlike membership of the Young Pioneers or the Youth League, which was dictated by the teacher's decision and peer popularity, Red Guard membership was being screened by family background only. The first enrolment comprised children from families of exalted rank, such as high officials of the Chinese Communist Party. Later on any rabid action would secure membership, so almost everyone could join. Being a member of the Red Guard granted legitimacy to torment any teacher they wanted to. On the teachers' part, as long as they were together, most felt safe. They had been through several political movements, and had learnt a crucial lesson: if you failed to keep your head down, you would be sure to end up in Xinjiang province or one of the Great North deserts, while if you didn't speak out you might just save your skin. Others stoically accepted this latest political movement as a fresh test or experience which would make them tougher. Most believed that they would be forgiven, provided that they studied Mao's books hard, self-criticised and confessed their sins vigorously; that they demonstrated self-negation. Recently more teachers had been taken out from their study sessions to be ritually humiliated at struggle sessions, and tensions between teachers and girls had been ratcheting up, with teachers sometimes being pushed about by increasingly strident girls. However, they strongly believed that one day they would be exonerated.

"The girls are imitating other schools' students. Our girls should have known better," Party Secretary Hu was optimistically discussing the situation with the maths teacher in the school office.

"But at this age, they are so pliable," the maths teacher said apprehensively.

"Eh, you may be right. Let's hope for the best," Hu sighed.

Suddenly a group of freshly-joined Red Guards burst into the office. Totally ignoring the teachers, they started pulling down the noticeboards, reward pennants and certificates of achievement from the wall. They turned out all the drawers of the filing cabinets and desks, and swept off everything, including the trophies on the shelves, to the floor. Concentrating on the contents of the filing cabinet, Li Xiaohua was looking for the results records: to destroy them as a consolation for not being able to change them.

Hu made as if to reason with the students, but the maths teacher discreetly tugged her by the elbow, and led her away.

"Next week we'll have our first school struggle session; we were assigned responsibility for the Year 3 speech, so we need to be prepared. Here is a list of the teachers we should attack. Yang Lian and Ma Huifang take five girls with you to search these teachers' offices for evidence on the first floor. Li Xiaohua take five girls to do upstairs. You three, go to the Red Guard headquarters to get more paper and ink," commanded Fan Ping.

The girls trooped off to ferret around from one

office to the next, going through school files and records, searching for incriminating evidence. There was a sudden burst of excitement from Ma Huifang as if she had found real treasure.

"Read it out loud, come on!" her companions encouraged.

Ma Huifang cleared her throat and read from the hard-cover purple notebook in her hands: "I went to the bureau today to fetch recruitment documents. On the bus, a beautiful woman stood next to me. My arm touched hers and I felt an urge to squeeze her breast ..."

"Oh, disgusting!" the audience squealed.

"Dog shit!" someone shouted.

"Whoever wrote it? Put him on the black list!"

"Put it in a poster, let everyone see how rotten he is!"

The girls went to the Work Group office to get approval but found nobody there, just a note on the door: "The Great Proletarian Cultural Revolutionary Work Group has been withdrawn from school by order of Chairman Mao. The replacement will be announced accordingly." Fan Ping read the notice through again, but could not comprehend. Who would be in charge?

"Great! We've got rid of the Work Group. No more grown-up interference. Down with the Black Gang!" Li Xiaohua exclaimed.

The girls went silent. Li Xiaohua climbed up the steps in front of the office building and faced the crowd.

"What are you afraid of? The Work Group was just an obstacle to the revolution. I hated them; who were they to tell us we shouldn't do this or that? Look at the other schools. They've made great progress, but our work group held us back," Li Xiaohua said fervently.

"But who will be in charge?"

"We are. We are the vanguard of Chairman Mao's Thought and the apostles of the Cultural Revolution. At this moment we are being tested; this is the moment to show we can do great things and remake history. We cannot afford to be lagging behind."

At moments like these, the decisive and confident win respect. The girls nodded and concurred.

"Who wants to come with me to visit No. 8 Middle School?" Li Xiaohua asked. "They are holding a struggle session this afternoon."

The girls cheered wildly, and from that moment on, they were hers.

At the Beijing Shida Middle School for Girls' struggle session a week later, Party Secretary Hu was thrust roughly onto the stage along with the other teachers who had their names on the list. She looked wan but composed. One of the organisers, a Year 5 girl with transparent framed glasses, snapped curtly: "Tell everyone who you are and confess your crime."

Silence. The packed assembly room watched intently.

"I'm a member of the Chinese Communist Party and I have not committed any crime," Hu stated. In the audience, Fan Ping felt unsettled and her fists were clenched. She had always liked and greatly respected Party Secretary Hu. She knew she had to make a decision soon, to declare where she stood, and the party secretary's reply gave her confidence that she had done nothing wrong and was still her role model.

"What did you say?" said the girl with glasses.

Hu said in her usual satin voice: "I have always dedicated myself to give all you girls a good, solid education, to ensure you can all go to a good university and make the best of your lives. I do make mistakes, and I hope for your forgiveness. I joined the Communist Party over twenty years ago. I would never do anything against the Party or Chairman Mao and harm –"

A Year 5 Red Guard on the stage interrupted her: "Shut up, you liar! You are a hidden enemy with a black heart. You come from a rich landowner family; you were always our class enemy. Fellow Red Guards, comrades, Hu has depraved and corrupted us to become white intellectuals, she has discouraged class struggle, she has used university education as a decoy and made us follow bourgeois ideology and become her docile tools. Chairman Mao never went to university. We don't want university. She has suppressed and bullied us with tons and tons of exams."

Another girl, tall and skinny, stepped forward on the stage, waving a piece of paper at the audience: "Here is a copy of her speech. When she quoted Chairman Mao's article, she wrote 'Mao said …', not 'Chairman Mao said …'. She is an inveterate counter-revolutionary, a Black Gang."

The horde was coalescing into a single entity, intensely focused on the hapless figure of Party Secretary Hu.

"Bow! Bow down to the revolutionaries!" it chanted.

Hu didn't move. In front of her was not just a group of recalcitrant teenagers, more like a pack of wild beings, possessed.

The enemy was right in front of her for the first time in Li Xiaohua's life. Like a newly-trained soldier, eager to battle, she shouted as loud as she could, but her passionate voice was drowned by the roaring clamour; like a drop in an ocean. She recalled the struggle session she had witnessed at No. 8 School and felt she would be nobody once again if she didn't act now. Hungry to flaunt her staunchness and anger towards the non-compliant attitude of the party secretary, she jumped onto the stage, and with a vicious swing, slapped her teacher's face. The air went taut, the clamour came to a jarring halt. This was a school which had never before witnessed an act of physical violence. A red weal developed on the face, four long fingers printed on the Party Secretary's cheek.

"I didn't know we had a boy in our school," a little girl whispered to her friend.

"Idiot, it's not a boy, it's a girl! She's called Li Xiaohua, she's in my sister's class. Yes, she does look a bit like a boy, but who wants to be a girly girl nowadays? It's fashion."

"He … she is so brave. I wish I could be like her."

Some girls came from backstage and the party secretary was pinioned by two Red Guards, another grabbed her dishevelled hair and jerked her head up. Her face was contorted in pain, the eyes pointing upwards, like a stone gargoyle on the roof of a temple. More girls climbed onto the stage, their caps turned back, buttons undone, sleeves rolled back, with belts and canes in their hands, shouting and gesticulating, waving their canes at the immobile teacher. The girl with glasses poured a bottle of black ink on the teacher's head and the horde jeered. Someone struck.

"There, you are black now. Confess! Confess!"

The clamour resumed, exploding in a paroxysm of anger. Released by her captors, Party Secretary Hu staggered, falling to her knees on the floor, bleeding. She was struggling to say something.

"Stop! Stop! Let her talk," the chair yelled at the girls and the noise receded.

"I confess, I'm guilty," she said faintly.

Fan Ping stood there, stunned, disappointed and distraught. How could she? A true communist, a venerable educator, surrender? All her respect towards the party secretary drained away. She felt bile in her throat. Everything in front of her made her sick. She abhorred the violence, but she was confused. She blindly pushed her way out of the struggle rally with a sense of foreboding. She stood outside, gulping lungfuls of parched air.

"There are no grown-ups in charge any more. What do we do? We are all on our own." Han Mei, panic in her voice, had followed her out.

Fan Ping couldn't believe that the adults had abandoned them at this moment. She led the way to the school offices, where they made increasingly desperate calls to everyone they could think of on the Beijing Standing Committee of the Party.

"Hello, we are calling from Beijing Shida Middle School for Girls. The students here are out of control, they are beating the party secretary. Please send back the Work Group, or someone to stop ... What? It's revolution? But ..."

"What did they say?"

"They told us to go back. They said casualties are unavoidable during revolution. What do we do?"

"What can we do?"

"It's not right."

"Who said it's right. But we'll be accused of being counter-revolutionists if we don't join in."

"I'd rather ..."

"Don't say it. You'll regret it."

On campus the atmosphere grew more hostile. Teachers were slapped, pushed and struck, ritually humiliated. Fan Ping couldn't help but speak out at the next Red Guard meeting the following day.

"We should keep calm and remain civil. If we are right we shouldn't need violence, violence is a sign of weakness," said Fan Ping, her voice full of passion, to murmurs of support from the girls around.

"I disagree," said Li Xiaohua, "we are the revolution's successors, we must strive against our enemies, be as cruel and merciless as the North Pole winter. Our great leader Chairman Mao taught us: 'A revolution is not a dinner party or writing an article, not embroidering or painting a picture, not so refined, so leisurely, or gentle; revolution is an insurrection, one class overthrows another via violence'."

She continued: "Our enemies are devils in our society, they are animals. Classmates, comrades, do we want to waste our lives being mere nuts and bolts, passively holding together a small part of a massive machine? No, we are the elite cohort, the revolution's successors, our destiny is to change the world, to do great things." She paused to absorb some of the growing adulation of the crowd, glanced at Fan Ping and continued, "Yesterday was a great success. Our current enemy, Hu, admitted her guilt. We should carry on the revolution to the bitter end."

Her words and bearing enthralled the crowd, heads were turned, lips parted and eyes focused on Li Xiaohua, whose existence most had been previously unaware of, now a rising star. Her shocking performance of yesterday had not only earned her recognition, but had granted her power and confidence beyond her expectations. Patriotic glory trumped reason. Fan Ping fell silent, too scared to push against this tide.

"I want to go home," Fan Ping said to Han Mei after the struggle session.

"Me too. I don't see why we can't," Han Mei said. "No one is in charge. The teachers and matrons are all concentrated in the Facilities Building, so who will stop us?"

"Li Xiaohua might. Didn't you hear? She led a group to catch girls who went home the evening before and accused them of shirking their revolutionary duties."

Suspecting that no one would notice if they slunk off home together after the others had gone to the hall, they left anyway. Their homes were in the same compound as each other, not far from the school. The empty street seemed full of tension.

"I'm scared and confused," Fan said. "From when I learned to talk I was taught to respect teachers, pursue knowledge and be kind to others. Now we beat teachers up, stop learning and are rude to each other."

"That's what revolution is all about. Don't you feel excited at being a true revolutionary?" Han Mei asked.

"Yes, I'm a bit, but …"

"The Politburo has given the Red Guards their full support, and Chairman Mao has praised the Red Guards' actions, remember?"

"I don't know, it just doesn't feel right," Fan Ping said, snatching a leaf from a tree in the pavement.

"Why do you sound so … reluctant?"

"Maybe because I'm a year older than you? But I don't know how to convince you."

"I'll see you tomorrow at school." Han Mei stopped by her home.

"Maybe."

"You cannot shun the Cultural Revolution. It's our duty."

Han Mei skipped into her apartment block. She told her father of the Politburo order and what had happened at school. Her father listened quietly and in the end said gently, "You are just children, yet have already learnt to hurt people."

"But they are bad people," said Han Mei. Her father lifted his eyebrows but said nothing. Han Mei fell silently into reflection.

The intensity of feelings continued to escalate at the school. From the steps in front of the administration building, Li Xiaohua was shouting at the throng: "Someone said to me we should be kind to our teachers – wrong! To be kind to our enemy is to be cruel to our friends. You will be our enemy if you show mercy to our enemy. It is crystal clear. We must strive to destroy our enemy!"

A girl rushed towards Li Xiaohua waving a newspaper in her hand, shouting: "The latest news! The latest news! The radio has broadcast Chairman Mao's letter to Qinghua Affiliated Middle School supporting the Red Guard movement, and the standing committee has supported the Red Guard's actions. The highest order is that there must be no interference with the students' actions and no investigation afterwards."

Li Xiaohua's vacuous speech, inflamed by this news, induced much louder applause than last time. It made their blood boil, fanning incipient resentments into hot-headed hatred towards their teachers and the school authorities. Once courteous and educated girls had lapsed into an ebullience of rioting and denigration of teachers. The message from on high was clear: aggression was to be glorified without challenge. Fan Ping, flummoxed, wilted into silence, her leadership contest thwarted.

Such were the vicissitudes of the many political movements, that one now took root in that most impressionable, and fertile, soil: the teenage mind. The school turned into a camp of savages, drunk on their emancipation. Girls cut their hair like boys, ran around half-naked with canes, bats or belts. Documents, books and records were fed into a voracious bonfire on the sports ground in front of the administration block. The trophies, certificates and banners of past glory turned into grey dust in the fire. Some girls even smashed their desks and chairs to bear witness to their determination that they would study nothing but Chairman Mao's book. Teachers and school officials were herded into lines, marching from one place to another, just as they used to march the girls between their classrooms, the canteen, their dormitory, the assembly hall, with a strict military discipline.

Li Xiaohua, exhausted after hours of rioting in the enervating high summer heat, walked away from the action and sat down alone under the mulberry tree. The windless air rippled with heat haze, the sky was deep and blue. She looked around; the school was not as intimidating as she remembered it and not a vestige of order was left in place. The walls had been replaced with black ink posters in primitive brush strokes: 'Down with the Black Gang!', 'You pig-faced bitch! Behave!', 'Confess your crimes!', 'Long live Chairman Mao!', 'Protect Chairman Mao with our blood and life!' ..., but she didn't want to read them. At the moment, she just wanted to read a letter from home.

"Hey, lunch?" Fan Ping and Han Mei walked past.

"Where did you get that?" Li Xiaohua noticed the shiny badge on Fan Ping's chest. The badge had Mao's portrait, with a red half-sun fanning upwards. It looked precious. Li Xiaohua had coveted one ever since they had first started appearing a few weeks ago.

"I'll get you one if you want," said Fan Ping, "and you," as she turned towards Han Mei.

"Thank you!" Li Xiaohua sang.

By the side of the path to the canteen, a line of teachers knelt down, heads bowed in the sun. Two girl Red Guards, equipped with canes, stood nearby. One figure in the line fell, so the guard girl ran at it, yelling and poking till the figure erected itself. Other girls, passing by, smacked them, some randomly, some choosing a particular target to attack. One girl, her cane held level, walked down the line briskly. The teachers' faces hit the stick one after another; laughter followed adding further misery. As she walked past her Chinese teacher, whom she hated most for her unjust punishments, Han Mei picked up her arm. She wanted to hit the teacher, but she just couldn't do it.

"What's your problem? Scared? Where is your revolutionary mettle?" Li Xiaohua caught up, poking her from behind.

"I felt someone watching, behind me, I heard them telling me it was wrong."

Li Xiaohua said nothing when she saw the tears.

The canteen was hectic like a village market, groups of girls swirling in and out. The placard of canteen rules had been daubed in black ink and trampled on the ground. The sinks were blocked with rotting food. The buzzing of flies mingled with shouts and laughter. Hardly anyone sat down at the tables, eating quietly like they used to. With a sudden shriek, a Year 4 girl ran out of the canteen as if she had seen a tiger.

"What's happening?"

"She stepped on a mouse and freaked out!" Laughter.

Li Xiaohua had a fleeting feeling of nausea as the scene evoked one of the times the warden had stood behind her to ensure she drank her milk, the bane of her life, at breakfast. "It is good for you," she was scolded as she ran off and vomited outside of the canteen, followed by the sound of laughter. Right now, this is like living in heaven, I can eat as I want, she thought.

As dusk fell, the air cooled, the girls gathered around the dying bonfire on the sports ground in the crepuscular light, occasionally feeding chair legs into the cinders. They danced and swirled around like a revolving lantern; some were playing tag or fighting, some falling or rolling on the ground. As the night wore on, the gyrations and shrieking subsided, replaced with a soporific aura of mystique and obscurity.

"Don't know why, I feel great, so free."

"Me too…"

"I feel I'm a true revolutionary now, like my parents fighting the Japanese, fighting the Guomindang, risking their lives for a good cause."

"It's thrilling to be in charge; we are ordering teachers around. Could you ever have imagined it before?"

"I agree some teachers humiliate and bully children, but to beat them? It's gone too far," Fan Ping protested.

"If Hu had truly confessed her guilt and repented, this wouldn't have happened. She has to be right all the time, hasn't she? Why can't she be wrong just for once?" Li Xiaohua's eyes flashed by the light of the embers.

"Can you stop now?" Fan Ping asked. She didn't know what to do and was afraid of being accused of sympathising with the enemy.

Li Xiaohua's resolution wavered, but then she felt her conviction surging once more: "Chairman Mao taught us that: 'The good attacking the evil is obligatory; the good attacking the good is a misunderstanding; the evil attacking the good is a challenge and the evil attacking the evil is – deserves them fucking right!'"

Applause crackled like a popcorn machine, testifying to the respect for this audacity, intelligence and foresight. The air had cooled down further from the summer heat and the buildings, normally lit up, now stood about them like black mountains. Han Mei said, "I wonder how many stars are up there?"

"As many as the class enemy," Li Xiaohua retorted sulkily, objecting to the sudden changing of subject. "Anyway, why should we care right now?"

"I want to go to the moon, like the lady Chang E."

"No, you don't. We need to clear out our arch enemies first, it's our greatest mission," said Ma Huifang.

"They don't look like the enemy to me," a Year 1 girl murmured.

The bright August moon was hanging overhead. As a cloud wafted across it, it cast a shadow on the girls' faces. Someone was playing the harmonica and a sweet voice joined in:

The waves of Lake Hong are rippling;
Nearby my home country;
Early in the morning the boats go out to fish;
Coming back at night the boats are full ...

The flags nearby moaned soft laments in the wind. A low year girl started to cry, and others said they missed home.

The next day Party Secretary Hu arrived at school at eight o'clock, as usual, despite the incipient menace, intending to take full responsibility on herself in the hope that the other teachers would be let off. She was horrified with the sudden eruption of teenage ferocity, seemingly indomitable, incited by Mao's first big poster, and replete with hatred and malice. However, she still remembered the girls as they had been just a few weeks ago and believed that she could depend on the fundamental goodness of the children to channel their behaviour away from this violent aberration.

The Red Guard girls, their vitality recharged, were ravaging the campus, hunting down teachers. As a group of girls dragged Party Secretary Hu out of the office building, others swarmed over, chasing and tormenting her like a pack of hyenas. Most girls just watched.

"Beat down the Black Gang!" the chant grew louder and louder, reverberating between the buildings as more joined in.

Belts lashed Hu's body, the girls painted her head and arms in black ink. She was shocked to her core by this extraordinary hatred; but she endured. She had loved these girls who were always so graceful and sophisticated, had thought of them as her own, had felt fulfilled by their every achievement. What had changed them from clever and courteous girls to delinquent teenagers in the blink of an eye? Being on the receiving end, she couldn't see, however, that this extraordinary hatred was mostly a show, contenders competing for a revolutionary title.

Fan Ping was in the crowd, watching, at the beginning. "What are you waiting for? Scared? Where is your revolutionary mettle?" She remembered Li Xiaohua's goading of yesterday. She felt uneasy. It was an absolute that she should never be discourteous to any grown-up, but in following the others she found a shaky excuse and made her first strike. To her surprise, she felt invigorated.

"Beat down the Black Gang! Smash her pig face!" the chants were more and more demanding.

Party Secretary Hu tried to appeal to the girls. "I take full responsibility for the wrong this school has done to you," but her voice was buried in the barracking from the mob of girls.

Strike, whip, thrash, beat, lash; belts with metal heads, the wooden rifles used for military training, bats from the gymnasium, flailed at the figure. Three girls whipped her in turn, and each one was harder than the other, as if they were in a race. They laughed, showing off, proud of their brutality. Hu yielded and cried out, "I'm Black Gang, I'm guilty, I deserve to die ..." but the beating and chanting carried on. Yang Lian spat on her face and yelled, "You, fucking black-hearted snake, if you dare to stand against working people, we will draw your pig tendons, dig out your pig heart, cut off your pig head. Fuck you, do not even think you can fight back, we will never let you free!"

Yang Lian swung her bat and hit her teacher's shoulder. Hu's arms were wrapped around her head, then her back was hit. She staggered forward, the mob chased after at once and a new ring was formed. Her eyes, filled with abject terror, met Fan Ping's, but Fan Ping drew back, looked away and stood there disorientated.

As she struggled to run towards the office building, Hu's legs were kicked out from behind. Her arms windmilled to regain her balance but in vain. She fell, grovelling on the steps to the building, while through the cacophonous sound of the baying pack of girls could be heard the thwack of metal buckles and sticks on flesh. The crumpled figure was now motionless. Ma Huifang kicked her head and shouted into her ear: "Get up! Don't you play dead. Bow to the revolutionary youngsters!"

The others eagerly joined in: "Down with the bourgeois running dog!"

"Long live Chairman Mao!"

"Long live the Great Proletarian Cultural Revolution!"

She could not hear and could not feel.

Someone shouted from the crowd, "Stop, stop. She is not moving."

Han Mei surged forward and grabbed Li Xiaohua's arm. "Tell them to stop."

They didn't stop; they poked and prodded the body

into action with their clubs and wooden rifles, like cats playing with their prey.

Han Mei bent down, touched the party secretary's body and shouted to Li Xiaohua, "Get an ambulance, quickly." Li Xiaohua elbowed Han Mei aside and beckoned Yang Lian and Ma Huifang to fetch water. The buckets of water failed to bring her back to life, only washed away the foam and blood from her mouth.

"Get up! Get up! Don't think you can get away by playing dead!" Li Xiaohua exhorted.

"She's not moving, can't you see?" someone murmured.

"It can't be, she was talking just now."

"The party secretary is dead!" a piercing squeal burst out.

"Shut up!"

Li Xiaohua was not convinced about the death but was visibly shaken. She, with her impassive face, vacillated between sympathy and further cruelty. She knew she might have got herself into serious trouble, but as soon as she saw Fan Ping appear, she decided to take the risk. She kicked the body and declared without a hint of remorse, "Whoever refuses to reform will end up like this!"

"Come on!" she beckoned the girl gang.

After a momentary freeze, the gang suddenly flew exhilaratingly away, off to hunt other targets, as if they had won one battle and went on to another. Fun and celebration at a carnival of violence.

"How could you?" Fan Ping caught Li Xiaohua by the arm as she brushed past.

"What? Be better than you?" Li Xiaohua challenged without a trace of a scruple and ran off.

Fan Ping and Han Mei stared at the twisted lump on the steps then at each other. They were obviously outcasts now, every girl's nightmare, as if they had lost their grip on the lifeboat in the middle of a storm. Li Xiaohua was in the boat, grinning, but they were in the water, drowning.

"She isn't moving."

Fan Ping nodded, wiped off the water on Party Secretary Hu's face and fanned away the gathering flies.

"What have we done?"

"We didn't do it."

"It's murder."

"But we didn't do it."

"What are we going to do?"

"She cannot be dead, can't be."

"Did you see?"

"Yes."

"I saw."

"It must have been an accident."

Fan Ping paused. The air was sultry, still. She panted as if she couldn't breathe, "I saw it, not an accident."

"But what do we do now?" Han Mei looked around, a few furtive faces appeared behind the windows of the building, but no one had come out. At least the building had kept the lifeless body out of the scorching sun.

"Just two of us? I don't know." Fan Ping buried her face in her palms.

"What about our doctor? He might be able to help," Han Mei said and ran off.

Han Mei came back with the school doctor and a flat-bed cart from the kitchen. A flat-bed cart, covered by disused posters, slewed along the street towards the hospital, pushed by two breathless girls and a grown-up in white.

Two weeks later, Mao, accompanied by His full Politburo in army uniforms, stood on the Tian An Men Gate to rally the Red Guard youth. One million Red Guards assembled at Tian An Men Square, under the never-setting, blazing sun, to worship, to vent their gratitude to their greatest leader and the father of the nation. Forty of the girls from the Beijing Shida Middle School for Girls had been invited onto the gate to be personally greeted by Mao. "Be violent," He said to the girls.

The Great Free Travelling

It was the third time we had come to Xian Central Railway Station in a week.

Hui and I sat on the bridge over the tracks, jetting out our legs between the banister bars, watching trains rumbling under the bridge, in and out of the station like snakes leaving a cloud of smoke, black and acrid, that stung our eyes, sooted our long plaits and made us cough. It was a warm October day in 1966 and the station was burned black in the searing sun.

The station grounds were swamped by avid Red Guards, each carrying a large backpack with a pannikin dangling at the side. They were darting across the square, gambolling for joy, tears of laughter mingling with revolutionary songs and slogans. Red flags and banners voicing: 'Revolution is Irreproachable; Revolt is Applaudable!', 'Go to Destroy the Four Olds!', 'Great Travel: Ignites Revolutionary Fire and Sparks Riot!', flapped in the wind like fire. I had never seen so many teenagers gathered together in one place before and my heart seethed with excitement.

Chaos ruled the platforms though. Our eyes tracked from one train door to another, where the squabbles turned into full blown physical fights, followed moments later by the station staff, the only grown-ups at the scene apart from a couple of middle-aged women standing next to their snack carts, rushing out of the building, helping to placate the angry parties. Finally, the train was loaded, the doors closed and it moved out of the station. Then another one arrived, loaded up with Red Guard teenagers, and left.

How we wanted to be like them, the Red Guards, travelling anywhere we wanted; no need for money for accommodation, transportation or food. Everything was free. Just one year older and we would have been Red Guards ourselves, and taken part in *Chuan Lian* – The Great Travel: Chairman Mao's plan to spread the Cultural Revolution out across the country. The prospect of travelling by train without grown-up supervision had sparked a burning desire among us. The thrill of a real adventure had kept me awake at night. For days at a time we had got together, drawing maps of the routes and selecting the cities that we'd like to go to, but we had known for sure that the hardest task was how to catch the train.

Turning to our Red Guard brothers and sisters, pleading with them for help, was our natural solution, but it had all been without success.

"You won't be able to board the train without a ticket," my sister Ke had said.

"But you don't buy a ticket."

"We have a reference letter from school with a big red stamp on it, and we have the Red Guard armbands. But you have nothing. I cannot take you."

"But you said that boy in your class was good at carving stamps out of potatoes."

"It's against the rules. Absolutely not, and anyway you would be a nuisance to us all."

"We won't, we'll do anything you want."

My sister had been adamant. I even went to Mama for help as a last resort, but she had said I was too young to travel a long distance without an adult's company, totally ignoring the fact that some children of my age had already gone. I was nearly thirteen, old enough to get married in old China, so we had been told in the class struggle lessons before the Cultural Revolution. We had been in the final year of our primary school, a boarding school for the children of high officials in Xian. If I had been only a few months older, or had been the brightest and been promoted a year up, then I would have been in secondary school and become a Red Guard.

With the primary schools now closed for good and our parents away for the unforeseeable future, the restraining control of school and parents was a thing of the past. The new freedom had initially brought euphoria; we played as and when we wanted, and what we wanted. But it became apparent that the true adventures beyond our compound were what we were really longing for, and the only resolution was to go away by ourselves. The two of us had sworn to each other to keep this secret from our families and our other friends.

That morning as I sat on the wall near our compound entrance gate, waiting with my canvas shoulder bag clenched in my arms, my heart beating savagely, there had been no sign of Hui. Had she changed her mind? The thought had made me sweat. I had to go away now; so many things out there I had to see and this was my only opportunity.

The autumn morning had been calm with a clear blue sky and no whisper of wind, the night-cooled air not yet heated by the sun. I had restlessly stared at my brilliant white gym shoes that I had powdered last night. They were extremely fashionable, and hard to get, costing me three hours' queuing, and being scolded for asking if I could try them on. I hated shopping; it was like you were begging even though you were paying for it.

The street outside the gate had been almost empty; only sporadic propaganda trucks passed by, leaving multicoloured leaflets swirling in the air. It was the longest morning I could remember. As I had begun to wonder what to do if Hui failed to turn up, her thin figure appeared in the avenue. Instantly re-exhilarated I hopped off the wall and ran over to her.

Suddenly copious steam clouds, sharp hoots and whistles shocked me out of my reverie. On the platform teenagers, myriads of them, continued arriving, departing, jostling one another. The ticket inspectors were shouting and struggling to herd the crowd. Hui spotted a train door on the platform that had no attendant.

"Come on, let's catch the train." I pulled Hui to help her up.

"We didn't bring our bedding; look at them, everyone

has a backpack," Hui said, "and we don't have the Red Guard armbands either."

"He doesn't have an armband, he's just part of a group. Let's find a group."

I feared the worst, as Hui was wavering. I had lost the whole month's worth of coupons for meat, sugar and flour in my frenzy of excitement. How was I going to tell my parents, and see the despair in their faces?

Perhaps Hui saw the panic in my face. "No matter, we'll go, it will be fun," Hui said with an offhand gesture.

On the platform, I followed Hui closely. Before I realised it, Hui had vanished onto the train, but a force from behind brought me to a jarring halt as I mounted the top step of the carriage. The inspector's cranelike arm lowered me to the platform as he said, "Hey, girl, where are you going?"

"*Chuan Lian,*" I replied, The Great Travel. The magic words to open a world of adventure.

"Reference letter?"

"I'm with them." I pointed to the group ahead of me on the train.

"No, you are not, I counted," the ticket inspector scoffed, "and you," he beckoned at Hui, who was peeping from behind the train door, to come down. He pushed us to one side and bellowed: "Lao Li, take these two kids to the office and keep them in."

We were led into an office and the door was locked from outside.

It was a large office that had seven or eight desks strewn with papers, leaflets and dirty teacups. Dust and waste paper carpeted the floor. In contrast, the wall was decorated immaculately with Mao's portrait, colourful posters of the sun, flowers, festoons and red flags. The place was sanctified. I rubbed the window on the platform side with my sleeve and looked through it, reflecting on our failed attempt and what to do next; then I saw the man called Lao Li leading three more men towards the office.

Hui spotted a cupboard door by the corner and pushing mops and brooms aside we squeezed in. The office door clanked open, followed by a cry: "What the hell! Where are they?"

It all went quiet.

"Gone through that window perhaps?" someone said meekly.

"I can't imagine anyone getting through that hole."

"You couldn't, of course."

"They shouldn't be far, come on."

The door slammed shut and the office fell quiet again. Quickly we slunk out of the office, blending into the crowd on the platform. Before long, we discovered another carriage that had no ticket inspector. A man with spindly legs came out of the carriage pushing a sack truck away. Grabbing the opportunity we scrambled up into the carriage. Piles of cardboard boxes, suitcases and packages lay all around, but there weren't any seats. While we dithered over whether to stay, footsteps on the ramp made us quickly duck behind some shelves. Watching through the gap between the tops of the boxes and the shelf above I saw a man in a black hat, searching around some boxes, bending down and marking certain boxes with a red ink cross. He was concentrated, agile and furtive.

"What are you doing here?" The man with the spindly legs pushed his sack truck full of boxes up the ramp.

"What are YOU doing here?" the black hat man retorted.

"I saw you marking those boxes, what is the meaning of it?"

"You keep your mouth shut, or I'll have your dog head dislocated from your shoulders," he snapped in a harsh rasp of a whisper.

I clutched Hui's ice-cold hand and bristled like a hedgehog. We wanted to get out but it was too late, as the door was pulled shut from outside. After that the whistle sounded, the steam engine puffed, the train jerked into motion, and before long it was thrumming away. The city soon faded, the buildings and bustle of people vanishing into the distance. In no time we were embraced into unfamiliar green; trees, fields and rivers, scenes we had not seen before. Our fears receded.

Sitting on a high box where we could see out of a barred vent, we snaffled up our bread and pickled cucumbers. Inside, the carriage was only half full, with a variety of boxes, luggage, parcels and barrels. The floor was coated with thick black soot and in one corner lay those boxes marked with a red cross.

"I wonder what they are," I said.

"Me too, but we aren't allowed to open them, you

know," said Hui. She had a habit of following rules, and for that she had always been chosen by teacher as our form prefect at school. It was my triumph that I was able to persuade her to come at all.

"But there's no one here to tell us off, so come on." I couldn't resist the temptation, I opened one.

"Oh, cigarettes!" Hui exclaimed. "They are very valuable you know. My father said cigarettes are more valuable than money."

"Why?"

"Because you cannot get them with money."

"But what are they for?"

"Are you being serious? Smoking, I suppose? Or buying things, anything. Juan's mother bought a case of apples with two packs of cigarettes. And I saw my father give the driver a pack of cigarettes, not money, when he drove my mother to the hospital."

"Yes, I remember now, my mother asked uncle Zhang to get her some cigarettes, and I did wonder as I know my parents never smoke. Can we have some?"

"That would be stealing."

"Oh yes and the man in the black hat, he sounds scary." I carefully closed the box. We turned our backs on the cigarette boxes and kept our distance after that, as if someone was watching us from the shadows. Instead, we busied ourselves building a den, or perhaps a castle, out of cardboard boxes, cases and parcels from the carriage, and then we tucked in to our new bed blissfully.

"I wonder if our mothers have noticed we're gone," I said.

"Perhaps not. They are only allowed home on Sundays. I left a note for my mama, I don't want her to be too worried."

"Oops, I forgot. But, but they won't have time to worry, will they? Last time my mother came home, she was in a stinking bad mood and a big hurry. It wouldn't have mattered if I were not there. She was looking for some kind of files. She said she was accused of being a traitor and she needed to prove what she did in 1939 in the Red Army. She was only fifteen then, not much older than me. Most of the time she was worrying about my father."

"Yes, my father said they all had to write confessions again and again, otherwise they would be sent to prison or banished and have our home ransacked."

"I guess confessions are deadly important. My parents often talk about it. It always makes my mother cry."

"Of course, if they write a good confession, they will be forgiven."

"My mother does worry about my sister; she is my mother's favourite. My father cares about me more but he is not a worrying type, so it's OK," I added. We concurred that our parents didn't have any time to worry about us.

We looked out through the window when the train slowed down while passing a small station. The platform was empty, but a few decrepit shacks stood behind the platform along with a wall covered with fresh posters and graffiti of revolutionary slogans. The station name was so unfamiliar that I forgot it straight away.

"We don't know where we are and where we are going, do we?" I asked.

She shook her head and her tired eyelids drooped.

The dusk fell gently and darkness soon filled the space. We huddled together. Occasionally lights swept the carriage through the narrow vents as we passed a station.

"These boxes are so hard, I miss my bed at home," Hui moaned.

"But isn't it exciting? We're going to see the Bund by the Huangpu River, the West Lake, the Great Youngzi Bridge and Tian An Men Square ..." I tried to cheer her up, feeling responsible for her suffering. Hui remained silent, but I carried on talking till I heard heavy breathing. My eyes grew sticky.

When I woke up, the outside was already bright.

"Hui, wake up! It's a big place, we can get out, maybe."

The steam engine hooted suddenly and Hui opened her bleary eyes and jumped up.

"Where are we?"

"A big city I think."

"We need to get out," Hui said.

"That's what I just said."

The train began to slow down, we packed up our belongings and gathered by the door. The door was seriously shut and we couldn't find any handle inside. We kicked and pushed but the door didn't budge. I crashed on the floor in despair. The train had completely stopped. Hui said someone would come to open the door. I stared at her with misgiving. No one came. I looked at the air vents.

"If I can get out through those holes, I can open the door from the outside for you."

At the time it seemed the only resort. I popped my head through the hole, saw the chaotic platform swarming with Red Guards, and no one looked at our carriage. Apart from one missing button, I landed on the platform rather easily. But I shrieked when I saw a big padlock on the carriage door.

"Hui, come out through the hole like me, the door is locked, I cannot open it."

"I'm much bigger than you, it's not possible."

"Try it! The train will leave soon." We heard the whistle.

"I cannot get through, oh the train …"

"Give me your hands, let me up," I shouted and started to run along with the train. But the train was gathering pace and I was suddenly seized by a uniformed man.

"What do you think you are doing?" he rasped.

In the station office, I was trembling, frightened and distraught at being separated from Hui and with absolutely no idea what would happen to me.

"You don't look like a Red Guard, far too young, so why were you trying to get into the luggage carriage?" a tall station staff member said aggressively.

I shook my head and refused to cooperate. Being alone, I was beset with poignant regrets, beginning to doubt the freedoms that we so coveted. Perhaps school life wasn't that bad; I was good at keeping myself out of trouble, although I never managed to gain teacher's approval. While I hated certain activities, like marching back and forth on the sports ground in the blazing hot sun, I didn't mind at all our three times a day, school wide, strictly supervised gym stretches. So in the end, everything balanced out, as long as I could avoid being scolded or humiliated by a teacher.

A uniformed man with grey hair came in with a bowl of hot noodles and put it in front of me. I looked at it suspiciously as though it were poisonous. He smiled, gesticulated at me to eat and began to chat; he was friendly and asked me where I was going and where I was from. I refused to say a word.

"My daughter has gone on the Great Travel for over a month now. She sends letters back every time she arrives at a new place. She's really enjoyed it. She said it was a mind-opening experience," he said in a soothing voice.

My eyes lit up, but I kept quiet.

"My second daughter, a bit like you, was too young to join the Red Guards. She pestered her sister to take her, but I put a stop to it," he said apologetically and continued, "I'm very impressed. You are very brave to go travelling by yourself, seeing the country."

I started to eat the noodles. Haltingly, I told him about Hui and how we ended up in the luggage carriage because the ticket inspector would not let us get on the passenger coach. He listened in a quiet and sympathetic way. As I became more relaxed I told him about the man in the black hat and the boxes with red crosses. His smiley face clouded over, and he got up and went out of the office. I saw him pick up a phone at the side of the platform rather than use the one on the desk in front of me. My stomach churned. I sidled up to the window and held my breath.

"You listen … another girl … the carriage … dangerous …"

When he returned he told me that I would catch the next train and meet Hui at the next station. I was too relieved at the prospect of being reunited with Hui to protest, although I had my suspicions.

As I squeezed into the passenger coach, I found myself plunged into the world of exuberant teenagers. The coach was packed solid with them, on the luggage racks, under seats, between the seats and in the aisles; zealous, rackety, swearing, sweltering, like in a film scene of refugees during the Anti-Japanese War.

As the train started moving, to gentle music suffusing the carriage, the platform glided away. The myriad faces, taut with excitement and mesmerised by the spirit of revolution, were framed within the red sea of flags, banners and posters. The floor pulsated to the beat of music; someone began to sing and others joined in:

Sailing the seas depends on the helmsman
All things grow by the sun
Rain and strong seedlings moist
Revolution relying on Mao Zedong Thought
Like fish with water
Inseparable melon and vine

Revolutionary masses cannot be without the party
Mao Zedong Thought is the sun that never sets.

I was soon dissolved into the unity as if my self had ceased to exist. I was standing by the door, resting on the Red Guards around me, contemplating, when I was brought up short by the sight of the black hat among hundreds of Red Guard green caps. The man in the black hat turned his face away as soon as his calculating eyes met mine. I couldn't move or scream in a swelter of terror. I felt as powerless as when I was being chased in my nightmares.

There was a sudden burst of tumultuous noise from the neighbouring seating block: two groups of Red Guards, one from Beijing and one from Shanghai, were having a fight, bawling at each other; verbal assault turned quickly physical. In the struggle some bags were thrown up producing a shower of raisins and sultanas. The Shanghai group, on their way home from Xinjiang, had brought with them bags and bags full of the precious dry fruits, so rare everywhere else in the rest of China that they were only available with a doctor's prescription. I cupped my hands to catch as much as I could of this free gift falling from heaven and forgot about the man completely. When I next remembered, he had gone.

The train drew into the station; I became agitated. I looked out through the gaps between the heads and I caught a glimpse of Hui, standing there with my bag in her hand and a uniformed man near her. We shrieked in delight as we came together on the platform, and I threw my arms

around her and whispered: "We are in trouble. They know."
I vacillated between being frightened and thrilled.

"Who knows?"

"The man in the black hat. We need to escape." I could feel she was shaking.

"Oh, he is walking towards us, what do we do?" she said.

"Pretend not to notice him and give me my bag. There is the door of the train two metres behind you. Don't turn. You say 'Go', we'll run and get into that door together."

We darted between the slow-moving people on the platform before the uniformed man could catch Hui, and leapt onto the train. I crawled on the floor, squeezing in between people's legs with my bag hugged close to me. We found a space for ourselves under the seats, and held our hands together, willing the train to leave before they could find us. But we heard that dreaded guttural growl, "Away, away, quickly …"

"Stop pushing, no way … What do you want?" a girl squealed.

"Looking for two kids."

"Here are nothing but kids. Which one do you want? What have they done?" a boy intervened.

"It's none of your business."

"Hey, you have gall. Open your eyes, you idiot. We are Red Guards, want to mess with us?"

"Er …" after a little hesitation, a voice said: "They are our daughters, run away …"

"They don't look like you at all. Are you kidnapping

them?" The boy in the seat opposite to us spoke out and winked at us. "Now get out before it's too late! Come on, kick them out of the train, imposters!" The crowd started chanting: "Roll away like an egg, roll away ..." before descending into a peal of laughter.

We crawled out from our hideout after the train left Hefei, under the scrutiny of many pairs of curious eyes.

"What's your name? Where are you from?" a girl Red Guard said superciliously.

"I'm Hui, she's Anni. We are from ..."

"The moon. What's your name?" I barged in, annoyed by the interrogation.

"Hey, she is sharp," a boy said to laughter from the crowd.

The coach was crammed, heated up by the Autumn Tiger temperatures and revolutionary fever, an acrid stench emanating from a hundred sweaty armpits. Surrounded by a mass of jaunty teenagers, we were no longer terrified and we told them all about those people in the luggage carriage and the mysterious cigarettes.

"I wonder what they are doing with those cigarettes?"

"Smuggling? Stolen goods?"

"We should report them to the authorities."

"Hongwei, don't be silly. Who are the authorities? We have smashed authority, haven't we? We, the Red Guards, are the authorities."

"And we cannot find these people, let alone stop them."

"You are right, our mission is to destroy the revisionists and reactionaries, and reinforce class struggle, not waste time on petty criminals," said Hongwei, her stern face framed by short-cropped hair. I stared at her in admiration, but she outstared me rather hostilely. I lowered my eyes.

"So, what are you two girls doing here? You are not Red Guards, are you?" Hongwei said.

"We'll do any revolutionary job you want. We have done propaganda, reciting Chairman Mao's quotations on buses. We just want go to places like you, to see the country," Hui said proudly.

"Oh yeah? Free sightseeing? I'm sure you don't have a train ticket. Exploiting the country? You aren't a Red Guard, you're not entitled to free travel. It's kind of stealing, you know."

"Hongwei, give us a break. How high do you want to sing now? G sharp?" said a boy's voice on the luggage shelves sarcastically.

"What do you mean?"

"Isn't that your speciality, singing your goody-goody tune? OK, I'm enjoying free sightseeing too, just travelling to visit places, I didn't buy any tickets. As a matter of fact, I don't have to pay for my accommodation and food either. You say it's stealing? And I didn't see you doing anything revolutionary."

"More than you did, I wrote reports, copied big posters, distributed leaflets, condemned our enemies, stirred up the local revolutionary masses wherever I went. I spread revolutionary spirit."

"Of course, you are the one and only, wow, a true revolutionary, apostle, most loyal ..."

"Are you being sarcastic? I'm sure you don't want to be accused of obstructing the Cultural Revolution, do you? There is a right and a wrong, you need to decide where to stand ..."

As her voice became increasingly intense, more Red Guards joined the squabble while others tried to placate with little success, and the hostility continued to fester. Hui and I watched and listened, totally engrossed in their heated exchange, as if we were watching a play. I was fascinated by the way they talked, so passionate, so sure, yet completely fulminating with rage. They spoke as if in a different language, using much longer sentences and plenty of complicated words I had never heard before, such as 'bourgeois', 'sanctuary', 'sacred place', 'kleptocrats', 'audacious rebels'. Their bursts of exuberance and energy never seemed to subside, as if they were about to set fire to the world. It overwhelmed me.

I was intrigued by a group of four girls who seemed a bit out of place in this raucous discourse. Unlike the others, they seemed discreet, taciturn and uninterested, though from time to time they whispered into each other's ears. Were they just shy? The tallest girl of the four was pretty while the smallest one looked so skinny and young, not much older than us. They didn't have Red Guard uniforms although they all had the green army caps.

"Hey, you two girls, do you want to sit by the window for a while?" said a boy. He must have felt sorry for us being so completely out of our depth, and, although amazed by his generosity, we accepted the offer with alacrity. He introduced himself as Pingan from Dalian. Sitting by the window, we gazed in rapture as verdant hillsides, valleys and forests flew past; we waved at horse carts or cyclists on the road in the hope they would wave back. I had to refrain myself from shouting and screaming. It was bliss.

With daylight fading, the coach became more sedate. A skinny boy was sleeping in his self-made hammock, dangling underneath the luggage rack. I was amazed at his ingenuity. The luggage shelves and space beneath the benches was all taken up in every direction. Still, I could just find a space for my feet, and reposing on those around me, I dozed off in the fug.

We were woken by the crackling noise from a loudspeaker; a woman was announcing the time for the Morning Consultation, a ceremony requesting Chairman Mao's guidance for the day. Most passengers, if they could, stood up, clutching their little red books to their chests as the woman enunciated clearly from the loudspeaker: "Comrades, first, let us wish, from our deepest hearts, Chairman Mao, the red of the reddest sun in our hearts, live for ten thousand years!"

"Live for ten thousand years!" the crowd echoed.

"Secondly, we wish His closest comrade and best friend Vice Chairman Lin, good health forever!"

"Good health forever Vice Chairman Lin!"

After three readings from Mao's book, the voices led by the speaker coalesced into a joyous chorus. The invigorated Red Guard body moved as one to the music, and if there had been space, a full-scale Red Guard loyalty dance would have been performed, like in the street parades; but it was so cramped no one could brandish their arms, let alone kick their legs in the air. Much to our amusement, the worship kept us entertained for nearly an hour.

After the Morning Consultation and when the passengers had calmed down, I plucked up the courage to chat to one from the small group of quiet girls. She hesitated, and before she could respond, a boy next to her butted in: "She is called Feng – phoenix. Don't hassle her, she is Black Five, all of them are."

It was now clear to me why those four girls clumped together like a rejected group. Feng smiled at me faintly and didn't seem to be upset at all.

"Her mother worked as a cleaner in the teaching college. She was arrested and publicly humiliated, and later was convicted of being a counter-revolutionary because she threw away a copy of a Chairman Mao pamphlet by accident."

"The sad thing was that Feng's father was the first to condemn her mother."

I couldn't believe they said that in front of her. I would have punched the boy's face, yet Feng just hung her head and veiled her emotions. She must have been through a lot worse than this. I felt guilty that I had been a pest, and brought her misery.

The two groups of Red Guards on the left side were deep in conversation. Each group, the boys from Beijing No. 8 Middle School and the girls from Beijing Teaching

College, was trying to impress the other. The boys were gloating about how they had raided Ma Lianliang's home.

"Who?"

"Ma Lianliang. Don't you know who he is? Where have you been all these years?"

"Spare her!"

"He is a superstar, the most famous Peking Opera singer in the world – ha, really just China – who used to perform for the Politburo Standing Committee leaders."

"Haven't you heard the story? He volunteered to go to Korea to entertain the People's Liberation Army during the war. It was a great success; the army loved him. After he got back, Ma sent a four million yuan invoice to the Communist Party and it upset Chairman Mao, so he was one of the first targets of the Cultural Revolution."

"My parents were fans; they used to follow him and his shows around. They never missed a single one even if they had to queue overnight. I felt bad when I went with the Red Guards from our school to raid his home, though I was curious. I know, I know you don't like it, but he was supposed to be a counter-revolutionary."

"We went for evidence and a hoard of money, gold or gemstones, but only found rooms full of junk; old books, piles of yellow papers, paintings. It all went in a fire, Ma nearly threw himself into the fire with them. I didn't understand it, not at all. He was badly beaten of course. Everything that was removable was thrown out and we smashed anything we could find: old pots, vases, blue china, jade figures, ugly old furniture and dirty paintings."

The narrator, aiming to impress, continued in an increasingly florid style: "This guy from another school had found a jade figurine; he was staring at it, stroking and admiring it, when his face so pleasingly sweet suddenly changed to wrathfully bitter. In an outburst of anger he hurled it through the window as if it had just bitten his hand. The bedroom was overflowing with girls, the sound of smashing all around; the room became filled with a luscious aroma and I heard this shrill cry: 'I wanted that!' One girl was jumping on the huge bed as if it was a trampoline, while another one was posing in front of a mirror in a carmine taffeta dress; two other girls were fighting for a hat with an ornamental bird plume, and there was another one in the corner spraying perfume on herself."

"One of the students rescued a bottle of Maotai just before it went into the fire. He took a swig and his face went crimson red as if he was about to choke to death, so we all had to try it, and the bottle got passed around. None of us had had alcohol before, so you can imagine. It was all rather fun though," the boy continued. "Yes, you might have guessed, we didn't find any gold or valuables and we couldn't find anything that would incriminate him either. After we had emptied his house and nearly everyone had left, I found him hiding in the toilet. I felt very bad for what we had done. His clothes were torn and blood was all over his face. I carried him to bed and covered him with a curtain. It was a pretty harrowing scene. When I told him my parents loved his show, his face became drenched with tears. I'd never seen such a renowned mighty hunk crying like a baby before."

Hongwei's idiosyncratic, high-pitched voice stirred the moment of silence. "To be cruel is to be good. He needed to be taught a lesson. Good to destroy his arrogance and pompousness. He will never learn, otherwise, to respect and serve the common people. Our school took part in cleaning our streets. The residents' association gave us the black list and we went through it one house after another. Of course we beat the hell out of those baddies, old bankers, factory owners, rich intellectuals. Our boys chased a rogue who was resisting reform. It took so long to catch him that they smashed his head in anger and frustration."

"Did he die?"

"I think so, there was blood everywhere and the body was just left in the street."

"How utterly appalling!"

"Is it?"

"Does it have to be so cruel? There must be some other way."

These words left me feeling mortified, reminding me of last Monday, when we had gone to the market. On the way home, we saw a woman walking stealthily, dodging around to avoid the pedestrians, with a scarf covering her head, barefoot and holding a pair of high-heeled shoes with the heels chopped off. It was obvious that her hair had been shaved by Red Guards, perhaps because of her fancy curly hairstyle. We had chased after her, chanting: "Stinky tart, stinky tart …"

"Someone's passed out!"

It was a girl from Xian who had collapsed from heat exhaustion. Hongwei imperiously commanded the crowd to back off and water to be delivered. Water bottles flew overhead back and forth from the ends of the coach. We kept some but only sipped a little to avoid the trouble of having to go to the toilet. We poured most of it on our heads. It was truly delightful to wash the sweat away with a burst of cool freshness. The sick girl was carried out of the train and her group left with her at the next station. Everyone in the coach joined in to help, generating a real spirit of camaraderie.

The train moved on.

The scenery outside changed leisurely as the dawdling train proceeded, but before long the train halted altogether. We looked out to investigate. It was quiet outside, no sign of platforms, buildings or any human existence, only steaming rocks and bare land. Half an hour later, the train still hadn't moved. I felt drowsy, feeling like mould would soon grow on me.

"What's going on? Why aren't we going anywhere?" Pingan grumbled agitatedly and continued, "I'm going to find out."

"Are you crazy? If the train leaves you'll be left behind and never find your way back. Wait a bit more. Remember, patience is virtuous."

"It's too hot, not enough air!" someone complained.

"Where are we anyway?"

"No idea. It's been nearly three days and we are still nowhere near Nanjing. It will be next year before we get to Shanghai."

"Oh, look, they have got out of the train. Let's go."

A huge herd of teenagers had already scattered outside; some vanished behind bushes and rocks to relieve themselves, some took the opportunity to stretch out on a flat piece of ground or rocks if they could find them. The area was strewn with motionless bodies like a scene from a battlefield. I was stunned by how all these people could have come from just one train.

Before long a pall of dark clouds obscured the sun and rain began to pelt down. The boys pranced along the train, shouting jauntily as if they were being baptised. By the afternoon, the rain had stopped and the setting sun touching the tips of the hill tops in the distance, painted half the sky scarlet.

As the train finally got back under way its passengers were thoroughly re-energised. In thrall to the spirit of revolution, differences of colour, background, personality and ideology were all set aside. The Red Guards were united and banded together with one voice, even the quiet ones. Slogans and Mao's quotations were shouted out, led by Hongwei: "We are Chairman Mao's Red Guards, we have missions to accomplish. We must live up to the great expectations that our greatest leader Chairman Mao entrusts upon us. The future of China has landed on our shoulders; we are now revolutionary torch bearers and it is our duty to light the revolution's flames and to struggle for victory …" Hongwei's oratory accentuated her already striking demeanour as a true apostle of Maoism.

Together they sang:

We are Chairman Mao's Red Guards
Bearing revolutionary flames in our chests
Class struggle has forged our red hearts
With iron conviction and bright goals
We endeavour to overthrow.
With utter devotion to the party and our leader,
We are Chairman Mao's faithful Red Guards …

Hui and I grabbed the opportunity to have a good sleep in vacated seats while they stood up singing, until someone woke us up. The Red Guards had calmed down, turned their attention to us, and asked us why we wanted to travel. We gave out the standard sanctimonious excuses, such as joining the revolution, following Chairman Mao and so on. Hongwei barely concealed her thoughts behind her sour smile and the others looked at us and waited for the real answer.

"Actually, she lost a month's worth of coupons …" It was too late to stop Hui. To my surprise, they gave up interrogating us and spared any further embarrassment by starting to argue about the coupons. Everybody agreed the coupons were stupid. I learnt that the coupons were introduced after the start of the Cultural Revolution to cope with a standstill in the economy. So without the Cultural Revolution, I wouldn't have been so miserable at losing the coupons, but then I also wouldn't have been on this adventure!

"Your parents will be so worried," Feng said quietly.

"Our parents are all locked up, away from home." I covered my mouth as soon as I said it.

"Oh, the children of Black Fives as well?" Hongwei searched my face.

"Leave them alone, they're just kids. You wouldn't have dared to come by yourself if you were their age," Feng retorted, entirely out of character.

"My father was denounced too." A boy, who had never had anything to say, broke his silence. "I was at the school one day when I heard my father had been taken away. I rushed home and found no one was there, not even my mother. My friend sat me on a chair, asked me to lock the door and not let anyone in. An hour later, he came back along with four of our classmates and a placard saying: 'This house has been thoroughly cleaned and properties have been sequestered by the Red Guards from Beijing No. 8 Middle School'."

"Are you from No. 8 Middle School?" A girl on the table next door said.

"Yes."

"Are you Li Nan?"

"Yes, how do you know?"

"My brother talked about you. My brother is from No. 8 too."

"Who is your brother?"

"Lei Shan."

"I don't believe it. He saved my life and my home.

It was him. He came back and rescued me. His trick worked, as not a single Red Guard came to my home. And I didn't even know he had a sister, such …"

His face was full of emotions. I guessed he wanted to say " … such a beautiful sister."

Feng said it reminded her of her friend Aiying. After her mother was denounced, Feng became a child of Black Fives. She was bullied and excluded from all activities at school. Worst of all, her roommates refused to let her into their dormitory, swearing at her and pushing her out if she attempted to get in at bedtime. She didn't have anywhere to sleep. Aiying, a girl from her class, took Feng into her own dormitory and Feng shared Aiying's bunk-bed for three nights. But later Aiying was reprimanded by a Red Guard official for sympathising with a Black Five. Under pressure, Aiying could no longer provide Feng a refuge. Feng ended up sleeping on desks in the classroom.

"Lucky it was summer time, I didn't need much to eat and I had some meat coupons to sell on the black market," Feng said with a sad smile.

Hongwei sat next to us, mellowing a little, fiddling with her short shiny hair with its straight fringe. She told us her father was a colonel in the army, and illiterate. He wanted his daughter to be a teacher so she could teach him. I tried to imagine her as a teacher. Would she be a good one? She certainly appeared bossy. Before long, most of the boys near her were completely under her thrall. It was both amazing and interesting to see how she put herself into a leadership position, winning trivial arguments or suggesting inconsequential ideas that others couldn't care less about. Wouldn't it be ideal for her to be in a position of control, but in the name of helping? I always felt teachers bullying children was unfair.

Everyone was talking about their families, their fathers, their siblings and I could feel the incipient friendships growing. Pingan became particularly interested in Hongwei; his gaze never left her face, quite embarrassing! They decided to travel together in a large team and even Hongwei was happy to accept the four Black Five girls as long as her assumed position of leadership grew, though she seemed keen that this didn't mean any increase in her actual responsibilities.

"What the hell!" An explosive caterwauling howl roused the whole coach. I stood up and saw that a tall, plump boy in a white vest, two sets of tables and seats away from us, was shouting in a swelter of anger, the back of his head dripping with vomit. The horror of the stench hit my nose and people nearby masked their faces, creating an empty circle around the tall guy despite the crowding. He pulled down a short boy from the luggage rack like a sack, and the boy, landing horizontally on his back on the seat below, let out a piercing cry. The tall guy, with one hand, lifted the boy by his collar as if he were holding a cat, and clouted him with the other hand. The onlookers circled around.

"Stop! It's not his fault," pleaded Li Nan.

"The little shit was sick on me!"

"He can't help it, he is ill. Can't you see?"

"Crass, useless," he seethed between his teeth.

"Let me," Feng said, and pouring water on some newspaper started to wipe the tall guy's head and back. Some other girls joined in to help and cleaned the floor.

Suddenly a voice let out a piercing shriek: "Look, Chairman Mao's picture!" Hongwei was pointing at the crumpled newspaper in Feng's hand. "That's outrageous."

Feng jumped up in fright, her face as white as cold marble. A circle of eyes stared at her in silence.

"I … I didn't see it, honestly, I didn't …" Feng cried.

Those silent eyes believed her, yet were thankful for not being in trouble themselves.

"But still … It could be a crime of active counter-revolution," Hongwei insisted in her astringent manner. Feng dropped the paper in shock. Her eyes were full of tears and despair, begging for forgiveness. I looked at the lump of wet paper, just like normal rubbish, so I picked it up and threw it out of the window. Hongwei goggled at me angrily as if I had just thrown her catch back into the river.

"You, you …" Hongwei trembled, "you cannot do that, it's evidence."

Li Nan turned around, moved slowly towards Hongwei, pulled her out of the crowd and said, pointedly, "I see no evidence, no crime here, has anyone seen it? Anyone?"

No one answered.

That seemed to settle the trouble and more people joined in the cleaning up. When all was done, and everyone was just about to return to their seats, Hongwei moved herself into the centre of the circle: "Comrades, fellow Red Guards, well done everyone. This has manifested the true revolutionary spirit. We shall be more united in fulfilling our obligation and ultimate mission …"

"Taking credit for doing nothing …" said a little voice behind us.

After three more days' train journey we finally arrived at Nanjing, the capital city of a few dynasties. Hui and I were elated. We were even more excited about getting off the train than when we first boarded it. We wandered about the platform hand in hand, taking in everything that touched our eyes. Suddenly Hui stopped me, and I saw her mouth opened and eyes focused straight in front us. He, the man in the black hat, was standing by a train door, smiling. A moment later, a Red Guard girl, not much taller than me, ran towards him. They looked like long lost father and daughter. I was certain they would have hugged if they had not been in public. She touched him and he ruffled her hair. He took off her backpack and they walked side by side to the exit.

"It cannot be," Hui said next to me, as astounded as I was.

"Yes, it's him, I won't forget his face," I said.

"I don't understand."

"Me neither."

"He got on the train just to go to meet her? Maybe he wasn't bad at all?"

"Maybe he just wanted to send us home out of kindness?"

Hui and I were trailing behind 'our' team after we had left the platform, hoping to be accepted. While waiting at the reception centre of Nanjing Railway Station, Feng put her army cap on my head and said: "It looks good on you. It's yours now." I didn't know what to say, wondering how she knew I would have given anything for that green cap. I wanted to hug her, but fear of embarrassment held me back.

To our astonishment, Hongwei then appeared waving two Red Guard armbands in front of us. In that moment I grew up. We had become real Red Guards. Like my sister Ke, they had faith; unlike Ke, they had accepted us. We were thrilled, proud, and couldn't wait to do our duty as Chairman Mao's Red Guards, with free bus passes, free meals and free accommodation of course. Although supposed to visit schools and universities, most of the time we visited tourist attractions; the Presidential Palace, Sun Yat-sen Mausoleum and Zhong Hua Gate. I wasn't disappointed. They were as beautiful as in their posters, as if they had been built just for pictures. Tourists came and went, but showed little interest in the history behind the sites. Hongwei was such a fervent Red Guard, insisting that we had not contributed enough to spreading revolution to the locals, that she had to write her own leaflets and distribute them.

"Go to buy a copy of *People's Daily*, be useful!" she yelled at me.

"You cannot buy the paper in shops, don't you know? It is all through subscription," Li Nan retorted.

"Go to find one in the school office then," Hongwei insisted irritably, "I cannot write without a newspaper."

With a copy of *People's Daily*, Hongwei quickly regurgitated the front page articles to create a leaflet entitled: 'To annihilate our enemy should they not yield', but it still wasn't enough for her.

The next day an open top truck, arranged by Hongwei, picked us up along with some local Red Guards. It was an important mission, we were told. We left the built-up area in the city on a tree-lined road, travelling many miles out, before the truck eventually veered off onto a dusty country track and stopped near a small hill covered with ancient pine trees. It was a picturesque and peaceful sightseeing spot I thought. Climbing up the hill we came upon a colourfully painted temple; inside several painted clay statues that we didn't recognise were enthroned on a large altar. As I was looking around for some clue to their identity, there was suddenly a terrible thud from outside and a deafening cheer. The massive temple placard had fallen to the ground outside. We ran out of the temple, getting out of the way just in time as the Red Guards went berserk. The statues of the temple gods were desecrated and then smashed into pieces.

"Why is everybody so angry?" I asked Hui.

"It's not anger, it's hate," the girl next to us said passionately. "The more we hate old thought the more we'll love Chairman Mao. That is 'show where you stand, articulate your love and hate', understood?"

"Do you mean like the factory owners or rich landowners …?" Hui said.

"Yes, like the Girl with White Hair," I butted in.

"Well, sort of," the girl replied, "but those are the hates we were taught as children. In the Cultural Revolution we must expand our hate to everything that caused such suffering. That's the Four Olds – old thought, old culture, old customs and old habits. We destroy the past to build the new future."

We nodded eagerly.

When everything that could be broken, was, the temple was set on fire. A pall of black smoke rose above us, as raging flames danced to heaven and the temple turned into dust. After the initial shock, the destruction somehow felt so satisfying, liberating. We were elated. The locals were gathering around the perimeter, looking gloomy and despondent. I heard someone murmuring behind me: "The devil, the devil has returned." A stab of guilt punctured my euphoria. The Girl with White Hair had been taken as a slave by a rich landowner when her father couldn't pay his debts. Raped, made pregnant and then cast out, she had taken sanctuary in a temple, living on the offerings, and her hair had turned all white. But hadn't we just burned her sanctuary?

That night Pingan and Hongwei announced that they would go travelling separately from the team. Unfortunately from then on the team began to fall apart. Hui and I decided to follow the Black Five girls heading towards Shanghai.

After we boarded the train to Shanghai, Hui was soon asleep. I felt tired but was too uncomfortable to sleep. I, with my eyes closed, was soon engrossed in a peculiar conversation from a group of local Red Guards sitting with us. Were they actually talking about the future?

"I think the best job is a shop assistant, as they get to distribute the meat, sugar, flour to their contacts before they even reach the public counter," a girl was saying.

"No good if they are ill."

"Well, they can trade with the doctor to get treatment."

Shouldn't we all be the successors of the revolution and do whatever the party demanded? I puzzled to myself.

The conversation was heating up and the boys started to take part: "A driver, I want to be a driver. I can get anything by trading with driving. No one has a car or truck. They will come to me and give me meat, sugar, food, clothes, whatever I want."

You want, just you want, how selfish … I stared at the speaker reproachfully.

"Steering wheel, stethoscope and shop scales are the most envious occupations now."

"What about being a revolutionary?"

"Revolution doesn't fill up your stomach."

That's true, isn't it? I said to myself.

"Yes, it does. Didn't you hear about that doctor who was kidnapped and forced to treat a patient?"

"You mean a revolutionary can rob, steal, intimidate?"

"Isn't that what revolution is all about? Violent redistribution of wealth?"

"If there was no wealth, there would be nothing to redistribute."

"Why does everything have to be about food and material things. What about cleansing our thoughts, purifying our souls and truly devoting ourselves to our greatest leader Chairman Mao?"

"Without food, you won't exist for long."

"I'd rather die for Chairman Mao."

After several minutes of eerie silence I peeped through my half-shut eyes, catching scenes of loss, confusion, sorrow and despondency. I woke up when the train stopped moving. The day was just breaking. I missed home.

That night at our allocated accommodation, I refused to wake up when I was shaken ruthlessly. The crashing of falling window glass sat me up. It was dark, Hui grabbed my hand and we ran following the other students through a soundscape of chaos. Hiding behind a toilet wall, we could hear shouting, screaming, crying, cursing and smashing. We were utterly disorientated. We huddled together in our hiding place, fitfully sleeping until daybreak.

When we saw our host in the morning, he explained that the events of last night were just one of those retaliation assaults from a neighbouring school. "Why?" I asked, but I didn't pursue it in the face of the icy stares; as if I was such an idiot to ask a sensible question in a nonsensical time.

On that day, in a searing terror, I discovered that lice had colonised my jumper. In the boiler room, I ran boiling water through my sweater and watched as the water flowed out like blood. For the first time in my life

I had lice. It frightened me and crushed my spirit. I told Hui I wanted to go home, but Hui said we had to go to Beijing first, we were Red Guards now and expected to go to Beijing to pay homage to Chairman Mao. It was what everyone lived for.

As Feng decided to go further down south with the boys, we had to part from our foster family and caught the train to Beijing by ourselves. We didn't have any trouble getting onto the train this time. The whole country had become orderless by now; Red Guards were ubiquitous and heading in all directions at once, frantically, like headless chickens. The railway system was utterly chaotic. Normal transportation was paralysed and all available trains, even freight trains, were dedicated to the shifting of Red Guards. There were no ticket inspectors or uniformed staff present at the train station. The platforms were in turmoil, like a street market, with a handful of food trolleys surrounded by a mob. It was one hell of a battle just to grab some bread and water. We were so completely exhausted, we couldn't enjoy the train journey.

Carried by waves of Red Guards at Beijing Central Railway Station, we found accommodation at a reception centre and two bowlfuls of tepid porridge at a food stall. Still, it was delicious. The middle school, close to Wang Fu Jing Road, that we stayed at was a small, messy place, completely unlike my school back home. All the classrooms were occupied by the Red Guards who had travelled hundreds of miles to Beijing to see Chairman Mao. Our room was dark and damp, the ceiling was low and had only two windows. The detritus from previous residents and a foul smell made the place seem like a refugee camp. The food came on time though. With a full stomach, we could endure any hardship. The following day, the army people came to train us, ten hours a day, marching in a square formation up and down on the school sports ground under the red sun. Hui said it was payment for the food and lodging. We agreed the revolution wasn't nearly as exciting as it was made out to be, rather as dull as our school assembly.

Eventually 12th November 1966, the day that everyone had come for, finally arrived. A torrent of Red Guards surged to Tian An Men Square. We did not, however, parade across the square, passing Mao on the Tian An Men tower. There was simply no room. Instead, we all lined up and waited by the street chanting slogans and singing loyal songs. The square was carpeted by an uncountable mass of eager Red Guards under the sunless, grey skies. Twelve hours we waited, for twenty seconds: that was all it took for His convertible to drive past. A haggard, emblematic statue of an old man, hardly recognisable from those smooth baby-skin portraits we always saw, turning occasionally towards the crowd. I was pushed forwards then back, surrounded by tearful faces, in a forest of arms sprouting little red books, amid the roar of a human sea. For some reason I stood there motionlessly, for a moment, my arm dropped down, my mouth closed. One army soldier came over and said: "What's wrong?"

I startled and lifted my hand to wave the little red

book and shouted: "Long live Chairman Mao! Long live Chairman Mao … "

Like the others, it was impossible not to do it.

What could I have hoped for, from that twenty seconds? Why wasn't I excited, shouting and crying like millions of others?

After the Tian An Men Square event, Hui fell ill. For two days I nursed her day and night; I missed Feng badly as she would know what to do. When Hui got better, we agreed it was time to go home. I bought a box of preserved fruit, a local speciality, at Beijing Central Railway Station with my last yuan, before we were homeward bound.

It was the afternoon of a grey sultry Sunday. I knocked on the door and held the fruit box to my chest. The door opened. Mama looked at me as if she didn't know who I was at that moment. I proffered up the box and said timidly: "Mama, I have lice, lots of them."

Mama broke her silence: "Take all your clothes off and leave them outside before you come in."

Po Xie

(lit.) broken shoes
(colloq.) slut

Jianping was sipping green tea from a jam jar, alone in the office, while staring at the empty yard. So far three scheduled deliveries had failed to turn up. For three months he had been unable to organise his team of five to operate the machines that compress coal dust into honeycomb briquettes. He was worried that there would not be enough coal for the winter and not happy to see the shed full of rubbish rather than a neat array of black briquettes.

He was a believer in honest living – you did your work and you got paid. It was obvious that if no one worked everyone would be starving. The others argued the revolution is everyone's duty, more important. Is it? He disagreed. He thought the revolution should be the cadres' job, they got paid to do it, to fight over power, to get rid of their opponents and to build their little empires. Why should we get sucked into their power struggles? He thought it was silly for those Red Guards to jump up and down, day and night, shouting to destroy those whom they didn't know anything about. Things were getting out of hand more and more. Last week, No.

2 High School Red Guards had tied a petrol can to a teacher and lit it. The teacher burnt like a torch. Then that was it, no one came to work any more in the name of taking part in revolution; like a state-organised strike.

Jianping didn't like the empty office. He wished at least one of the three women would be in the office, but what can you say? Ai preferred to play with her three children at home, Bei had a baby to look after and Dai would rather stay at home serving her husband than come to work. He felt piqued with jealousy. 'How can I make Lili homebound like them?' he thought.

Peng's office next door had been ransacked by fervent Red Guards, searching for incriminating evidence. Peng, the party secretary, was condemned, dragged in parade several times, and his home raided and possessions sequestered by the rebels led by Wei Dong, one of Jianping's workmen. Peng, despite his occasional sanctimonious and supercilious talk, was not a bad person. Jianping didn't at all like the way Peng had been treated. On the other hand, he had to admit to a hint of schadenfreude.

Jianping was grateful that his father's misfortune had turned out to be his good fortune. Before the first revolution, Jianping's father had inherited a small farm with over fifty acres of prime land from his grandfather and he made a good living by growing grain. The largest landowner in the area, Mr Hai, coveted his fifty acres of land and cajoled him into borrowing money to invest in textiles. When Mr Hai foreclosed on the loan prematurely, Jianping's father lost everything. After the liberation in 1949, Mr Hai was executed for being rich and nasty. Jianping's father became the head of the village and Jianping went to college and was able to have a job in the city.

Jianping was especially glad that his father's misfortune had accorded red status to him. Whatever happened, even if the whole world turned upside down, he was pure red and could never be wrong, unlike two of the people in his work unit who were branded as Black Five.

Suddenly he remembered the night, some of Lili's comments, such as wooden head, and useless. She had not been like that when they got married three years ago. Yes, the marriage did happen a little too fast, three months after the meeting arranged by the matchmaker. She was a high school graduate, tall and beautiful and she wanted to live in the city. So the marriage suited both of them: Jianping had a beautiful wife and Lili had a Huko, a city residence permit.

A group of people with red armbands appeared in the yard. He went out of the office to greet them.

"Is there anything the matter?" Jianping didn't expect any customers.

"Clean up the Black Fives," a middle-aged woman answered.

"We've finished it. We have two: Peng, the manager, whose nephew was an officer in the Guomindang army and Lu Dan, the accountant, whose father was a factory owner."

"We know, we know. We are looking for Zhao Jianping."

"That's me. Anything wrong?" Jianping was slightly alarmed.

"Don't worry. We would like your support."

"What support?" He relaxed a little, and responded with a suspicious glance.

"It's about your wife."

"My wife? Oh, she is red, her parents were poor peasants for many generations. I can swear that and …"

"Not about that."

"Oh, she is a good worker, always on time and actively taking part in the Cultural Revolution." Jianping was doing all he could to protect his wife. He knew the consequences if one fell on the wrong side of the rebels. The woman quelled him with a look.

"What about her moral behaviour?"

"How do you mean?"

"Your Residents Association Committee sent us a report, that your wife misbehaved."

"I don't understand. Must be a mistake."

"Is your wife's name Zhang Lili?"

"Yes?"

"Does she sleep with other men rather than you?"

Jianping thought it was absurd of her to ask a question like that.

"Can you confirm their claim?" the woman said.

Jianping's face was taut with knots.

"OK, call me at this number if you want to talk. My name is Miao." The woman handed a piece of paper to him.

So that was what it was all about, Jianping thought. Back in his office he started brooding.

'The first year of our marriage was good. The house was in good order and food was on the table when I got home. She learnt how to speak in a city way. I was planning to have kids. Then things changed after I found her that job in the shopping centre. She had new haircuts, new clothes and even painted her face. She said it was for work. I'm not that stupid. Gradually she came home later and later. She made it my fault that she flirted around. She was so arrogant when we argued.'

'She is my wife, I have a duty to protect her and I love her. I want her to be close to me but I don't know what to do. I can't stop her seeing other men. Why can't I just wave my fists at those men, threaten to break their legs and shout at them to piss off. I'm not really a man, am I?' Jianping held his head in his hands and started sobbing. He was torn between confirming and denying his wife's conduct.

The clock struck, it was lunch break. Jianping locked the office and walked towards home. It was a twenty-minute walk, which is why he usually just got salad noodles from the neighbouring canteen. Especially in this heat, he'd rather have his siesta at work than walk in the scorching sun. The street was empty except for leaflets, torn newspapers or posters dancing about, the air rippling as if it were alive. Halfway there, the oppressive heat made him regret, "Damn woman!" he growled through his teeth. Even rebels and Red Guards wouldn't come out into the noonday sun.

He was dripping by the time he approached home. He shambled along his lane, where a couple of heads popped out furtively. He had never liked the Residents Association, a bunch of nuisance housewives, snooping on others. It was none of their business really. But he was slightly thankful as he would never have been able to confirm his suspicions.

The door was locked and he was angry. He didn't unlock the door but went straight to his wife's shop, a five-minute walk away.

"She has gone home for lunch," the girl at the counter informed him.

"Thanks, I'll just go home," he said cheerfully, but he was really furious. He didn't want to sit in his empty home, being angry, so he returned to his office.

The office was like a sauna, so no one came to work in the afternoon. Jianping sat by his desk, panting and brooding over his anger, thinking what he could do. He couldn't send her back to the country, because she would kick up a big fuss which he would do anything to avoid. It took him a while to calm himself down. In the end he fumbled in his pocket and found Miao's telephone number. He picked up the phone and put it down without dialling. He stood up and sat down again. Then he took off his T-shirt, went out and poured a bucket full of water on his head. He felt better, not so much aflame. He turned on the radio, and started humming to the tune of 'The Story of the Red Lantern'. Then the news came on. There were announcements one after another and the names of those who were proscribed and expelled from the Party were read out. Jianping felt totally disconnected; he didn't care who was in power and who was not. At the moment he was troubled by his wife.

By the time the sun went down, he was a lot calmer and more confident. He decided to go to the shop around the corner to get something nice for his wife. He had determined to sort out the problem between them that night.

Next morning Jianping arrived at the office while the cleaner, Hua, was dusting his desk.

"Morning."

"Morning."

"You are the only one again?"

"Eh?"

"Are you all right? You look … ill."

He stared at her thinking: why can't my wife be considerate and caring like her?

"What's the matter? Do you need to see a doctor?"

"No, no, I'm OK, just didn't sleep."

"Why didn't you sleep? Anything the matter? Go home like everyone else, sleep. Go on …"

"I'm OK. Leave me alone." He was beginning to lose his patience.

"Shall I make you a cup of tea? Tea will calm you down and keep you cool as well … Tell me what's the problem."

He didn't answer, his eyes fixed on Hua perplexedly as if he'd never seen the woman before. Hua stopped talking and left the office as quickly as she could.

He was all alone again and glad he was alone. After a night of heated fighting, he was exhausted. The words, those piercing words, he couldn't believe came from her. Everything I have done for her, and all I got was "Worthless, moron, none of your business, gruesome, toilet brick – foul and hard."

He held his head and knocked it hard on the table. He should not have married a beautiful and clever woman. The biggest mistake. The stupidest thing …

There was a knock on the door. He stood up and went out to answer the customer's delivery question. When he returned, he saw the piece of paper Miao had left.

"Hello, can I speak to Comrade Miao please? In a meeting?" he said, frowning.

"My name is Zhao Jianping. OK, I'll wait." He dropped his jaw and twiddled his fingers.

"Oh hello, Comrade Miao, yes, my wife, … you came yesterday? Yes, she needs help, some lessons maybe?" He had an attentive expression on his face.

"What? You are too busy?" He drummed his fingers on the table.

"What about next week?"

"Could you let me know when? I can take you to her. Thanks. Bye."

He opened the door to let the breeze in and felt relieved and satisfied that he had found a way to solve his problems. He was much happier and even the heat was more bearable.

The once a week study afternoon went past without trouble. Chairman Mao's red book was read and discussed, then newspaper front page articles were also studied. Jianping knew how important these study sessions were as they set the tone of what he should say and do. One word wrong could land you in jail. On the other hand, he found the sessions boring and pointless. Those phrases, slogans and jargon were meaningless and a waste of time. Being so red, he was in no danger of becoming an enemy of the people. The only good part of the study session was to catch up with the news and gossip afterwards: the bus services had stopped completely on Wednesday and Friday; Lao Wang had been deported to his home village in the country; Fang's uncle came to visit from Beijing and said railway stations were packed with Red Guards who swamped the city; Wei Dong had moved into Number 8 Tower. He was now leading the Workers' Propaganda Team who had taken over the Central Provincial Bureau.

To them this was certainly the most shocking news since the Cultural Revolution had started. The grandiose Number 8 Tower, guarded by armed soldiers, surrounded by high walls and entered by cars only, aroused vigorous speculation.

Does it mean he's running the Bureau? Jianping thought – unimaginable! Three months ago he was shovelling coal dust, and not even good at it.

He was in a good mood and even the absence of his wife at home did not mar his mood. That night he had a nice dream that his wife hugged him passionately in bed and asked for his forgiveness. In the morning he began to doubt if he was doing the right thing. By the end of the day, he phoned Comrade Miao.

"When will she be back? Can she call me? It's urgent! Yes, yes. Thanks."

The next morning he was late to work. He was surprised when he saw a group of well-armed rebels waiting by the gate. What business did they have at a small coal distribution station? But when he saw Comrade Miao, he panicked.

"I called you yesterday to cancel it. I can confirm my wife is faithful."

"What? Do you want to mess the revolutionary rebels about? How many lives do you think you have? Hurry up," Miao said in a peremptory tone of voice. Two rebels pushed him forwards. He stopped resisting as he knew what the rebels were capable of.

On the way to his home, for the first time in his life, he wished his wife was not at home. It was such a relief when he saw the padlock on the door.

But they found Lili at her work. They dragged her out of the shop and hung a sign and a pair of broken shoes on her neck. "Po Xie" was hastily inscribed in large red characters on the heavy wooden board. She resisted in vain. Salvos of belts and cudgels showered on her. A throng was gathering, some jeering, some watching. Some simply shook their heads and left.

"Down with the whore!" Miao screeched.

"Down with the Black Five!" the throng echoed.

Lili screamed and fell when she was hit by a brick on her head. Jianping could no longer keep still and jumped in front of Lili to protect her.

"Comrades, she's not a whore! She's a proletarian like you!" Jianping shouted.

But the beating continued. Even though he was

terrified, anger overcame the fear. He went berserk, clasped the arm of a rebel in action and seized his cudgel. But he was outnumbered and his wife was still under attack. His contorted face aimed towards Miao, the leader of the rebels, and pleaded, "Stop them now."

"Who do you think you are?" Miao sneered, and beckoned for others to continue.

The mixed fury, regret, embarrassment reacted like a chemical explosion; he charged at Miao with the cudgel in his hand and aimed at her back. The rebels abandoned Lili and seized Jianping.

*

He was held captive for several weeks with other Black Fives until he was charged with assaulting revolutionary rebels and sentenced to be deported to his home village in the desolate countryside. He was transferred to a prison near the train station, ready to be deported the next day. The place was a disused warehouse, jammed with a few hundred Black Fives, and each had a dirty old shoe in their mouth to prevent them speaking. Dropping the shoe would trigger a beating by their jailers.

Jianping hadn't had any water for a day and a half, and he felt sick and exhausted. He missed and hated Lili. If it hadn't been for her, he would not be in this situation; even his red status couldn't save him from the diabolical Miao right now. It was a long night, children were crying, some people were moaning. He was indignant and depressed. They had no right to arrest him. The rebels were just a gang of thugs and they had no proof of anything. He had never had such longing to see Lili and to tell her that he loved her. He hoped that she would come to see him and say goodbye.

Miao was annoyed by the news that Jianping was to be deported. She resented it that he was being let off so lightly. A contusion on her arm had swollen and was throbbing; it exasperated her. "Bloody peasant, how dare he!" she growled, her slightly protruding teeth becoming more prominent. She was seething and pacing back and forth along the corridor. All of a sudden she stopped as if enlightened, returned to her desk and shouted at her telephone for half an hour. "Tonight!" a roar of triumphant rage echoed along the second floor corridor of the massive office building.

Lili had made up her mind to return to Jianping's village. Though her life's ambitions would consequently turn into dust, she was convinced this was what she must do to atone for her sin.

She sat between the half-packed boxes, staring at the grey sky through the tiny and translucent window. A thin piece of paper, its title printed in red "Death Certificate", wafted down from her hand. The bandages on her head were half undone, a long scar running the length of her left cheek was red and weeping. From her puffed eyes rivulets of tears dripped down her cheeks like rain down a cracked pane of glass.

An Autumn's Tale

Chongqing's autumn was swelteringly hot, especially that year, 1966, the year the flame of the Cultural Revolution had arrived.

Dawen was in front of the procession, hoisting a red banner with 'The Red Guard Fighter Team, No. 29 Middle School' stitched on in yellow. He was thrilled and extremely proud. Ten years of communist education had made him crave to be a hero, like the Gadfly, and had been an unremitting reminder that he had not been born in time for the liberation. Now he could hardly believe his luck to have this opportunity to be like his parents and those old communists whom he had learnt about from the plethora of didactic books of his childhood. Dawen had always adored the communist heroes, who had spilt their blood and lost their lives for the people, for the country, and for an ideal world. In equal measure his loathing of the class enemies portrayed in those same books was visceral.

His flushed and sweaty face bloomed with exhilaration; his tall, slender body bubbled with euphoria, despite him losing his voice, exhausted from chanting slogans. He led his troop, quickly immersing them into the flood of people arriving from all directions, singing and dancing their way towards

Chongqing People's Liberation Monument. A parade of decorated trucks slowly passed them. Abundant drummers, lavish red flags, banners and a Mao statue standing in the middle, filled the first float, followed by one decorated as a train, with painted cardboard and covered with slogans: 'Celebration of the Great Proletarian Cultural Revolution!', 'Follow our greatest leader Chairman Mao closely!', 'Long live Chairman Mao!' Next came a moving stage on which a group of girls in army uniforms were dancing to the beat of a military marching song. The crowd slowed down to watch, distracting Dawen from his mission. On his first glimpse of the moving stage, his attention was sidetracked by the sight of a familiar figure. He halted, almost mid-stride, as his eye followed the girl leading their phenomenal performance. It was her, Lingling, his classmate from primary school. He was certain of it. He handed the flag to his best friend Yang, and sped up to walk alongside the truck. He gazed at the girl, her every movement, her tall, voluptuous figure, as if she had just come out as a dazzling débutante, and compared this vision with his vivid memory.

*

It had been in a morning lesson in year four, that Dawen, dragged by the collar, was put next to a girl for having interrupted the teacher, to an outbreak of giggles. He was incensed at such an unfair punishment, which instantly made him a target for mockery and humiliation. To him, that day, the sun had stopped shining; the playground had stopped being an attraction; it was the end of his world. He blamed the girl, a skinny little thing with two silky long plaits and a pair of almond-shaped eyes. In revenge, he dubbed her 'Little Pigtails' from the well-worn idiom meaning to capitalise on somebody's vulnerable points, implying he would forever be picking on her. He congratulated himself on so subtly putting the girl in her place. After his anger died down, Dawen began to be intrigued by this new companion. His initial conclusion was: the difference between girls and boys was that girls had long hair. Wanting to test if there was a difference between long and short hair, he grasped his hair and pulled, while simultaneously stretching his arm behind the girl's back and tugging her plaits from the other side.

"Ow!" the girl squealed. He smiled.

Little Pigtails turned around to look for the source of the pain. She scowled at him. Dawen quickly shook his head. After class, he was summoned to the form tutor's office and ordered to do the classroom chores. He cheerfully put up with this punishment, considering it was a fair price to pay for his experiment, yet Little Pigtails felt sorry for the trouble she had caused and was willing to make reparation.

The next day the girl brought Dawen a pencil with multicoloured stripes. Dawen pushed it away and drew a line on the desk with chalk, declaring it to be the 38th Parallel, the Korean War settlement featuring heavily in their curriculum at the time. The girl cried.

"What's the matter, Lingling?" the music teacher asked.

Lingling looked at Dawen but said nothing. From then on Dawen began to acknowledge her name. He even became grateful to that pedagogue who had punished him, although he still preferred to call her Little Pigtails. Lingling, on the other hand, would bring him cigarette wraps or marbles from home, and Dawen would stand up for her when the boys got too rough. Once, in the playground, the boys shoved Dawen at Lingling and her girl group, chanting "Married! Married!" Lingling couldn't lift her head up in the classroom afterwards, but Dawen didn't mind.

It all came to an end in year 6, on the final day of primary school. She did well at the secondary entrance exams and gained a place at an elite school, while he didn't rise above the bottom tier.

*

Dawen stirred suddenly from his daydream as the mobile pomp came to a halt at the monument. The streets around were bubbling with life, gushing to the convocation in the square that had already overflowed with an ebullient crowd. Dawen searched around only to find that his troop had been swallowed by the throng.

"Hello, is that you?" a gleeful voice said from behind. Dawen turned to face her, astounded at how Lingling had grown and how sophisticated she had become.

"Oh, hello …" He sounded shy and embarrassed, his wits momentarily deserting him.

"It's so good to see you, Dawen, after so many years," Lingling's voice tinkled.

"Yes, great. You look … When did you join the Red Guards?"

"Three days ago," she said proudly, like a long-awaiting and just accepted postulant. "And you? You must be a founder of the Red Guards for your school, having a father like yours. I remember when your father came to our school to give us a talk. He was a true hero. I didn't know you then."

Dawen listened and his eyes fixed on her warmly, searching for any trace of Little Pigtails, the shy and quiet girl in his memory.

"Do you know you were quite naughty in those days?" Lingling said.

"You girls were just a bunch of teacher's pets."

"You can talk. Remember? I didn't like killing those poor sparrows, and you said that when all the sparrows were killed we will walk into a communist utopia. I bet you were just copying the teacher."

"That's not a crime, is it?"

On the moving stage, a man began to harangue the high-spirited crowd with frenzied slogans.

"I'm so excited, aren't you?" She didn't wait for an answer and continued passionately. "I never believed I could join the revolutionary vanguard; I feel as if I am on top of the world and my life has suddenly become meaningful. The Cultural Revolution gives me a sense of purpose; I have sworn to endure any hardship and to sacrifice my life for the cause, like a heroine. I believe we can make history, don't you?" Lingling said solemnly.

"Of course I do. I'm seventeen years old this year and I have done so little with my life. Sometimes I feel …"

"What?"

"Hard to describe. Er …, I feel life just slipping through my fingers."

"Exactly," Lingling concurred.

Tentatively he invited her to his home. The girl flushed, so did the boy. They quickly returned to their conversation, but despite their reserved demeanour, they each felt an undeniable attraction emanating from the other. They went on as if nothing was happening around them. A call for Lingling from the truck broke through their tête-à-tête, and a boy in a Red Guard uniform, slim, with a pair of glasses squashed onto his broad nose, jumped down to interpose himself between them. The boy's small mouth and his interruption irked Dawen somewhat. Lingling warmly introduced Dawen to her Red Guard comrade Weiguo whom she was grateful to for helping her join the Red Guards. Dawen, however, was irritated by Weiguo's solicitude towards Lingling. He hurled back a suspicious look when he caught Weiguo's furtive glance.

After being reunited with his school Red Guards, Dawen was soon once again immersed in the thrilling crowd of buoyant teenagers. The monument was surrounded by red flags and placards of Mao's portrait; the air was impregnated with the euphoric and exhilarating sense of triumph. A loudspeaker blared in front of the stage, dispensing hyperbole and bombastic messages. The crowd cheered, the usual slogans were chanted and the patriotic songs and dances were performed. The square was like a carmine poppy field, hundreds of thousands of little red books blooming on stems of green arms. Dawen looked at this mighty ocean of people with awe.

The day after Lingling's visit to Dawen's home, they met again by the Jialing River. As twilight flowed up the plain, they zealously exchanged their news and views on the new revolution they were privileged to take part in. They ambled along the riverbank. The moon hung high above. The lights of the boats, suspended in mid-air, drew lines on the dark screen of the hills to the thumping cadence of engines and, showering on the surface of the water, dazzled and scintillated like a thousand fireflies.

They chatted away, exchanging friendly insults, the attraction between them intensifying through their conversations. Lingling found Dawen easy to talk to, about her family, the bickering with her little sister, and disputes with their annoying neighbours. She liked his charm, non-judgemental character, and his light-hearted sense of humour, but she also wanted Dawen to share her passion and love for Chairman Mao.

"Dawen, I can hardly express how proud I am to be a real communist successor, Chairman Mao's adherent and a revolutionary fighter. When I saw Chairman Mao on the Tian An Men Gate, at that moment I was trembling, every cell of my body was quivering, my tears fell like torrential rain. The girl next to me collapsed because of the excitement, and heat of course. When it was over, I rushed to wire the news to everyone. It felt like my life's ambition was fulfilled. Afterwards my mind had grown so vast and was filled with such passion and heroism. Who but us can save the world? We can set the old world on fire, burning hotter than the sun." Lingling paused. "What are you thinking?"

"I'm excited with pride too Lingling, but sometimes I feel … Things aren't always as they seem," Dawen replied.

"Why?"

Dawen paused a little and said, "Do you remember in year 5, when you had an argument with Tao, the head boy?"

"No? Did I?"

"It was about when the sun is closest to us during the day. Tao said it was closest in the morning and evening because it looks bigger, but you disagreed. You said it was at noon because it is warmer. The debate was intense, some supported you and some supported him. He almost hit you."

"Yes, I remember now. You protected me… I couldn't believe the argument went on for so long, even other forms joined in. It's so funny. How did you come up with that idea to break the deadlock?"

"It's easy. If Chairman Mao said the sun is closest to us at noon, it must be right."

"It worked beautifully."

"I wouldn't dare do it now, it would be a counter-revolutionary crime to fake Chairman Mao's quotation. What if Chairman Mao said the sun rises from the west? Will everyone agree?"

"Of course, it's obvious."

"That is why I am so lost. Chairman Mao often contradicts Himself …"

"Sh …" Lingling put her hand over Dawen's mouth. He quickly grasped it and drew her closer. She shivered but didn't withdraw. She gradually rested her head on his shoulder and let him wrap his arm around her waist, as if she suddenly realised that tenderness and touch were what she really craved. The noise of the riverboats faded out, the Jialing River had gone to sleep and the autumn moonlight turned the river into a metallic surface, seemingly indestructible yet so soft and fragile. As evening darkened, they sat down and the sound of water swishing at the grass bank soothed them.

On the Wednesday afternoon, Lingling felt restless as the four, long hours of compulsory reading of propaganda circulars and newspaper articles wore on. She hadn't seen Dawen yesterday, and she couldn't wait any longer. After a failed attempt to find him at his school, Lingling cycled to his home.

A group of Red Guards had clashed with the compound guards as Lingling arrived at the gate of No. 2 Peace Street. As she stood irresolute outside the gate Lingling saw Dawen.

"Come," he said gently, guiding her through the heated squabble. Dawen's face was sullen and pale, his eyes red with unshed tears. As they approached his house, Lingling's discomposure came back; she caught sight of the posters on the walls and banners hung between trees. A large ash pile was still smouldering outside; broken glass, china and pieces of figurines were strewn nearby. Lingling wondered if she had come to the wrong place; she had a hundred questions but she did not want to pry. She picked up a half-burnt book, 'A Collection of Tang Poems'.

"It was my book. Lingling, we cannot get inside at the moment," Dawen said apologetically by the door.

"That's all right."

"You saw the poster, they said my father was a traitor and a capitalist-roader, but he is not."

"I know. He is a revolutionary hero, he liberated the country … But who did this?"

"What about you ask your friend, Guo …"

"Weiguo? Are you sure?"

"They beat my father up and paraded him in the street."

Her eyes opened wide in shock.

"We were ordered to move out in three days," Dawen added.

"I'm so sorry."

"Did you hear teacher Lin in our primary school committed suicide? At least we are not as badly off as that," Dawen said.

Lingling looked at him with deepest sympathy but didn't know what to say to comfort him.

Lingling arrived at the riverbank before sunset. The Jialing River was abnormally quiet, with no sign of boats or ships except for one light ferry carrying city residents across the river. While the peace and tranquillity held obvious attractions as a meeting place for them, the privacy was important to Lingling, obscuring them from prying eyes, concealing her secret. She didn't want to tarnish her glorious revolutionary image: a completely committed Red Guard should be free from any personal desire or happiness. Weiguo had been troubling her with obvious signs of jealousy, but the more he disapproved the closer Lingling was drawn towards Dawen. She never mentioned Dawen to her mother, not wanting to be bombarded with advice, judgements, petty instructions and criticisms. She wished her mother was pure red, someone she could be proud of. Dawen was different however, even though he wasn't as devoted to Chairman Mao as she would like, yet he possessed a strange attraction that she couldn't put her finger on. She leaned on a lamppost and started reflecting on what had happened that day. Cleaning out the Four Olds and Black Fives in her school had been an easy task, but clashes with local residents, triggered by a minor contretemps on where to hang a poster, were upsetting. The fighting had got out of hand. Reinforcements from a neighbouring school had been called in, and by the time it had settled down again a dozen people had been injured with three sent to hospital. Just like Chairman Mao said: 'The enemy will not back down without fighting, like the dust will not vanish without sweeping,' Lingling thought.

"Sorry I'm late. Had to take my mother to hospital. I couldn't find a pedicab so I had to push her on my bike all the way. It's the revolution, even the pedicabs have vanished from the street," Dawen complained.

"But … What do you think is more important, the Cultural Revolution for the country or your mother?"

"Of course my mother," he retorted. She was surprised at his selfishness, shirking his duty and forgetting his faith and loyalty to Chairman Mao.

"In the middle of the Great Revolution, you only think about yourself …"

"And you."

They both went quiet. After a while Dawen said, "On my way here I saw a dead body lying on the pavement, no one even took any notice."

"I know some people have been killed, but maybe it's necessary. They must have been our implacable enemies."

"It doesn't look right, too brutal, unjust. Look at them, some Red Guards, all teeth and claws like wild animals. Such a big mess. No one knows what will happen from one day to the next. We hadn't heard anything from my father for three months, but one day he suddenly turned up on the doorstep and couldn't get in. I only found out later from a note he left for me. My mother is the same. She could be at home for weeks, but be away for months, or perhaps just a day, for various random struggle sessions or study groups. My little sister is too young to join the Red Guard and is like a lost lamb in the wild."

"Chairman Mao said: 'Uttermost disorder will lead to uttermost order.' That's the beauty of the revolution, it's filled with life inspiration. Isn't it also wonderful? Dawen, please cheer up, show your commitment and vigour. Be presumptuous and outspoken! I just want to destroy the old world and follow Chairman Mao's thought with you side by side. Just think about it, we used to listen to our teachers, every word they said, religiously; now they listen to us. We tell them off for depraving us with revisionist rubbish. We tell them how they should behave. Don't you think it is great?" She didn't wait for an answer: "Last year, a girl in my school was strangled by her father with her young pioneer scarf. Her father was a Guomindang agent. So you see the class enemy is everywhere! If we aren't alert and don't beat them, they will destroy us. Our greatest leader Chairman Mao said: 'If the east wind doesn't beat the west wind, the west wind will beat the east wind, there is no middle ground.'"

Dawen said nothing but listened, and sensed the gap growing between them, although he was more confused than he was in disagreement with her. They parted gloomily that day.

Winter and insurrection had stripped the city bare. Spring arrived nevertheless, though largely unremarked. School classes remained 'discontinued', the Red Guards were still rampaging about the city, smashing things and beating people up, believing they were doing good deeds for society. More and more factories shut down, offices were locked up, buses rarely ran, and shops remained unopened most of the time. People of various ages joined rebel groups, taking control of the town hall, police stations, public offices and strong strategic positions.

Nine o'clock morning sun poured into the dormitory one Monday. Dawen was still lying in his bunk bed, mulling over his new role as a member of the revolutionary committee at his school. Although elected in absentia, he was feeling good with himself.

"Get up!" Yang poked and rocked Dawen on the bunk bed above and shouted, "Press conference today! You have to be there."

He sat up like a jack in the box, grabbed the half-eaten bread out of Yang's hand, and went out in haste. The conference hall was packed already. No one wanted to miss the news and updates from the top, which directed everybody's minds and determined everybody's actions. One mistake could be devastating.

"The flour price will go up from 8.3 cents to 9.4 ... Chen Yi, Tan Zhenlin are denounced ... Deng Xiaoping exiled ... The Foreign Office is closed ... A soap coupon is introduced ... Chairman Mao said: 'The rebels have a right to arm and to defend themselves.' He calls for the Cultural Revolution to be carried out to the very end." Bulletins from the Central Cultural Revolution Group were read out, then the internal Party announcements, which was a privilege for the students. At the end of the announcements, the audience received the sombre news that Mr Lan, the committee member and deputy head, had committed suicide.

The hall was in shock. The silence was broken as some girls started sobbing, more joined in shouting and the room coalesced into a howl of pain and anger.

"He was pushed!" somebody shouted behind Dawen. He turned around and found a familiar face, partially hidden beneath a cap, that he couldn't quite place. The man was in his mid-thirties, and didn't quite fit into this teenage world. He could have been a cadre, a worker or even a teacher.

"I just don't believe it's suicide, it must be murder, cold-blooded murder by the Red Squad."

"Murder! Down with the murderers!"

"Murder! We want justice!"

It was incendiary and unstoppable. Like water released from a sluice, the Red Guards of No. 29 School rushed out into the street, blocking the road, halting the traffic and demanding justice in a lawless society.

In the weeks that followed a new, relatively moderate normality was established in the city, with much marching and occasional scraps between factions that did little to upset the equilibrium. Then Beijing Red Guards started to arrive in Chongqing, and with the overwhelming endorsement of both Mao and the Central Cultural Revolution Group, they set to work prodding and goading the local Red Guards and rebels into further violence; more officials were condemned, and the last vestige of the local authorities was obliterated. Rioting grew in strength day by day. Within a fortnight, rebel groups and Red Guards had raided and pillaged every corner of the city; the schools, government buildings, the news agency, radio stations and factories. The mood changed. The city centre was painted red with a profusion of Mao portraits and poster graffiti. Men harangued impromptu mobs on the streets with frenzied eloquence. Little red books were carried as amulets in public to avoid physical assault or imprisonment. The badges of Mao's head were a must-have to demonstrate conspicuous staunchness. A boy from Lingling's class pinned a badge onto his chest through the skin, he didn't even blink for all the pain and blood.

By now, the internal power struggles of the Central Communist Party instigated by Mao had spread to the whole of China, such that all sides were seeking and snatching local rebels' support. In no time, China was pushed to the brink of civil war; the only restraint to full, armed conflict was the sheer diversity of opposing factions. The uprisings and disorder whipped up by Mao, and meant only to weaken his opponents, had gone so badly wrong that even Mao himself had to admit: "China is so divided that it is like the eight hundred vassal states of the Zhou dynasty," and commented privately, "It's no good, the whole world is in chaos, I have no control of it." Should he have thought about this when he was spurring the rebels on?

Half a year on from the start of the Cultural Revolution in Chongqing, the Red Guards, the Picket of Workers, the citizens and other rebels constellated and fragmented into a plethora of rebel factions. No surprise that in the political vacuum they had created, the bickering over who was the most left and most loyal to Mao among the rebel factions soon culminated in egregious violence and brutal murders. Armed with locally produced weapons, the rebel factions acted like district warlords. In a surprise attack, one faction surrounded the city hall, took over the telephone exchange room and the press printing factory, without too much of a struggle. Each faction occupied and barricaded their school, college, factory or government unit as their base. Each had its own petty agenda and its own backing from the top, and therefore had their target to destroy. Sporadic fighting between rebel groups was reported, and tensions mounted over the following months. All factions declared they had the strongest backing from the Central Party and, most importantly, from Mao Himself. Aside from the fratricidal strife within the rebel factions, they went out to create their fuss in the streets, marauding through the city. Any home, shop or office could be smashed and anyone could be dragged out, beaten up and humiliated in public. Many times the root cause was merely a personal grudge or some trivial dispute.

Despite the surrounding turmoil, Dawen couldn't stop thinking about Lingling; her ravishing figure in the moonlight and the melodies in her speech were the only things that would offer him solace. One day, in the grip of his obsession, he abandoned the customary secrecy of their too infrequent meetings and went to look for her – he had to talk to her.

"She is busy," Weiguo said, stopping him at the school gate.

"I only need a minute," Dawen said with growing distrust.

"Actually she is not here." Weiguo stood firmly, goading like a picador.

"Actually I don't believe you," Dawen replied.

What really galled Weiguo was Dawen's hubris. His face went white and he lost his wit to retaliate.

"What are you doing here?" Lingling appeared at the gate, looking surprisingly mortified.

"You didn't turn up … at the riverbank," Dawen said.

"Something happened, I couldn't make it, sorry," Lingling said.

"Can we meet up … What are you doing?" Dawen protested. He felt a pair of hands clamp onto his shoulder and he was pushed so harshly that he struggled to regain his balance.

"It's all right, it's all right," Lingling implored and freed Dawen from Weiguo's grip.

"You cannot just turn up here, like we are dating," Lingling whispered.

"Are we not?"

"We are in the middle of a revolution."

"So?"

"It's embarrassing."

"All right, I'll go, but just promise me we'll meet at the riverbank on Wednesday evening."

Dawen returned to his school just in time to hear the diktat from the top: Mao had eventually curtailed His love of violence and ordered an end to the internecine strife between rebel factions around China. The announcement received an immediate cheer from the Red Guards of No. 29 Middle School and they dashed into the street to deliver the good news. The next day moderate and extreme rebels, Red Guards and Picket of Workers were called to join the biggest rebel unification rally in the city.

Dawen ardently marshalled his troops for the rally that was designed to bring all rebel factions together and form a grand coalition. Although he welcomed the new direction, and hoped that it would be the end of the brutality, he could not help but grumble: "One day they want chaos, another day they want to restore order. Make up your mind." He had serious misgivings as to whether the violence could be just turned on and off like a switch.

The rally was progressing in full swing, and Dawen had secured a place close to the stage for his troops, though tensions from deep-rooted mutual mistrust crackled in the air like static. A middle-aged man in a grey Mao suit who represented the coalition was giving a long-winded speech. From time to time he picked up a little red book and quoted from it. The audience were not impressed. Those quotations should have been memorised. When the names of the newly-formed coalition committee were being read out, the audience started hooting and booing. Then a handful of Red Guards, coming from nowhere, climbed onto the platform. One of them snatched the microphone from the speaker and yelled at it: "The Red Squad are the real revolutionary rebels, we don't take orders from the Picket of Workers!"

One part of the horde cheered, and started chanting "Red Squad! Red Squad!", and others jeered. Someone wrestled the microphone off the intruder and shouted, "The Revolutionary Headquarters are the best ..." But he was immediately attacked by copious fists and pulled off the stage. People punched, kicked and wrestled with each other on the stage. No side was prepared to yield to any other. More Red Guards jumped onto the stage, swarming over the new would-be speaker. One group had seized a committee member, an ex-official, on the stage and pinioned him to the ground. Others rushed to rescue the official, turning their bawling anger into hefty thwacks. The melee escalated and started to extend to the crowd off stage. The rally was becoming a maelstrom of mobs.

Dawen, watching anxiously, felt the arrival of the crucial moment. Every aspect of his temperament screamed hesitation, yet despite his character, he jostled his way forward and jumped onto the stage. Struggling through the melee he managed to grab the microphone: "Stop! Stop fighting! Chairman Mao taught us: 'We should have debate and should not turn violent.'"

"We want peace! We want peace!" he chanted. Suddenly the microphone was ripped out of his hands, while someone grabbed his hair from behind and pulled him off balance.

"Bollocks! Chairman Mao said: 'A revolution is not a dinner party or writing an article, not embroidering or painting a picture, not so refined, so leisurely, or gentle; revolution is an insurrection, one class overthrows another via violence.'"

Dawen had regained his balance and made towards the speaker who was yelling at the microphone: "'The act of violence against counter-revolution is the only route to success…'"

"We want violence! We want violence!"

His attention was suddenly seized by the sight of Lingling who was on the other side of the stage. As he turned, a fist landed on his eye, and he fell in a burst of light and pain as a shower of fists and feet thrashed across and into him. He managed to curl up and hold his head, before the noise suddenly cut off.

★

It had been almost a month since the violent strife at the rally. Sitting on the edge of his bed Dawen was riveted by a book called *The Thaw*, one of the many books he wasn't allowed to read, but no one was around to enforce this. The room was small and dingy. An old wedding photograph of his parents in Western style dress, which was now considered bourgeois, surviving from the Red Guards' ransack by virtue of being hidden in a pillow case, was displayed above the bed, like a substitute for Mao's portrait. For these few weeks, he had been resting, convalescing from his injuries in his refuge. His family had been allocated two adjacent rooms in the block, little more than a ramshackle shed, a single-storey row of rooms, each with a small window to the rear and a door to the front, next to a small covered cooking area, that faced communal taps. His bedroom doubled as the sitting room and dining room, while next door his parents' bedroom had been sub-divided by a cloth screen for his sister's bed. He finally had time to reflect and to educate himself. He had become engrossed in the story. Koroteev's falling in love with Natasha set him dreaming about Lingling, their enchanting evenings by the river, and singing songs together. But right now he felt lost, stumbling in the twilight. He bitterly regretted he had wasted so much time on messing about in the street as a Red Guard smashing people and things before his own home was pillaged. He was dismayed at his inability to read another person's mind, even more frightened by the possibility that though happiness could be right in front of you, one more step towards it would inevitably send you over the precipice. He went over the rally in his mind, his narrow escape, curling up on the ground, encircled by ferocious savages and showered with punches and kicks; his last vision had been of those twisted angry faces. He had wanted to cry out: "What have I done wrong? Why do you hate me so much?" but his words had had no voice in the tumultuous throng. He had never been so terrified for his life. If it hadn't been for Yang, his best friend at school and closest Red Guard comrade, who came to his rescue, he would not have been here at all. His melancholy train of thought brought Lingling to his mind again. What had happened to her at the rally? He hoped she was all right. He couldn't help but worry about her safety and wondered if she felt the same. In the end he decided to continue reading rather than dwell on it.

The tussle for power at the rally had led to a consolidation. The Chongqing rebels coalesced into two main camps led by the Red Squad and the Revolutionary Headquarters respectively. Dawen's school joined the latter, which was characterised as a moderate and conservative faction. The Red Squad, their opposition and backed by the Central Cultural Revolution Group, proclaimed the Revolutionary Headquarters as class enemies and reactionaries, and were therefore determined to destroy them completely. Should they not have had the local army's support, the Revolutionary Headquarters would have been wiped out entirely almost overnight. The stand-off between the two rival camps had turned Chongqing, the main weapons manufacturing base of China from the time of the Anti-Japanese War, into a tinderbox. Dawen relinquished his Red Guard leadership post and sequestered himself in his eight-square-metre room, his haven.

Yang dropped in one afternoon, passing on gloomy pieces of news. The Red Squad had raided the *Chongqing Daily* newspaper offices to retaliate at a newspaper article. They had clashed with the army unit on guard duty and injured several soldiers when disarming them of their weapons, so the army unit had fought back by opening fire on the mob, maiming several people. The next day the Red Squad snatched four corpses from the crematorium; two had died in traffic accidents and two of natural causes in the city hospital. They had taken to the streets, carrying the four corpses, clamorously claiming the 54th army was responsible for their deaths. Afterwards their exhibition of the four decomposing bodies in the city centre had aroused further rancour and venom, and several thousand Red Squad rebels had rampaged through the city, shouting "eye for an eye and a tooth for a tooth", hunting down the conservatives.

At the same time the Red Squad had raided the artillery factory, killing and injuring thirty-five members of the Picket of Workers. Dawen was aghast and grasped onto Yang till he assured him that Lingling's school was not involved in the fight. He felt a surge of relief as if he had just been dragged out of a dark abyss. Dawen pleaded with Yang not to expose himself to further danger and to stay at home.

"Do you remember, Yang, the Central Cultural Revolution Group's memorandum with Chairman Mao's quote: 'We must give the Leftists weapons'?" Dawen said passionately, "That is when all these bloody fights started, isn't it? Of course everyone claims to be a Leftist, so everyone should have weapons, guns, to kill."

"Yes, guns are frighteningly common nowadays. You can see children wandering around in the street with guns in their hands. Guns are everywhere, so scary. The day before yesterday, two housewives were shot dead in the street," said Yang.

"Housewives? Why?"

"Some Red Squad youths had just got guns and were excited to try them out. Those unlucky women were their target practice."

"That's outrageous!"

"Do you know who knocked you over at the rally? It was the guy with Lingling at the square."

"Yes I saw him just before he hit me. His name is Weiguo."

"Well, they joined the Red Squad, including Lingling. I saw he went to two primary schools, to organise the youngsters: printing leaflets, distributing them in the street, throwing rocks at the opposition – that sort of thing. Those little ones are agile, manoeuvrable, loud and dare to swear, the ideal troublemakers. They'll go round shouting 'arsehole' at anyone in the street, destroy posters, which would be a crime for adults, and interrupt the opposition's conferences. You cannot catch them. They are loyal and pliable, perfect foot soldiers. In return, the Red Squad gave them Little Red Guard status and free travel passes and the kids were over the moon. They run around the streets shouting "Kill, Kill, Kill!", all very naive and childish, but they do stuff that grown-ups couldn't. We have to get together and fight back."

"It can't go on like this, it's got to stop. I don't understand why Chairman Mao wants disorder and violence. Why do you have to get involved? Please stop going to the school, come here and we can play Go Chess."

"But listen to me, the Red Squad ambushed our peaceful march yesterday, they injured twelve people and took away twenty-five. Do you know they sometimes kill their prisoners? I've come to fetch you to school, we need you."

Dawen made no reply but glanced at the internal-distribution newspaper that Yang had brought.

"Look at this," Dawen said, "Chairman Mao said: 'The Cultural Revolution is the continuation of the struggle between Communist and Guomindang; we must celebrate this nationwide civil war.' I don't get it at all."

"Why? Isn't Chairman Mao supporting us in our fight against the class enemy?"

"He said Liu Shaoqi was the greatest leader in China last year, but now He decided Liu Shaoqi is the No. 1 class enemy."

"How could you question Chairman Mao?"

"I used to know the answer …"

"You shouldn't say that to anyone, even me."

"I know."

"You've got to come to school with me, because we were assigned to draft a pamphlet to condemn the Red Squad atrocity. You are the only pen we have. Please don't abandon us," Yang implored, but Dawen gave no reaction.

"You hate violence, right? Here is your opportunity to condemn it," Yang said.

Dawen rested his chin in his palm, contemplating. Towards the end of the day, they set off towards the school with Dawen sitting astride Yang's bike carry-frame at the back. The sun had set and the evening breeze had cooled the air. There was no traffic in the street, not even bicycles or pedestrians. The two close friends chatted amiably and enthusiastically as if they had not seen each other for years. At the T-junction, Dawen stopped Yang, "This is not the way to the school."

"But this is the safe way. The Red Squad barricaded the main road. If we go the other way we have to go through their territory and you never know what will happen if they catch us."

"Oh really? It's a two-kilometre longer trip though

and look at you," Dawen said, watching Yang mopping his forehead.

"What about taking the armband off and denying we belong to the Revolutionary Headquarters," Dawen added.

"You really don't know how bad it is out there, do you?"

"It's only five minutes ride, we'll make it quick."

"Fine," Yang said unwillingly.

Yang pedalled along the deserted streets, scattered with debris of bricks, wood, glass and torn posters. They passed the dilapidated shop fronts, post office, and shoe repair hut. Dawen spotted 'Man and Wife Sliced Lung', the famous restaurant where you always needed to queue to get in, but which was now empty. Along the street, a telegraph pole had been pulled down as part of a roadblock, cables and wires left dangling, smoke rising from the wreckage. The gates of the mighty police station were chained by a heavy black padlock, with a drift of newspapers and leaflets at the bottom of it. Dawen recognised the restaurant where he had once had a meal with his family as a youngster. He had been deprived of the crayfish he had wanted – he was 'too young'. He had resented that unfairness at the time, but now it seemed so trivial.

Yang slewed to avoid some rubble but quickly lost balance. Off the bike they walked quickly and silently in the dusk.

"Stop! Hands up!" a crisp voice shouted behind suddenly. It made them quiver. Dawen could feel a hard cold object pressed into his back.

"Put your hands up," Yang whispered.

They slowly turned around to see three teenagers, no older than fourteen, touting sub-machine guns, standing in front of them. "Who are you?" demanded one of them.

"Wang Dawen."

"Li Yang."

"Shut up idiot! Which camp?"

"No camp."

"Rubbish. You must be spies."

"No, no, not spies," Yang said.

"You walked in a stealthy and sneaky way," the taller and older one said.

"I'm just scared," said Yang, "please let us go …"

"Scared? You must be a class enemy then, a true revolutionary could never be scared."

"Let us go, you have no right to stop us," Dawen fulminated.

"Shut up, you are our prisoners!"

The teenagers poked them with their guns, pushing them towards a five-storey building. Its entrance was obscured and barricaded by bricks and office desks, and the ground floor windows were boarded up. Yang didn't like the sound of 'prisoner' as he had heard horror stories about how the Red Squad killed their prisoners. He couldn't stop shaking. Suddenly he took flight, running to a passage on the right.

"Stop! Stop! We'll shoot if you don't …" the teenagers shouted and ran after Yang till he halted. Yang put both his hands up, but a gun went off. His hands dropped like a bird being shot in the air, blood was dripping, Yang shrieked. Dawen quickly torn a strip off his shirt and wrapped Yang's hand to stem the bleeding.

"What are you doing, you idiot?" the tall boy shouted.

"I … I don't know how, it just went off. I didn't mean to shoot, honestly. If he hadn't tried to escape …" the short boy said timidly.

Inside, the building was as dark as at night, like a bunker, except for a few fluorescent lights flickering. People scurried back and forth along the corridor, clear signs of preparation for an assault. The room where Dawen and Yang were kept was an ex-office; desks were piled up to block the window and next to them was a stack of bricks adjacent to a wall of certificates of awards. On the wall opposite a massive poster sported a revolutionary ditty:

砍头何所惧 *Never fear to be beheaded*
革命志不移 *Never falter in revolutionary spirit*
敢上刀山下火海 *Dare to climb the razor mountain and swim the flaming sea*
誓死保卫毛主席 *Swear to protect Chairman Mao to our deaths*

While holding Yang's injured hand, Dawen gazed at his friend's frightened face, desperately thinking how to get out of this hopeless situation. So Dawen was astonished when Lingling opened the door, followed by the tall boy who had taken them by force.

"Ling …" Dawen hesitated.

"What are you doing here? Joining the Red Squad?" said Lingling.

"We were just passing, your friends invited us in with a gun shot," Dawen said and pointed at Yang's hand.

"They are spies. You said we needed to be extra-vigilant, that the Revolutionary Headquarters would send spies before the battle," the tall boy defended himself.

"All right, leave them to me," said Lingling to the boys.

"This is my friend Yang. We were at school together, we're like brothers," Dawen said after the boys had left the room.

"Yes, you told me about him before. So have you decided to join us?" she teased.

Dawen, normally inclined to tease her back, had no mood for it.

"Lingling, we need to go urgently." He pointed to Yang's hand.

"Well, if you aren't spies, I'll let you go."

"Can I see you sometime at the riverbank?"

Lingling looked at Dawen intently for a moment, and then said: "Same time?"

"Yes."

"I thought we'd never come out alive," Yang said when they arrived at his dormitory, and were able to examine his hand.

"It was close," Dawen sighed, "This will be OK, the bullet has grazed your hand, it didn't go in."

"It hurts like hell."

There was a long silence as they recovered from their ordeal.

"Riverbank eh? Are you going out with her? Do you choose to consort with the enemy?" Yang asked suddenly.

"She is my friend, like you."

"They have killed our people, and she is part of it ..."

"She is not our enemy! I like her. She is awfully good-looking. Even you have to admit it. She is smart too. It doesn't have to be personal."

"But everything is personal, Madam Mao and the new leaders in the Central Cultural Revolution Group are supporting the Red Squad camp, the old cadres support us."

"Quite."

The sun was setting when Dawen arrived at the riverbank. He was early though. He sat down on a rock under a willow tree listening to the plash of water beating the grass bank, and looked at the Jialing River and beyond. A cluster of utilitarian grey buildings on the opposite bank painted a dull background to the silenced river. No boats, not even river-crossing ferries, were in view, as if the river had stopped flowing. A gust of wind ruffled the surface of the water. The leaves had mostly fallen, the skeletal trees ready to endure the harsh winter. He stood up, pulled up his collar and strolled along the riverbank as dusk fell. He felt so lonely in the gloomy twilight. Nightfall gradually drew out the darkness, and his hopes for a moonlight tryst were dimmed.

"Boo!" A voice behind him made him jump.

"You are late," Dawen teased, "and that deserves a punishment." He commented on her pretty blouse, a contrast to her normal Red Guard uniform. Lingling blushed and dismissed it strongly, protesting how much she hated vanity, as if her true desire lay exposed and she was vehemently fighting her own cravings.

They took a stroll along the path side by side, humming their favourite songs together. After the turmoil and confusion of the day, they found this tranquillity at the riverbank both pleasing and refreshing. As night fell, he offered his hand. Lingling paused a little and took it. Dawen told Lingling that his mother had taken his younger sister and fled to his grandparents' home in the countryside.

"Good. The city is now too dangerous for them. Pedestrians often get caught in the middle of fighting," Lingling said.

"But their letter said the countryside was as bad as the city; people were dying every day in fights between rebel groups as well. I don't understand why life has become so worthless. What is the point if we will all die in aimless strife in the end?" Dawen said angrily.

"I don't want to live like my mother though; she just obsessively saves money. But what is money good for? You cannot wear pretty clothes because you will be shouted at or laughed at. I yearned for a bicycle, but my mother couldn't get me one because she doesn't have connections. Not everyone has your privilege," Lingling said rather resentfully, then continued. "So what's money for? I could buy sweets or glossy craft paper when I was little, but what now? My mother always said she was saving money for a rainy day. Isn't it pouring now? Power cuts, water cuts, the shops are empty, what good is her money now? We cannot buy anything. My mother thought gold and jewellery were safe, but the Red Guards got it all. It isn't a bad thing though, it's made me feel more proletarian and more revolutionary," Lingling said with a sad smirk.

"I remember your grandparents were rich. Was it true?"

"Yes, my mother's father was a banker, but he left Shanghai before the liberation. Mama stayed because of my father. He's a musician and composer. He said he loved his country more than his own life and his own family. He wanted to make China strong. He put his life and soul into building the new China …"

"Lingling …" Dawen spoke softly.

"You know what? He killed himself … with a broken heart." Lingling started sobbing.

"I'm so sorry," Dawen said.

"It was 1957, the Anti-Rightist Movement. He was condemned. I was seven. I have never told anyone at school as I was too ashamed … Until, recently, I found out that so many of my classmates' parents were rightists too."

"I remember when my uncle was sent to prison along with many of my parents' friends, my mother criticised them in public but cried at home," Dawen said.

"That is what I don't understand. Your parents are the very original communists, yet they suffered no less than my parents who aren't at all red."

"Yes, by joining the revolution so early they were as good as dead – they like to say they held their heads on with their hands. Against all the odds they succeeded, but they are still just struggling to survive; how ironic. It seems the purpose of life is to survive, just to stay alive."

"That's pathetic, no more than an animal."

"I used to sometimes wonder, who am I? Where am I from? Having seen what happens makes it even less possible to answer. I've become a nihilist."

"I don't think that way. I want to be someone who lives with a purpose and to be admired by many."

"A hero? Like a shooting star? Like the Gadfly?"

"Do you mean the book? Have you read it? Everyone is talking about it, but it's so hard to get hold of a copy. Tell me more about it."

"It was an Irish author, writing about a young English revolutionary. It's a tragic and complicated story, you'd better read it yourself. I have a copy, but I've lent it out at the moment."

"Please keep it for me when you get it back."

"Of course. But Lingling, please keep away from the Red Squad. You put yourself at risk with them. They are fanatics, no brains. You have brains and you have a future."

"So what will you do then? Since you don't belong to any faction."

"I don't know. I'm seventeen but I don't know myself. So I read, looking for answers from books. I'm reading Aristotle and Plato," Dawen said.

"Who?"

"Greek philosophers, Plato was Aristotle's teacher."

"How could you do that, running away from your Cultural Revolutionary duty to hide at home reading Western bourgeois books!"

"They are not bourgeois. There was no bourgeoisie in 300 BC, don't you know?"

"Whatever … You know you only need to read Chairman Mao's book."

"I just don't want to waste my life on those nonsense feuds and enmity, it's pointless, there is no right and wrong in fighting. It's all wrong."

"Yes, there is. The Red Squad representatives came back from Beijing last week and we have full support from Madam Mao and the Central Cultural Revolution Group," Lingling said.

"So? The Revolutionary Headquarters have local government and army support."

"How could you be on their side?"

"I'm not on anyone's side. I don't agree with this internecine conflict. It's absolutely stupid," said Dawen passionately.

"We should not shirk our responsibility for the people and for the country. It is time to test our fortitude, our deeply held convictions and beliefs. I have pledged my life to protect Chairman Mao."

"But we are killing the people, not for them. We are destroying the country, not for it," Dawen said.

"You are beginning to sound like our enemy."

"Not if you don't put that hat on my head."

"You are incorrigible," Lingling said irritatedly.

"You are so ignorant. You cannot know you know nothing unless you know something. How many people have died since the Cultural Revolution started?"

"We've lost people too. A couple of days ago, an anti-aircraft gun fired at us from boats on the Jialing River, seven people died and fifty-two were injured. We had to fight back. The battle went on the whole night. The next day, you could see the bodies floating in the river, hard to tell which side they belonged to. But if there is revolution there will be loss of life."

"Chairman Mao said to an Albanian visitor: 'China has a lot of people, so it doesn't matter if it loses half of the population.' How can you trust a leader who is sending half of His people to death and has no shame for it?" Dawen said. At that moment his love towards Lingling turned into frustration and anger. He continued, "Can't you see this revolution has brought misery to everyone and landed us in a great mess? I thought you were intelligent with keen discernment and good judgement, but you have stopped using your brain, and are so deluded that you just blindly follow."

Lingling stood there, flabbergasted, staring at this suddenly monster-like Dawen with his dilated and bulging eyes. She turned around and walked away. Dawen ran after her and shouted, "Please keep away from the fighting, I cannot bear to see you harmed!"

"I'd rather die to protect Chairman Mao than be a traitor!" she shouted back and disappeared into the darkness. Her strong rejection plunged him into the deepest despair, yet her tenderness and charm lingered behind the revolutionary façade.

Chongqing's autumn, over a year into the Cultural Revolution, was red hot. The city was still engulfed by violence. Bitterness and acrimony were fanned by rumours and news from the top; violence and mayhem broke out like a chain of increasingly violent volcanic eruptions; the perpetual pandemonium wreaked more havoc, yet no one seemed to know who was fighting whom and why.

On a hot afternoon, the door suddenly crashed open while Dawen was busy having his siesta and Yang burst in. His dishevelled hair was mixed with dust and sweat and one sleeve was torn on his mud-bathed, crumpled, green uniform.

"Failed … failed, massacre …" he gabbled between snatches of breath.

"Blood … What happened?"

Yang said nothing but the tears couldn't stop running down his cheeks. Dawen held Yang's shoulders to support him till he calmed a little and could speak.

It was about two weeks before, just after Yang and Dawen were released, that the Red Squad had launched a concerted assault on the Revolutionary Headquarters in Beipei and Shiba districts. The Revolutionary Headquarters fought back with any weapons they could find: metal bars, truncheons, batons and stones, but faced with real guns, they could do little but run away. One night, shortly after, a small group of the Revolutionary Headquarters sneaked into a military factory where the Red Squad stored their weapons and stole some machine guns, rifles and ammunition. On their way out, they were ambushed by the heavy fire of anti-aircraft guns and machine guns.

"The plan must have been leaked," Yang said.

The Revolutionary Headquarters suffered heavy losses that night, five dead and seven wounded. The next day, they staged a mass demonstration in the city centre. They carried the mutilated bodies of their comrades at the front of the procession, condemning the brutal atrocity that the Red Squad had committed. Seeking to redress the imbalance of power against their faction, the army issued weapons to the Revolutionary Headquarters.

At night the fighting resumed, quickly escalating and extending to the Yangtze River. Artillery salvos lit up the river overnight and the exchange continued into the next day. Three gunships were sunk and many damaged. The ammunition depot containing tens of thousands of anti-aircraft gun rounds and artillery shells, destined for the Vietnam War, was emptied. Hundreds of people were killed, by their friends, comrades, family members, neighbours. Thousands from both sides were duped into this gratuitous savagery and violence, yet clung on to the fallacy that they were protecting Mao with great fortitude. The Revolutionary Headquarters were defeated in the end, by politics – proscribed as conservatives by Mao and the Central Cultural Revolution Group. Aggrieved at this turn of events, yet still united, the Revolutionary Headquarters buried their over two hundred dead, and amassed three thousand of their people to march up to Beijing, to petition the party for a fair judgement. Yang joined the march.

The marchers were stopped by a convoy of open-topped trucks near the railway station. Without any warning, machine guns started to fire at the crowd from the trucks. Many fell instantly, others ran aimlessly; some, Yang included, plunged into the river, a cover for protection from the bullets. Desperately looking for his girlfriend, he saw with horror that she had not followed, and had been grabbed by her plaits by a large thug, who was striking her across her face again and again, till the blood came out of her mouth, nose and eyes, and yet she refused to surrender. As Yang swam frantically back to her, the exasperated thug shot her three times. A boy from his school, hit by a bullet as he jumped into the river, was dragged out of the water and sliced open because he refused to switch sides. Hundreds of dead bodies were strewn on the road and surrounding area and the ground was bathed in blood. Yang had escaped by diving under the water and allowing himself to be flushed down with the current.

Exhausted, Yang collapsed onto Dawen's bed, occasionally screaming and twitching violently in his sleep. Dawen put two benches together to make a bed for himself but he fretted and worried so much that he couldn't sleep. Midnight passed. The moon shone through the window, casting ghostly shadows before cloud obscured it. Faced by such adversity he felt defeated. A succession of pictures passed through his mind: Lingling's silhouette in the autumn moonlight, free from provocative red; the pair of them surrounded by cool tranquillity chattering vivaciously about the films they both loved; 'Heroes and Heroines', Lingling flitting onto a huge rock and standing erect like a statue, taking the part of the protagonist, shouting into her fist, a pretend microphone, "Fire at me! Fire at me! For the people, fire at me …"

He dreamed about travelling around China with her after the Cultural Revolution was over and wondered where she would prefer, the Yellow Mountains, the West Lake or Suzhou Gardens. He fell into despondency, then just as quickly swung to anger. He hated this current precarious situation, he hated everything: the disruption and madness, his family's misfortune, and lack of a future ahead of him. He was still furious at Lingling's stubbornness, but what he needed most was love beyond politics. He had not seen Lingling since they had quarrelled. He regretted being so harsh and upsetting her. It might just be that she had to be even more radical than others to compensate for her inferior background. He felt terrified of losing her like Yang had lost his girlfriend. He was tormented by anxiety. He sat himself up at the dining table, laid a blank sheet of paper in front of him and started chewing the pen in his hand.

"Dear Lingling," he wrote.

He hesitated, wondering if this was just another futile attempt to reach her, but he continued: "It has been a long time since I last saw you at the riverbank. I know you probably won't want to see me unless I join the Red Squad, but I have to tell you that I miss you and worry about you, especially with the incessant and brutal battles fought between rebels." He stopped again thinking about the words to use, as he didn't want to sound reproachful. "I'm not a coward, but I find slaughtering your friends, your classmates, your brothers and sisters is inhumane, sad and wrong," he wrote. "How are you? I would have visited you if there had been no checkpoints set up by the Red Squad on the bridge. I heard the fire brigade was attacked while passing the bridge on their way to put a fire out. Do you think that was the right thing to do?" He scribbled the last sentence out and continued: "I am sorry I upset you the last time we met. All I want is for you to be safe because I love you. I will protect you wherever you go. Can we meet up at the riverbank sometime next week? Wish I could see you soon, Dawen." He folded the letter, slotted it into an envelope and put it into his pocket.

Yang left Dawen's home the next day. He said he could not sit around while his friends were being slaughtered, despite his injuries, and he vowed to avenge his girlfriend.

Early in the morning the sun broke out after an overnight thunderstorm. Two thousand soldiers from the 54th army were parading on the street towards the city centre, supporting the Revolutionary Headquarters. The spectacular march was a display of pomp and circumstance led by neat blocks of soldiers with their 56 style semi-automatic guns and machine guns, followed by rockets, cannon and tanks. Thousands of spectators from the Revolutionary Headquarters hurrahed and cheered. The parade stopped at the square and people crowded over to watch the demonstration and admire the machinery. A group of youths took over a tank and broke out for a joyride. They drove towards Red Squad territory to flaunt their prowess, but they were stopped by an angry mob of the Red Squad before it reached the bridge. The tank tried to escape, but in panic it reversed into the crowd and killed a rebel from the Red Squad. The enraged mob dragged out the occupants of the tank and smashed them to pieces.

Dawen learnt that the Revolutionary Headquarters was planning revenge. He begged Yang for more detailed information.

"Cannot do it, no, no." Yang shook his head violently.

"Why not?" Dawen asked.

"I cannot betray my mates and comrades, I'll be cast out if I help the enemy. No one will ever talk to me again."

"You have me."

"You? Look at you, hiding in a cave like a rodent, shrivelled like a dried turnip."

"OK, that's enough. Will you help me or not?"

Yang made no reply.

"Think of her as your own sister."

"Oh yeah? Helping my own sister would be an absolutely selfish action. Haven't you been told 'sever all relations'? Why her?"

"Because she holds the secret of life."

"What is that?"

"Hope."

"You are talking nonsense again. Are you in love with her?"

"Maybe, I don't know. Maybe she is my fate, or nemesis …"

"Stop being so philosophical, so … premonitory."

"Think about your girlfriend. I don't want to wait for her to be captured, tortured or killed as if there was nothing I could do."

Yang's face darkened.

"I'm sorry … I shouldn't …" Dawen said.

"I'll see what I can do," said Yang and left.

Yang didn't return for three days, which agonised Dawen, and eventually he went out to look for Yang. To his dismay, Dawen was stopped at the school gate by two of his classmates, one of whom was famous for getting zeros in the mathematics exams, as he recalled.

"Look who's here?"

"Shirk, traitor I would say."

"I'm looking for Yang," said Dawen, ignoring the sarcasm.

"Hey, quite demanding. What have you been doing these days, escaping from the revolution, enjoying yourself while we are fighting for Chairman Mao?" the voice turned hostile.

"You know, if I see you again, I'll break your leg," the other one added.

Just as he was leaving, Dawen heard Yang's call. The two Red Guards stared at Yang grudgingly. Yang said to them, "He is on our side, doing undercover work for me …"

Dawen looked at his best friend who used to be bullied on the sports ground while he had been the leader of the class, admired and followed by so many. He understood why people wanted so much to belong. He could see that Yang's inflated vanity, finding expression in dedication, had deformed his good character. Deformed, but not destroyed, and friendship won out. Having extracted the information he wanted from Yang, Dawen hurried ahead to look for Lingling.

Finding her was no easy matter, but convincing her was even worse.

"I cannot just abandon the new world Chairman Mao is creating; an equal, rich and ideal society where everyone lives a wonderful, easy and happy life with no social stratum, no rich and poor. One day we can have everything we want and contribute as much as we can. That is a goal worth dying for, don't you think?" Lingling said.

"Please don't go to the Architectural College today, I beg you," Dawen said.

"I'm not scared of death …"

"That is suicide, you know? You don't want to be like a lemming …"

"What are you talking about?"

"Nothing," Dawen said. He didn't want to make things too complicated, but he was utterly astonished by her ignorance and stubbornness. Dawen was thinking he may need to knock Lingling unconscious and kidnap her, but he could not do it himself.

"What if you get caught? They will torture you till you switch allegiance."

"We have to take an outright stand against the class enemy. Firstly we must not be afraid of hardship and secondly not afraid of death."

"Do you know the naked body of a girl was dumped

in the street near the stadium? The body smelt foul in the sun, yet people walked past like it was a piece of rubbish waiting to be picked up by the truck. This is insane."

"I know, but we cannot compromise our class roots for a few deaths," Lingling said rather indifferently.

"If you died, how could you build the new world you want? And who is going to look after your mother and your younger sister?"

These words made her pause.

"I'll think about it," Lingling said reluctantly.

"Don't think about it, just don't go there today."

There was only a mute response from Lingling.

"Promise me," Dawen turned around and said on his way out.

His nerves kept him awake that night. He switched the light back on and tried to read. He scanned through the lines, but read nothing. He was distracted and unsettled. He jumped at a gentle, hesitant tap on the door. It was Lingling's little sister. The girl was panting, unable to speak clearly. Dawen sat her down and put his hands on her shoulders.

"She left home this morning but didn't come back …" the girl managed to say, "Mama couldn't stop her, now she is crying."

Dawen knew she wouldn't have stayed at her school as it had been all but destroyed a few weeks ago. The only place she could have been was the Architectural College.

"I'll find her and bring her back, I promise. Can you go back home by yourself?"

Dawen ventured out on his bicycle in the darkness, dashing towards the east side of the city where the artillery barrage was still going on. After he passed the Revolutionary Headquarters checkpoint, the bombardment began to die down. He abandoned the bicycle and followed the source of the gun shots. It suddenly went eerily quiet. He moved forward cautiously, debris and detritus crunching under his feet. Suddenly a flare spat into life overhead, lighting up a battered building that seemed somehow stubbornly alive. Dawen took in the defaced library block; on one side the front had collapsed to reveal debris of office furniture and dangling cables. He recognised those columns that he had admired so greatly during his school visit to a potential university. It was precisely this architecture, the grandiose stone façade, columns, pediments, portico and vestibule that had made him want to be an architect.

Yang was shocked yet excited to see Dawen in the middle of the battlefield. The Revolutionary Headquarters had surrounded the library building early that evening. He proclaimed that they had successfully vanquished the opposition, victory was in their hands, the enemy had stopped resisting just a few moments ago and they would advance into the building to clean everyone out at dawn. He explained how they had cut power and water to the building, how they had ambushed the enemy's reinforcements. The enemy was weak and any survivors would surrender.

"Where is Lingling?" Dawen asked, playing down the true reason for his presence.

"Don't know yet, have to wait till dawn." Yang paused, he fully understood his best mate. "Don't worry, we'll find her. But are you sure she is here? Didn't you tell her?"

"Her sister turned up at my home; apparently she ignored my warning," Dawen said.

"No point in fretting now, let's get some rest." Yang ushered Dawen into a room adjacent to their battle HQ that had long settees.

Dawen was wide awake and he could not help but contemplate the images of their riverbank strolls playing back frame by frame. Lingling was telling him about Debussy's Clair de Lune in the moonlight. He had never heard the music but he enjoyed her description. What he liked most was when Lingling invited him to her home so she could play the piece for him. He had hurled some names like Freud, Hugo or Dickens around to impress her. As he had become rather carried away, he had said, "What do you know about Marxism? I wonder if Chairman Mao ever read 'Das Kapital'. Maybe He didn't need to read it, He just knew everything about it, or perhaps just picked a few words and regurgitated them to suit His own interests."

"It's our duty to love and to respect Chairman Mao," Lingling reproached. Such an easy solution for all things, to simply agree and follow, Dawen thought.

When the east sky started turning pale, the Revolutionary Headquarters loudspeaker blared out at the ruined building: "You are completely surrounded, your reinforcements will not come! Your only way out is to surrender! Come out immediately now, one at a time with your hands raised!"

The loudspeaker repeated itself, but only silence responded.

"You have fifteen minutes to surrender unconditionally."

Five minutes passed, there was no movement from the building. Suddenly a small silhouette emerged on the rooftop. A girl in a Red Guard uniform was waving a Red Squad flag frantically, then she put down the flag, walked to the edge of the roof and shouted: "Long live Chairman Mao!" She flew off the building as if in a hero film.

While the surrounding witnesses watched stupefied, Dawen leapt out of the shelter and ran towards the building as if he were trying to catch the falling girl. Too late to stop Dawen, Yang shouted after him, "Come back, Dawen! It's too dangerous." That was Yang's fruitless plea.

"I can talk them through it," Dawen shouted back. Having seen no one following him, Dawen slowed down, he took off his white shirt and waved it in the air as he walked cautiously towards the entrance. Terrified by the eerie silence, he plucked up his courage and called out: "Lingling, I just want to talk!"

Thirty metres of rubble-covered ground lay between him and the building. There was no sign of life but bodies and body parts were scattered about. Dawen didn't have time to investigate, he wanted to find Lingling fast, and had to move on. He called again and this time he heard

Lingling's voice respond, "Dawen, don't come here, I'm fine. We won't -"

Dawen felt a heavy blow slam into his chest before he heard the gun shot. He wobbled a little and fell.

Time seemed to stop.

A familiar voice called out in his dream, "Dawen, wake up, Dawen." When he opened his eyes, Lingling was bending over above.

"Is that you, Lingling? You are here … I'm so glad, but … it's too dangerous for you …"

"I had to come. I couldn't stop him, I am so sorry …" The tears rolled down her face.

"The day is old," Dawen muttered.

"What did you say?"

Dawen didn't reply and he looked in great pain. He gesticulated towards his pocket. Lingling delved into his pocket and pulled out an envelope.

"It's for you …" Dawen said.

Lingling rubbed the tears from her eyes and was immediately engrossed in the letter. Her hand began to shake so violently that she could no longer continue. She looked at him in complete devotion, and his bleached lips arched upward weakly as if he was satisfied that his love was requited. Lingling then was slowly pulled away, the air between them was dispersed and thinned and his eyes became blurred and started to stray. Dawen heard three gunshots and a faint bawling from Yang: "Who the fuck did that? You bastard! I said -"

Then he heard Lingling's sweet voice, "If I could live again …"

The voice faded as if it were moving further away. Dawen was holding his last breath.

★

Winter had come again, bringing the temperature down to below zero in an atmosphere impregnated with death. Mutilated bodies were scattered in and around the ruined buildings, on the piles of debris and in the streets. The city seemed apathetic and indifferent. Its citizens were completely desensitised, death had become accepted as normal, and they moved on. Some were even proud at showing no emotion. "It could have been me" had never crossed their minds, like a herd of prey; when one of them was taken down the rest did not look back.

In a street on the outskirts of the city, children were chasing a scraggy young man, pelting rocks or mud at him, but he didn't dodge nor even twitch when he got hit, as if he had lost the sense of pain. His glasses were cracked; his hair was long, matted and rumpled; his green uniform was torn with some buttons missing, fluttering in the chilling northerly wind. He shambled along the street, over the ruins, rags wrapped around his feet in place of shoes, occasionally poking into the rubble and rubbish piles, muttering "Lingling … lost, lost, Chairman Mao's badge." He had a dark brown canvas bag in his hand; within it was a half-eaten pear and a hunk of cold steam bread. He stopped, lifted his head and listened to the crepitation of gunshots in the distance, like the crackling of squibs. He turned sharply

131

into a narrow path between the houses to hide, where he was confronted by the residents' hostile stares. Some shooed at him and others gossiped among themselves.

Guilt is always isolating, it separates us from other human beings.

"They said Lingling has taken away his soul," a middle-aged woman whispered.

"Really?"

"Who is he?"

"Weiguo, one of the rebel leaders of the Red Squad."

"That rabid extremist."

"No way! It doesn't look like Weiguo at all."

After Weiguo was out of their sight, the excitement diminished; the crowd dispersed into the houses and narrow paths, back into their normal lives. The street went dead again while the silent echoes of dirges wafted unheard on an icy breeze.

*

Chongqing's autumn was still hot fifty years later.

On a pleasant September morning, Yang, recently returned from the United States where he had become a professor at Princeton University, and his five-year-old granddaughter, Tiantian, strolled along the riverbank heading towards the park. He wanted to spend some quality time with her before starting his new professorship at Chongqing University.

Tiantian was elated, prancing about like a puppy, dodging the early runners along the path, then she stopped at a group of old dancers, moving with the music, mimicking their steps. As soon as her grandpa caught up, Tiantian set off again.

"Can we go in there, Grandpa?" Tiantian asked, stopping suddenly in front of a pair of black iron gates, solemn and indestructible.

"No, it's locked."

"Why?"

"It's a cemetery where the dead are buried. Those are tombstones, they tell you who is buried there."

"Are they heroes, Grandpa?"

"I'm not sure, darling," Yang said.

"Who are they?"

"Some of them were my friends, my classmates and my best friends, Dawen and Lingling."

"Are they in the picture on your desk, Grandpa?"

Yang nodded.

"How did they die?"

"Dawen died for saving Lingling and Lingling died for saving Dawen," he said sombrely.

"Why you are crying, Grandpa?"

"It was a long, long time ago."

"How long, before I was born?"

"Long before."

"Why, Grandpa?"

"Because … Because we were dumb heads, because we only read one book."

"I don't want to read that book."

"Because we followed."

"Why?"

"You ask me such a difficult question that I cannot answer."

"But Daddy said you are very clever, no question you cannot answer."

"I'll tell you all about it when you are a bit older. This should never be forgotten. We will never let it happen to you."

"Grandpa, I'll never forget it," Tiantian murmured, then stood seriously when she saw her grandpa's face.

"It's raining, Grandpa …"

Yang felt nothing, as he watched through the gate at the rain beating on the untended mass grave that he had helped dig fifty years ago; the snakelike vines entwined around the ancient trees; the sharp tang of blood and explosives in his nostrils. He stood there, gazing at the epitaph on the tombstone: 'Heads can fall, blood can be spilt, Mao Zedong Thought can never be lost,' now covered with lichen and moss, obscured. Evocative memories gushed into his head, it was so ridiculous: hateful posters, uniformed fashion, stupid marches of passion, crazy colossal convocations with their rows of pinioned humans, being treated like animals, no, worse than animals. The phrases bit his lips; everything to regret, to love, to hate; the spike stabbed into his calf; the brick he had thrown at his classmate. There might have been some reason in the madness, but while insanity is rare in individuals, in groups, in nations, it is rife. Those malicious moments, he chuckled ironically to himself, muttering, "How astute we were, how shrewd, yet we were so deluded; how we defied, yet we so blindly followed …"

"Grandpa, you are wet …"

Mango

Xinhua News Agency 1968 August 5: This afternoon at Zhongnan Hai, Chairman Mao Zedong received Pakistan's Foreign Minister Mian Arshad Hussain and a warm and friendly conversation was held between them. …

In the pitch black summer's night, piercing police sirens travelling at full speed along the West Chang An Avenue ravaged the city's sleep before flashing on towards Qinghua University in the North West of Beijing. A few lights were switched on in the apartment buildings along the avenue and windows opened to investigate. Some sweet dreams ceased and some nightmares were set off. Inside the police car, a uniformed middle-aged man repeatedly turned to the back seat where a cardboard box sat in the middle.

"Slow down, you'll break them!" he urged.

"What are we delivering?" the driver asked.

"Chairman Mao's supreme instructions."

"Will they break?"

"These ones will."

"I don't understand."

"You don't need to understand, you just need to drive – carefully."

"But you told me to hurry?"

"I know, it's only twenty minutes to midnight, and …"

"The supreme instructions must be delivered the same day."

"Exactly."

Another blaring of sirens, the black car vanished into the darkness.

*

The following morning at the gate of the *People's Daily* compound, Yifeng, a junior reporter of Xinhua News Agency, dismounted his bicycle, as was his habit, to greet the guards, armed soldiers. Yifeng, an ordinary man in his mid-thirties, of average build, with an average brain, and wearing an average outfit, was nevertheless something of a rarity, a young reporter in Xinhua News Agency.

Inside the building the offices were teeming with activity: people rushing up and down the long corridor, passing copy to each other, telephones ringing and being answered, the clattering of a telex, chattering and shouting above the noise – like a bustling marketplace. The boss's office was already packed with eager volunteers.

"You agree I'll go to the Politburo meeting, Commander?"

"But I've been there before, let me go."

"I've got a contact …"

Employing his aptitude for making himself unnoticed, Yifeng sidled up to his desk. As he ran his finger along the surface, a line appeared. Someone had left a window open last night. Yifeng grumpily dusted his desk with a freshly printed *People's Daily*, then settled into his chair browsing the paper, his mail and the calendar. He looked around to see if anyone was still in the office on whom he could eavesdrop for gossip, then he stared through the window. The sun had risen nearly overhead giving out a burning heat, the sky was cloudless, no sign of rain nor even a whisper of a breeze; from the street below came sporadic bursts of tumultuous noise and the blaring of horns from passing trucks and buses. It was not a good day to be out, he thought.

Yifeng came from Baoding, a city 150 km north of Beijing. His father was originally a street trader, selling household essentials, occasionally door-to-door, but more usually from a kiosk in the city centre. Just before the Communists came, he had made a bad deal and had lost everything: his business, his home and his wife. Facing penury, as soon as the Communists arrived and without the slightest hesitation, he had sent the sixteen-year-old Yifeng to join the People's Liberation Army. No ideology was involved, it was purely a source of income. He couldn't possibly have foreseen that this was to turn out to be the best decision he would make in his life. In his misfortune he had also lost his class; he was no longer petit bourgeois but penniless proletarian. Yifeng thrived in the army. Not only did Yifeng have a natural aptitude for staying out of trouble, but not knowing how to fill in 'Family Background' on his enrolment form, he had put down 'factory worker' because he thought this would sound good. With this solidly proletarian background on his records, Yifeng was subsequently hand-picked, promoted and sent to college to be trained as an officer. While still at college, he had been put forward by his regimental commander in a university affirmative action recruitment drive. Thus two birds were killed with one stone: the university ticked off on its proletarian quota, while Yifeng's regimental commander moved someone on who would never be officer material. Yifeng was assigned to study journalism. Gradually he came to believe he was a worker's son and kept discreet about his fortunate misfortune. At university, his lack of intellectual capacity had dragged him down to below average, but he applied himself and was never bottom. He kept well out of the rivalry among his classmates. He didn't have many of his own opinions, accepting whatever the predominant view was. If he was pushed into making a decision he wouldn't rush, but watched and waited as long as possible. He would wear what the majority wore, say what the majority said and feel what the majority felt. His passive contrivance won him many competitions, as he understood that he need not be brilliant so long as he made fewer mistakes than his opponent. He was proud of being the tortoise in the race.

He narrowly escaped being convicted as a rightist, unlike fifty per cent of his university classmates who, during the Anti-Rightist Movement, were hunted down, accused, convicted and sent to prison. At graduation a further thirty per cent, deemed to be sympathisers, had been assigned to factories in remote mountain areas while he rose through this process of opposition attrition, to become second in his class. As if he had won first place in the Imperial Examination, he landed a job in Beijing, at the *People's Daily*, principal newspaper of Xinhua – the most prestigious media organisation in China. His astonishing feat validated his belief in keeping his head down. A by-product of his success was that he earned the reputation of having strong backing in high places, which he never denied nor confirmed. Since the start of the Cultural Revolution, many of his colleagues at Xinhua had been accused and sent away, yet he had survived by being invisible; never standing out, either for or against, never a sycophant for any camp, never showing up a colleague to promote himself, never a monger of office rumour, never one to escalate a trivial dispute: neither foe nor friend.

Feng, a plain-looking secretary in her blue cotton trousers and white blouse, appeared at Yifeng's desk and knocked him out of his torpor.

"The Commander wants you." Yifeng picked up his shorthand notebook and followed her out of the office.

"Commander Zhao. You want me?"

"You, go to Qinghua University before 2pm, get me a report on *Mangguo*," said Zhao, without looking up. Army Commander Zhao, Yifeng's line manager, was a square-faced, broad-shouldered army officer of forty, part of the management team sent in by Zhou Enlai as the Centre struggled to maintain some level of control over key institutions, after nearly all the Party cadres had been denounced.

"M … *Mangguo*?" Yifeng held up his notebook and pen.

"Hurry up, will you! Something to do with the WPT. Go, go," Commander Zhao barked peremptorily.

"Can I …" Yifeng stopped as his eyes met the Commander's. At the door, three people halted their discussion and whispered into each other's ears, smirking. Yifeng breezed past them and went back to his desk.

'The WPT – Workers' Chairman Mao Thought Propaganda Team? I wonder whether there might be a proper story in this,' Yifeng thought, but he didn't hold out much hope as Commander Zhao only ever assigned Yifeng to report on the most trivial affairs, such as a local residents' association putting up a shrine of Chairman Mao on their street. His one really interesting assignment had been spiked. It had been on Beijing's crime rate. He had diligently spent four months visiting half of the police stations in Beijing, but the Party censor had blocked his report despite the simplicity of his findings: the top two categories had been counter-revolutionary crimes – 82%, and adultery – 12%, while there had been no reported murders, and theft and robbery were virtually non-existent.

He took a dictionary off the shelf, and flicked it open – his finger gliding across the page to the entry: '*Mangguo*: A fleshy, oval, yellowish-red tropical fruit, not grown in China.'

"Fruit?" He shook his head, unable to comprehend the importance of it. He looked at his watch, it was just after one o'clock. 'Not enough time to get there by bus, and not enough time to have lunch,' he thought, knowing full well that his assignments never came with a car, unlike for the others. He called his wife Ying to tell her he would not have time to go to the shop. Ying was at her station on the production line in the Beijing No. 1 Textile Factory when her foreman shouted over the clatter of the machines to take the phone call in his office.

"I have to look after Pingping after work and the coupons will expire this week and we don't know when it will be in stock again. We haven't had any meat for two weeks. Can you go tomorrow?" Ying said, "Where are you going anyway?"

"Qinghua, and yes I can go tomorrow morning."

"What, Qinghua? You can't go there, haven't you heard? The rival Red Guards in the university are fighting each other with guns – rifles and real ammunition. What if you get hit in their crossfire? Please don't go." Ying continued anxiously, "You will be careful, won't you? Bullets don't have eyes, believe me! You don't have to go ..." she pleaded.

"What if I say this might get us a flat in the new building?" said Yifeng. Ying went silent.

Yifeng was concerned by the violence too but he didn't feel he had much choice. He grabbed his bag and left the office. It was the hottest time of the day, siesta time, the sky was high and empty, no whiff of a breeze. He peddled out of his work unit apathetically onto the sticky tar road. The street was deserted, posters were hanging off the walls, litter and papers were strewn around the pavements, and banners and flags were draped forlornly as if the city had been abandoned. Freewheeling down the empty street, the breeze in his hair, Yifeng was thinking about his wife Ying and their seven-year-old daughter Pingping. Ying had worked at the Beijing No. 1 Textile Factory for nearly ten years on the packaging line, cutting towels from a cloth band that came out of the machine, folding them and packing fifty of them to a box. At the beginning of the Cultural Revolution everything had been shut, and she had spent most of her time at home playing with their daughter. It was only recently that workers had been summoned back to the factories and students back to school. Ying missed her two-year-long holiday and felt aggrieved to be back at her packaging line again. Liu Shaoqi and his supporters had long gone, and the Red Guards or rebels had lost their quarry; but they couldn't stop, for the fighting spirit had been engraved into their minds by Chairman Mao Thought. To Mao's dismay, the Red Guard factions had provoked feuds among themselves; violence had spread out across the whole country. Two weeks ago, the Workers' Chairman Mao Thought Propaganda Team, or WPT, had been created and deployed to every school, university and college in Beijing to stamp out the violence.

He scanned his watch and swept across Jianguo Gate before turning onto the main road. Suddenly there was a truck crawling at the same speed next to Yifeng's bike. A burly, bald man wound down the window, and waved his fist at Yifeng yelling: "Bloody fool, you deserve to be squashed under a wheel one day!"

Yifeng was rattled: What did I do? he thought. Why is everybody so horrible nowadays? Perhaps the driver had been shouted at by his leader that morning. He shook his head and moved on. He passed some Red Guards who were splashing glue onto a wall to put up posters. On the pavement under the shade of the trees a middle-aged woman selling ice lollies had no customers.

Yifeng zoomed past a bus and some cyclists on the Qinghua Road, the Qinghua University buildings visible ahead. Some people had recently daubed 'Greatest gratitude to Chairman Mao for His solicitudes' on the compound walls. Qinghua University gate was festooned with multicoloured lights and ribbons, and people were crushing through the gate as if going to a festival. Yifeng left his bike and sounded out the herd.

"To see a magic fruit."

"I don't know, I want to see what's going on."

"Why so many people?"

"A special gift from Chairman Mao to our WPT, my whole factory has come here."

"What gift?"

Yifeng joined the flood of black heads surging towards the campus; scattered blockades stood in front of the buildings, bullet holes pockmarked the windows and walls, debris was scattered everywhere. 'It was a hell of battle,' Yifeng thought. On the road to the event centre, bands of people, thousands of them, congregated, moved forward slowly, shouting, crying and waving the little red book. The loudspeakers were broadcasting a panegyric on the rapture of the mangoes.

"Excuse me, excuse me, I am a reporter from Xinhua News Agency!" Yifeng shouted to gain a path forward as the crowd grew thicker and slowed. He was surrounded and squeezed with the sweat dripping off him. "Please let me through."

"No way, we've been waiting since eight o'clock," someone moaned.

"But I have a job to do!" However, no one responded. As soon as a gap opened up it would immediately be filled by someone blocking his way. The crowd was barging forwards and backwards. Yifeng was pushed around on his tiptoes but was fascinated and, after abandoning any attempt to be at the venue on time, was enjoying the festival spirit.

"It is our greatest honour ... Our greatest leader Chairman Mao enlightens us with the knowledge that the factory workers class is the leading class. All factions of Red Guards should surrender their weapons and hand over power to the WPT and ... " a speaker shouted through the microphone on a temporary stage in the campus. The crowd cheered, chanting "Long live Chairman Mao!" At last Yifeng got close. A performance troupe danced exuberantly behind an altar on which the mighty fruits were displayed; two dozen golden mangoes glittered in the sun on a large flowery plate covered by a glass container like an upside down fish-bowl. In front of the altar was a barrier manned by soldiers, while arm-banded WPT guided the crowd. People stood staring at the mangoes tearfully.

The stream of spectators continued to file past the

mango shrine, more speeches were made, songs were played. Yifeng dodged among the crowd taking notes, interviewing, taking pictures. After the rally, he went up onto the stage and introduced himself to the man who looked like he was in charge.

"From Xinhua News Agency? Welcome, I am Yang, leader of the WPT for Qinghua University. People just call me the chief," he said, "Can you believe it? There were over forty thousand people here viewing the mangoes today."

"That's stupendous," said Yifeng and offered his hand.

"We needed Chairman Mao's support. We lost six colleagues last week. The mangoes came at just the right time. The rebel factions have backed down, and we can now move into the administration building," said Yang triumphantly.

"It's bloody well time, the Headquarters Corps won't dare stop us now, even if they eat leopard hearts," boasted another member of the WPT. This raised a laugh.

"What happened?" Yifeng said to the chief and took out his notebook and pen.

The chief cleared his throat, straightened his back, and started reciting in a somewhat stilted manner, "Eight days ago Chairman Mao sent us, I mean the WPT, and thirty thousand fellow workers from over sixty factories, here to Qinghua to dissolve the Red Guard factions and to put a stop to their fighting. When we arrived, the 414 Camp, they're the moderates, were under siege in the Science Museum by the Headquarters Corps who are the militants. To be honest, the 414 Camp were pretty grateful to be able to surrender to us. After the Headquarters Corps had set fire to the Science Museum the 414 Camp had tried to tunnel out, but the Headquarters used some fancy scientific detector to find their tunnel and blew it up! Bloody kids, not using their learning for proper purposes. Anyway, the Headquarters Corps refused to give up their weapons, instead fired at us. Six workers were killed and hundreds injured."

Yifeng lifted his head up, the chief's face writhed in fury, but he wiped his clouded expression and said in a restrained voice, "Let's celebrate the success of the day." The chief turned to the people gathered around the table on the stage: "What are we going to do with these precious gifts?"

"Keep them in a glass jar?"

"In salt water?"

"Dry them in the sun?"

"We could eat them."

"Who said that?" the chief demanded. Heads turned towards the corner of the table, where a young man, in blue overalls, smiled proudly for the attention he had received. The chief looked him in the eyes and said, "Easy, isn't it?"

The young man nodded suspiciously.

"Tell me one good reason."

"Well," the young man calmed down slightly, "it's fruit, isn't it?" and he looked around for approval. "We eat fruit, we don't do anything else with it, right? We don't play with it, we can't wear it, we can't ride on it?"

Most people around the table were nodding slightly, even Yifeng. Suddenly there was a loud bang as the chief brought his fist down on the table furiously. Tea cups jumped, so did the people around the table.

"Such an idiot!" the chief roared.

He gestured towards the mangoes, succulent and golden, at the centre of the table and cleared his throat before launching into a diatribe: "Did you say fruit? Mango is not fruit. It is a precious gift from our greatest leader Chairman Mao and these are divine objects and symbolise Chairman Mao Himself. We must treasure it, cherish it, adore it and worship it. My heart was thumping when we received this gift from Chairman Mao last night, and I was so moved and overwhelmed that I couldn't sleep. And the people couldn't stop crying. These mangoes are magic, they give us ultimate power to accomplish our mission of ending violence between rebel groups, destroying counter-revolutionaries, and carrying out the Great Proletarian Cultural Revolution to the bitter end. We must not forget our duty and earn the trust placed in us by our greatest leader," the chief said sanctimoniously. Everyone went solemn and there were no more suggestions involving preservation.

"Stop tapping the table!" the chief ordered curtly.

"But is it wrong to eat them?" A quiet voice responded from the corner.

"There is no such thing as right or wrong, only should or should not. For instance, beating people up is wrong, but we should beat the hell out of bad people because Chairman Mao has instructed us to."

"Yes, I kind of agree, smashing old temples is wrong, but …"

"We should wipe out the Four Olds, right?"

The chief cast a disapproving look at the interruption and said: "We should love Chairman Mao and defend His reputation whatever is needed regardless." The chief went on speaking in this way for half an hour.

It was getting late, yet there was no sign of any kind of decision. Five core committee members of the WPT stayed behind to talk over the options and strategies, but they could not come up with a sound solution, even after the long-winded and heated conversation. As night fell, impatience was apparent and it became more trouble than it was worth, but no one dared to say it. Yifeng stood up to say goodbye but was stopped by the chief.

"What do you think we should do?"

Yifeng hesitated, "Well, I'm only a reporter, I shouldn't …"

"Just tell us what you think," the chief demanded.

"Ahem, maybe … you could give the mangoes to your factories as a gift?"

There was a moment of silence. The chief gave a gleeful chuckle. "Yes, we can share our fortune with others, how wonderful!"

"And we don't have to worry they won't last any more."

"Why didn't we think of that?"

The chief held Yifeng's hand and shook it violently before Yifeng left the WPT. When he got to the university gate he found his bicycle had gone. He was in a red hot rage as no bus would operate at this hour and he needed to write a report for today's event. Yifeng made his way back to the office on foot; it took him two hours and he worked well past midnight.

Xinhua News Agency 1968 August 7:
The Greatest Solicitude; The Deepest Conviction; The Profoundest Support and The Most Overwhelming Endorsement

On the afternoon of the sixth, when the great happy news of Chairman Mao giving mangoes to the Capital Worker and Peasant Mao Zedong Thought Propaganda Team swept out from Qinghua University campus, people flocked to crowd around the greatest leader Chairman Mao's gift. They cheered, sang, and indulged their tears over and over again, sincerely wishing our beloved great leader Chairman Mao long life! Long live Chairman Mao! Long live Chairman Mao! The good news was on everybody's lips; a variety of celebrations were held through the night and crowds marched in the rain to Zhongnan Hai, to proclaim their utter devotion to the great leader Chairman Mao.

As he stepped into the office building the next morning, Yifeng was swamped with congratulations from his colleagues and became the cynosure of all eyes, the pivot of their attention. He stared at the freshly printed *People's Daily* in someone's hand; his mango report was on the front page! Despite the exultation and

149

curiosity of his office mates, he maintained a calm and collected exterior. His phone rang. It was Yang, the chief of the WPT.

"Do you remember we agreed we would give those mangoes away?"

"We?" Yifeng said, extricating himself from responsibility.

"I'll come to pick you up now, it will be a good story for you," Yang said.

The black limousine glided through the gates of Beijing Xinhua Printing Factory escorted by a pickup truck. The workers lining both sides of the road waved their red flags, holding up their little red books, shouting and cheering as if Chairman Mao Himself were coming. Yifeng got out of the limousine and took a few pictures of the crowd, while the chief, holding a glass reliquary with the golden mango in it before him, organised his guard of honour comprising members of the WPT and four armed soldiers. As they processed towards the stage, a wave of jubilation engulfed the crowd.

The stage had been erected outside the administration block which stood at one end of the expansive factory yard. Around a thousand workers, assembled in their uniforms, stood solemnly in formation, facing the shrine of the mangoes. They listened with habitual stoicism to their leaders' lengthy sermons.

"Comrades, I now present you with the mango, the ultimate gift from the greatest leader Chairman Mao. These mangoes were originally given by our foreign friends to our greatest leader Chairman Mao, and

Chairman Mao gave them to us workers as a symbol of His benevolence and love for us. Comrades, look at this beautiful succulent fruit, it is as rare as gold. I had never heard of mango before; is there anyone here who has heard of mango? Hold up your hand?"

"No one, that was what I thought," he continued. "It was us, the workers' community who have been marked out to deserve such great honour. The mangoes represent Chairman Mao's affection, trust and support. Let us make a solemn vow ..."

After a couple of the factory dignitaries' triumphant speeches, the workers filed past the mango shrine, bowing respectfully to the precious fruit. Some were in tears, some were curious: what did it taste like? But it was a place for worship and respect not for curiosity. Suddenly the procession broke out and formed a ring in front of the altar. A worker in his late forties was on his knees, clasping his hands before him, he sobbed: "Please our Greatest Life Saver, my mother is very ill, I cannot find a doctor. Please help!"

Xinhua News Agency 1968 August 18: More than twenty major factories in Beijing have received Chairman Mao's mango in the last few days. Over one hundred thousand overjoyed workers, the pillar of our society, congregated at Tian An Men Square ...

He basked in the novelty of attention and success, but the more Yifeng revelled in it the stormier Army Commander Zhao's face became. One morning the storm broke: "Who said you can come to work at nine?"

"…"

"Who approved you to go to those factories? In and out in a car like a VIP?"

"Commander Zhao, I lost my bicycle at Qinghua, and I don't have a full month's salary to spare. Can I borrow one please?"

"That's your own fault."

"But it was so crowded that I couldn't get into the Qinghua gate, so I had to leave it outside of the gate in order to do my job. I did lock it."

"There is no need anyway, you are suspended from mango reporting; you are going to these primary schools from tomorrow, the mango is too important now."

"But … it was already arranged, the trip to Shanghai with the chief of the WPT, it's tomorrow." Yifeng said timidly, yet with a hint of annoyance.

"Without consulting me? Cancel it."

"Yes, can you … ?"

"Don't try."

Yifeng had been salivating at the prospect of flying to Shanghai since the chief of the WPT had told him the day before: "A specially chartered plane, you know. It leaves the day after tomorrow. The No.1 Machine Tool Factory want to send their mango to their sister factory in Shanghai. I told them I could arrange to have you as the reporter covering the event. You will go, won't you Yifeng?"

"Of course!"

"The whole country is hysterical. I'm getting

hundreds of phone calls, everyone wants a mango but I don't have so many and you know they will go off eventually."

Yifeng had been quiet for some time, reflecting.

He had begun to like the chief better; he found him, beneath the sanctimonious exterior which had been shaped by the Cultural Revolution, to be an honest and moderate man, though stubborn and with little leadership skill. He did not like to give instructions to the people he led, rather he expected them to do what he wanted them to do, and in this way he avoided confrontation or disengagement if the order were not received well. So the consequences were often undesirable, as one could get away with murder if one wished. However, he could also be the most dogmatic, stubborn person Yifeng had ever met. When he had made up his mind, even on the most trifling matter, he would fight to the bitter end, especially against people he knew well. He had insisted on coating the mangoes with wax to preserve them, despite Yifeng's protestations that it would not work. He would never let himself lose an argument, even if it was as trivial as an interpretation of the weather conditions. Arguing was his main joy in life. He treated all people, whether family members, friends, colleagues or even strangers, absolutely fairly and equally, and found it hard to have the passion or desire to care for any one person in particular. He didn't love anyone, except Chairman Mao, or didn't show it if he did, not from selfishness, but as if loving were a sign of weakness. He was phlegmatic, popular at work but not at home. Yifeng got on very well with the chief as he was an honourable man. Yifeng's reflections had suddenly come into sharp focus. The wax may not stop the mangoes from rotting, but: "Make some wax replicas, they won't go off," he had told the chief. The chief had loved the idea, and even expanded upon it – why couldn't everyone have a mango?

Yifeng sat at his desk, eyes fixed on the empty wall, contemplating how to broach his dismissal from mango reporting to the chief. He didn't want to start a feud or conflict, as he believed any hostility would eventually come back to haunt him, yet he desperately wanted to go to Shanghai. He decided to leave it to the chief. What was said, he didn't know, but the note on his desk the following morning demonstrated the chief of the WPT had changed Commander Zhao's mind.

The Shanghai trip was a spectacular experience for Yifeng. He was stunned by the crowd, the flags, the band and dance troupe gathered at the Shanghai Hongqiao Airport, there to greet the mango. Yifeng and the WPT delegate were taken in a Red Flag, a prestigious shiny black limousine, red flags rippling from the wings, escorted by six cars and a truck, towards the Shanghai Machine Factory. A crowd had congregated in the street outside, and the whole factory had rallied to pay homage to the mango in the assembly hall, each person carrying their little wax replica before them. After the ceremony, Yifeng was driven along the Bund, passing grandiose stone-faced European style buildings and was utterly impressed.

Xinhua News Agency 1968 August 20: To date,

factories in eight cities have received the divine mango.
Up and down the country, millions of workers are
filled with a euphoric sense of pride and triumph …

For a whole week, Yifeng wallowed in the luxury hotels, and sumptuous receptions with the WPT, travelling to Xian, Chongqing and Hangzhou, presenting the precious mangoes. The mango mission had bestowed upon him VIP status everywhere they went, along with the title 'Mango Reporter'. Little had Yifeng ever anticipated that one day he would become so famous. Every day his report would be printed on *China Daily*'s front page, and instantly reprinted on the front page of thousands of local newspapers around China. Back at the office he was inundated with phone calls, letters and telegraphs reporting relevant news and rumours from the whole of China.

Two days after his return Commander Zhao called an emergency meeting.

At the meeting, Yifeng was accused of stepping out of line, disrespecting a superior and making false claims, etcetera. Yifeng remained silent throughout. He was not to be tempted out of the shell of his silence. He didn't defend himself, as if he had been expecting that this was going to happen. After the hour, he headed home.

His one-bedroom flat was on the top floor of an old four-storey building set back from the main street. He held his breath while passing the entrance of the building. The rubbish was piled up as if it had not been collected for a year. The stench from refuse simmering in the high summer heat was the worst, then the flies and bugs made the site a health hazard. Yifeng took a deep breath as soon as he got inside the building; here the air possessed a pungent odour of rancid cooking oil and suspended dust. He switched the light on and carefully climbed the stairs without touching anything. His flat was like an oven, baked through the poorly insulated roof from above, while the mean window opening onto the cacophonous road brought little relief. He dusted off the flakes of burnt-brown white paint on the windowsill, and went to the basin to wash his hands, but there was no water. It happened sometimes in the summer when there was a water shortage. He had been eligible, based on his rank, for a one-bedroom flat from the *People's Daily* for the last five years, since Pingping was two. He buried his sweaty face in his palms, distraught.

"What's the matter with you? You look, ill," said Ying, putting down her handbag on the chair and closing the door behind her. Pingping disappeared into their bedroom.

"I'm all right, it's just too hot," said Yifeng, wiping his damp face with a flannel. "How are you?"

"Fine."

"Anything the matter?"

"The mango you brought to our factory? It turned brown. You know it was coated with wax to preserve it. Those idiots didn't sterilise it before coating it. The factory's Party Committee held an emergency meeting today and decided to boil the mango in water. I had a sip of the water this afternoon, in fact, everyone in the factory had."

"Did you really? What did it taste like?" Yifeng burst into laughter.

"Don't be sarcastic. I didn't want to drink it, it's so silly, just a rotting fruit, but I couldn't stand out and make a target of myself."

Yifeng recalled a report that he had received three days ago from Sichuan province. He told his wife about an old dentist there who had gone to welcome the mango to his town. The dentist had been disappointed in what he saw and commented casually: "It looks like a sweet potato, what's the fuss?" The old dentist had been arrested and accused of viciously insulting the mango. They were both plunged into a sorrowful silence. Yifeng got up to check if the water was back on, as their water storage was running low.

"When can we move? This place is driving me mad," Ying said.

"I'm working on it." Yifeng didn't want to get into the topic.

"What have you done? Five years we've been waiting."

"I did my best."

"What have you done?"

"I tried to work long hours, and be in the good books of my boss. Don't you remember you bought Maotai and meat, even used up our ration?"

"But why have your office mates moved, and not you?"

" . . . "

"Why can't you pester the real estate manager every

157

day and stab others in their backs like they do? Such a wimp."

Mosquitoes were whining, Yifeng slapped his own face and cursed.

Xinhua News Agency 1968 September 5: Plastic mango replicas have been presented by local revolutionary committees in remote rural provinces and counties to rein in the rival Red Guards and rebels, while in Beijing the people continue to give thanks to Chairman Mao at the Mango display in Tian An Men Square ...

Yifeng had been excluded from reporting the mango stories for a week, despite the agency assigning a dozen reporters onto the topic. Coming back from an interview on the start of the new school term, a Red Flag limousine parked by the office building caught Yifeng's attention. As he came onto his floor, he was called in to Zhao's office where two men dressed in Mao suits introduced themselves as being attached to the General Office of the Politburo. They invited Yifeng to Zhongnan Hai to provide a brief on the current situation of the mango affair. Yifeng looked at Zhao meekly to seek approval, Zhao's face twitched a little but he waved his arm in acquiescence at Yifeng.

*

On the way back to his home in the Red Flag, Yifeng was still panting and throbbing with the stupefaction of meeting Chairman Mao and so many important figures.

In the beginning he had been at a loss for words and stuttered, but he had quickly regained his composure as his stories seemed to stun the audience, who listened quietly with open mouths and wide eyes, and who sporadically burst out into laughter. Yifeng could still feel Chairman Mao's warm and friendly handshake, and no words could reflect his great reverence and respect for Chairman Mao.

"Look what I got, Baba!" said Pingping, running towards him as he opened the door.

"Wow, a mango. Where did you get it?"

"School, teacher said we should place it in front of Chairman Mao's picture."

Yifeng felt he had nothing to say.

"A collection too, one yuan for the mango please. We learnt the mango dance today, let me show you," Pingping began to sing and dance:

Every little mango portion,
received in our adoration,
facing towards our Golden
Sun …

"The school is going to Tian An Men Square tomorrow. We'll dance and sing for workers. I want to be a factory worker when I grow up Baba," Pingping said solemnly before she went to bed.

A week later Yifeng found that Commander Zhao's desk had been emptied, seemingly cleared overnight. Yifeng felt drained, 'It must be heatstroke from the Square,' he thought.

"It's because of mishandling the mango affair, he's had to return to his army unit," someone explained. Yifeng felt uncomfortable, but then he had seen so much injustice lately.

Xinhua News Agency 1968 November 23: Beijing No. 2 Plastics Factory has successfully produced lifelike Mango replicas in large production volumes to meet the increasing demand and jubilation.

Autumn came and went, taking the colour with it. Winter was just around the corner. Mango was still a topic in the office, although no one could explain why or how, it had just happened. Yifeng's office, consequently, had moved from a four-shared, to a two-shared and then to his very own office. Dubbed the Mango Office, it was strewn with a panoply of mango replicas, images and art pieces, and even a trophy in the shape of a mango.

It was a quiet news morning, but Yifeng clutched his hand struggling to control his elation. He had got the key for a three-bedroom flat in a new building next to the *People's Daily*. 'What more could I wish for?' he thought. He kissed a wax mango on his desk and ensconced himself in an office sofa in the corner to plan his home move this weekend. The phone rang, it was Xiao Zhang from the sub-office in Guizhou Province.

"A fight broke out …"

"Sorry I am not doing fights or any violence," Yifeng said.

"No, no, a fight for mango …"

"Fight for plastic? You must be joking."

"No joke, got a pen? Yesterday the revolutionary committee of Guizhou Province went to Wengan County to give mangoes. The suppressed faction of Wengan County resented it and organised a few thousand supporters to waylay the mango. There was a stand-off between the two camps, both armed with sticks, metal bars and farm tools, at a crossroads outside the town. A serious clash could have started at any moment, but both camps had Chairman Mao's picture held up in front, and no one dared to make the first move. As it turned out, it was only a picture of a mango they had been waiting for."

"OK, not a good story for publishing though. Did anything actually happen?" Yifeng said.

"Fighting? Yes, but not too bad. A dozen of them got injured, but no one died."

"It hardly seems worth the effort, for a picture of a mango?"

"You want to know something interesting? You know my cousin works in Zhongnan Hai? He told me Chairman Mao doesn't eat mangoes, He thinks they are too posh. Normally when He receives mangoes He gives them to my cousin to distribute among the staff straight away. Funny, heh?"

Yifeng could not sleep that night, he was too excited about his new flat, his new life. He experienced a euphoric sense of freedom. His reflections turned back to what Xiao Zhang had told him earlier. Strange the twists and turns of fortune, how he had finally achieved his new flat simply because Chairman Mao doesn't like mango.

Yanzi

(Little Swallow)

"Baba, I'm home!" Yanzi, a skinny girl of twelve, shouted after the door clunked shut behind her. "Look what I've got, you won't believe it, it cost five packs of Da Zhonghua. I offered the farmer three packs, but he said it wouldn't do; he said she was still laying, so I gave in, because Mama needs it to recover. Did I give in too easily, Baba? I'll just have to work more for Dahei, but when I saw him open one pack and light up, I was dead worried; what if he doesn't give me the hen? Am I being stupid? He did give me the hen and some lettuce to compensate. Maomao and I raced all the way there, and on the way back we got so tired we had to stop. We played with dandelions, like a hundred little umbrellas, but that's when I lost the button off my shirt. Sorry I'm late home, but you've got to help me, she's flapping, look how big she is? Baba? Are you there? Am I talking too much? How is Mama? She'll be better after she has this chicken, I'm sure of it ..."

Yanzi stopped in the doorway to the bedroom and let out a short but excruciating scream. The hen won the freedom of the flat. Mama was on the floor, partially wrapped in her bed clothes, unconscious. The table and chair were tipped over and the medicine bottles, broken pieces of glass, paper and books were strewn across the floor. Yanzi stood paralysed by inexperience. As she knelt down and bent over her mother, her tearful face gradually regained colour.

"Mama, Mama, wake up, I'm scared, wake up …"

Yanzi lay down next to her mother, one arm wrapped around her waist, sobbing, "I'm sorry Mama, I am sorry I play too much, where is Baba? What has happened? What do I do? Please don't leave me alone …"

Someone was at the door. Yanzi went to answer it. It was their upstairs neighbours.

"Juan Juan said your father was taken by rebels. We came to check if you are both OK."

"Oh no, let's put her back in bed."

"Juan Juan, go and get a doctor, she's passed out, quickly."

In the twilight, lying motionless in bed, Mama's breathing grew regular. The neighbours had left. Yanzi was worn out and fell asleep next to her mother. She woke up in Mama's warm, invigorating embrace.

"You are back Yanzi. Baba was taken away by rebels; I clutched onto his clothes but I fell. I have no memory of anything after that."

"You fainted. The doctor came and said you needed rest after your big operation, especially because your wound is not healed. Don't move. Do you want something to eat?"

"No, just come closer, let me hug you."

"I got you a hen and I'll cook it for you."

"Just let it go, you couldn't stand to see it killed."

"What has happened to Baba?"

"He was dragged away by a gang of rebels."

"Why?"

"They didn't say."

"When will he be back?"

"Don't know, I'm sorry."

Yanzi looked at Mama's pallid face and began to snivel, "I'm going to find him …"

"No Yanzi, it's too dangerous, Baba will come back."

Yellow leaves started falling, rolling and racing along the street in gusts of wind. Baba didn't come back and no one knew where he had been taken to or where the rebels had come from.

One morning Maomao was shouting her name outside, so Yanzi opened the window and looked down.

"What's the matter with you? Five days I've waited? Where have you been? I got those badges … Oh, don't cry, I'll come up," said Maomao, brandishing her skinny arm.

Yanzi and Maomao, as scrawny as each other, sat there, their faces propped on elbows resting on the worn wooden table, the only piece of furniture that was theirs and which had been inherited from her grandma, staring at each other in silence. Yanzi and Maomao, although not in the same class, had become friends after their school was closed the previous summer. Yanzi was never popular at school, never spectacularly good at any subject, but she had a reputation for being clever, though hot-tempered, and troublesome, yet taciturn. She had disliked her form teacher, whom she feared, and who had silenced Yanzi through petty humiliations. In the Cultural Revolution, the popular cliques of her school had dissolved, and the boundaries of the social hierarchy fragmented; someone's powerful, chauffeur-driven parent from one day could be emptying a septic tank in prison the next. No one really knew whether you would ride on the top of the wave or drown at the bottom of the sea in this tempest. Yanzi, however, unfolded. She seemed unable to stop talking.

Maomao pulled her face a little, two dimples popped in, framing her glimmering white teeth, but Yanzi didn't laugh. Maomao placed her fist in the centre of the table, then revealed the contents in her palm, a glittering Yan An badge. Yanzi's eyes lit up like a match then flickered out; she was too engrossed in her sorrow. Yanzi glanced at the clock on the wooden shelves and got up. After the two girls had sat her up to take her medicine, Mama closed her exhausted eyes and nestled back into her bed.

"Have you lost your tongue?" Maomao whispered as they walked out of the bedroom.

"Baba was taken away the day we got the chicken. I don't know what to do."

"What happened?"

"Mama was on the floor, unconscious, when I got back … I was so scared, and Baba was gone. I've been to all our neighbours but no one knows who took Baba. They said there was a large green truck, like those army ones, parked in front of the building, and around twenty people jumped off it. They said they didn't have red armbands, no flags, banners or any signs that had names. And they looked older than student Red Guards. Uncle Zhang upstairs asked where they were from, but a big ugly guy punched him and his nose bled. There were a lot of people watching but no one dared to question them after that. Then they pushed Baba onto the truck and drove away."

Maomao grasped Yanzi's hand firmly as she continued through the tears welling up in her eyes: "You know when we were watching the parades, struggle sessions, I was worried about my parents, but Baba said he would never be in trouble because he is not in a high position, he doesn't have a black background, he's not an intellectual, and he keeps away from the rebel factions; he thinks the Cultural Revolution has nothing to do with him and he just needs to look after Mama."

"What are you going to do?"

Yanzi withdrew her hand, blotted her eyes on her sleeve and a note of determination crept in: "I'm going to find him, I will."

"I'll come with you if you do all the talking."

The two girls hooked their little fingers together and shook solemnly.

The next morning Yanzi got up early while Mama was still asleep. She cleaned the kitchen and dishes left from last night. The kettle was boiling, but as she poured the steam startled her, and her arm went red and hot but she didn't cry out in case it woke Mama. As Yanzi soaked the Chinese medicine in an earthenware pot, the porridge boiled out.

"Slowly …" she said to herself, "Don't burn Mama's medicine like last time!"

The morning went smoothly, Mama had breakfast, her morning wash and her medicine. Yanzi put on a newish yellow and blue checked top and the blue trousers that didn't have patches.

"I'm going, Mama. Aunty Liu will come to check on you. I'll be back later," said Yanzi as soon as she heard Maomao was at the door.

It wasn't the first time the two girls had set off on adventures since that long, early summer holiday had started over a year ago; joining the other girls, prowling around the compound, climbing up walls or onto roofs, following the parades and propaganda performances, throwing rocks at boys, or playing hide and seek with the estate manager. It was wild sensations they were seeking in a disordered world. But this time it was pretty incredible; they had a real mission, like in the films, a purpose. The girls were high-spirited. It was a sunny autumn morning, the sky was blue and the air fresh. They pranced out of the gate and skipped along the path till they came to the bridge where a food cart was selling snacks, with a tinker's bench next to it. Nearby, a flock of squalid boys were throwing rocks in the channel. The girls slunk past the bridge before the boys could identify the new targets, then walked on the Weixiuyuan Road towards the North Gate of Peking University.

Totally unexpectedly, they passed the gate unchallenged, entering a maze of posters; above their heads, on the walls, on the ground, on top of the buildings and trees, rattling in the wind and raving into empty space. Yanzi found everything so different from the last time she had come to Baba's office, that she began to wonder if they had lost their way. People scurried to and fro, taking no notice of the posters brushing their faces. The Weiming Lake appeared and Yanzi recognised the rockery and the willow tree.

"Yanzi? What are you doing here? Is your Mama poorly? Haven't seen your Baba for a week, how is he coping?" said a middle-aged man in his blue Zhongshan suit. "Oh, don't cry, what's the matter?"

"Uncle Qin, Baba was taken away."

"By whom?"

"Don't know, no one knows, he's not come back. I came to look for him."

"But he isn't here," said Uncle Qin and paused a little. "Let's go to the WPT, they might think he was a Passive Resistant."

The WPT officer – everyone deferred to him as Master Tan – bellowed down the phone as they entered and forced the receiver to rest in its cradle. The wax mango model in the centre of his desk jumped as if startled by the sound of his fist. Yanzi quailed before his fierce gaze, but finding no resistance to her halting introduction, picked up her stride. Her long-winded explanation of how her father had been taken by twenty or so rebels in a truck, while she was out, and how they nearly killed her Mama, was rounded off with confidence: "I've got his pills, he will go crazy without them, and his glasses. I know he has to write confessions, and he can't write with no glasses, right?"

Master Tan, a lathe operator by trade, since his deployment to Peking University by Chairman Mao two months ago, had rapidly gained a reputation as a despot. To everyone's surprise he patiently listened to Yanzi before he nodded gently and picked up his phone.

"Is Lao Ma there? Get him now. Hello Lao Ma, how is it? I need a favour. Can I have a list of the cowsheds in the university? Twenty-one of them, so many? Thanks."

"Cowshed?" Yanzi whispered.

"Where the baddies are kept for thought reform – my father is in there," Maomao said.

"So they cannot be baddies then, logically," Yanzi retorted.

"Go home now kids. Wait for news. At least your father's absence won't count as anti-Cultural Revolutionism," Master Tan said as he put the receiver back.

"But I need to see him now, I've got his pills and glasses. The cowshed won't suit him at all, don't you agree? He's a nice person like you, he wouldn't hurt anyone, not even an ant. Everyone loves him, in the whole building: Uncle Zhao, Aunty Jin, … you name it. And he works hard and is loyal to our great leader Chairman Mao. He loves the PWT …, don't pull me …"

"It's not PWT, it's WPT, the Workers' Chairman Mao's Propaganda Team," Maomao said quietly.

"Yes, WPT, he loves the WPT, he said the WPT saved them …" Yanzi stopped as she saw Master Tan's face twitch. "Am I talking too much?"

It was lunchtime when the girls got sent out of the

office. Yanzi bought some Baozi, steamed dumplings, from the staff canteen, and they sat down by the Weiming Lake to eat, watching the people hurrying back and forth wearing their gloomy and contorted faces. On the other side of the lake, two groups of people were arguing and shouting slogans at each other, as if eager to have their voices heard above all, and then they started to push each other on the chest. Others attempted to placate them by waving Chairman Mao's little red book and reciting his quotations.

*

Qingming was dragged out of his home with his hands tied by rope and pushed onto an open-top truck. He tried to stand up and ask, what is this all about, but was knocked back with a shower of fists. He was confused and furious, though relieved that his daughter, Yanzi, hadn't been there to witness his treatment. He couldn't comprehend. He had always been proud of having a squeaky clean background – three generations of poor farmers; he had no criminal history and had never been in the slightest trouble in any of the previous political movements. He used to work in a factory before moving to the facilities department at Peking University and being put in charge of purchasing lab equipment. He couldn't think how he had ever made any enemies. He felt hilariously important with some twenty people coming to get him, but he concluded it was either for show or these people had just come for a day out, and he would be straight home after the mistake had been identified. The journey was longer than he had anticipated and the truck bumpier, they were far out of the city centre.

He was pushed into a sparsely furnished room, a chair in the centre, facing a desk at the other end, behind which sat a middle-aged, blue-suited man with a scowl on his face. Two brawny men stood behind him. In one corner a metal frame was populated with a few whips, cudgels, chains and some metal implements. A frieze of white posters sporting large black characters decorated the room, reminding the reader of 'leniency to confessors', 'resistance severely punished', though Qingming, from his vantage point in the chair, wondered whether it would have been more appropriate to have had a Chairman Mao portrait to confess to.

"Wang Jingming: do you know why you are here?"

"I'm Wang Qingming," he corrected, "I don't know why I am here. Where am I anyway?"

"Don't try to insult us, you are Wang Jingming."

"Do you think I don't know my own name?" Qingming said.

The blue-suited man flicked his two fingers, one of the men advanced towards Qingming and punched him in the face.

"I think – you know how to behave now."

"There must have been a mistake …" The blow knocked over the chair. The big man set the chair into its position, and gripping Qingming's hair in one hand guided him back into his place.

"A wise man would confess."

"But what do you want me to confess to?" Qingming said.

"What you did five years ago."

Qingming looked surprised at the question but managed to respond: "I was … working at the department of …"

"Chicanery! You think you can get away by deception? Take him away to the box till he is prepared to confess."

"Please – can you tell my family?"

"When you confess!"

Qingming couldn't stand up in the cabinet. He curled up on the shelf that smelled of cleaning chemicals, fretting about his sick wife and young daughter. He was disorientated, not knowing what was going on or what to confess to. He missed his family; how were they coping and how worried they must be. Why he was here, he did not know, although it seemed to be a mix-up of identity. The night was long and the cabinet short. He had plenty of time to evaluate his options, and vacillated between confessing and not confessing. However, to him the long-term outcome would be the same: convicted as an enemy if he did not confess, or convicted as an enemy if he did confess.

In the morning the interrogation was repeated, with much the same result. An honest man, he just couldn't bring himself to admit to being someone he was not, and this he clung to in the blur of pain, sleep deprivation, hunger and humiliation.

It was never his malefactors' intention to kill or maim. While sometimes boundaries were inadvertently crossed through revolutionary ardour, or opportunities created for those disposed towards unwarranted cruelty, the purpose was to break and remould. The victims must participate in the act of revolution. Qingming did not crack in that initial shock, and so after two days he was moved to the cowshed where the other denounced, incorrigible ex-officials were kept pending their change of heart. He was soon familiar with both the twenty-odd inmates and the daily routine: get up; recite Chairman Mao's quotations; hard labour; listen to a recital of Chairman Mao's writings; admonishment and goading; bed. The work ranged from cleaning toilets and emptying septic tanks, to carrying bricks or repairing roads. If they got lucky they were given the canteen's leftovers, otherwise they were fed cold, hard cornbread.

★

One sweltering night, Yanzi was woken up by the whining of mosquitoes. There was no way she could get back to sleep with them in her net, singing their lullabies next to her ear. She switched on the light with eyes half opened and squashed three, big, juicy specimens, before turning off the light and lying there. She was still unable to sleep, fretting over the failure of her quest. "Where are you, Baba?" she whispered, but the darkness responded with silence, and she eventually slipped into a fitful sleep, disturbed by amorphous fears.

It had become her routine these days to get up early and prepare the morning for Mama, before going with

Maomao to Baba's work unit to see Master Tan of the WPT. And every day she was sent away. "Cannot find him, he isn't here. Has he run away for some reason?" That was all she got out of them. I've got to do something myself, Yanzi concluded, her thoughts churning over this resolution.

"Yanzi, you're here again. I've called all the cowsheds on campus but no one has him. See this list? It is all marked, I checked every one of them. Your father is a good comrade and a true revolutionary, but there is not much more I can do, go home to your Mama. He'll be back," said Master Tan.

"How can I go home? The home with no Baba isn't a home. Can you imagine your kids without you? And can you imagine being stuck somewhere and unable to go home to see your kids?" Yanzi's high-pitched staccato voice rang out fast, as if someone were chasing her.

"He will come back, I'm sure."

"How can you be so sure? He has not been home for two weeks. I won't leave unless Baba is back."

"That's not an option," Master Tan said irritatedly.

"Can we go and check the cowsheds ourselves then?"

"No."

"Why not?"

"Because I said so. Because everyone here obeys me, including your father. Go."

Yanzi's eyes rested on Master Tan's desk, on that piece of paper. "All right," Yanzi winked at Maomao and, snatching the list from the desk, ran out of the office.

They arrived at the first cowshed on the list, that

was for the Department of History. They climbed up the wobbly steps and entered a sequence of shanties and shacks thrown up out of corrugated iron and reed matting. Inside was clammy and dank, with no windows except a glass pane on the door filtering in a mean natural light. On the floor were rows of straw mats, about twenty of them, one next to another, but nobody was there. Yanzi and Maomao recoiled from the acrid stench of dirt, sweat, and mould. Back on the main road they sat on the kerb, watching people pass by, and not knowing what to do next.

At the sight of a small parade of prisoners approaching, Yanzi stood up, eyes dilated, scanning the stumbling lines like an eagle hunting her prey; for she was convinced they were the residents of the cowshed. They scanned the faces. A tall lanky man of fifty with dishevelled long hair veiling his gold-rimmed glasses, wan and bleary-eyed, had a pickaxe on his shoulder. He was dressed in black trousers six inches too short. The next man, undersized with grey hair, his face mottled with age spots, wearing a shirt that covered his knees, was carrying a shovel. There were two women dressed in men's boiler suits, holding a large basket full of tools between them. Maomao nudged Yanzi with her elbow and asked, "That one?"

He did resemble Yanzi's baba, same build and similar height.

"No. He would recognise me."

"But he didn't lift his head up."

Yanzi took another closer look. The man's face was

covered with a beard, he had a fresh wound next to his nose and one of his eyes was so swollen it had become a line. But the other eye wasn't as large as Baba's. Then there was a sudden burst of tumultuous noise from up the road and a horde of raving Red Guards marched into view. The parade of prisoners stopped and moved off the road warily.

The girls made their way home in silence. The next day they went to the cowshed for the Department of Eastern Languages and were glad to find someone in the guard's office.

"Go, go, go away!" shouted a pale young man with hollow cheeks from behind the door window.

"Please, I'm looking for my baba, and I've got this," Yanzi said, waving a piece of paper at the door.

The girls squeezed in through the reluctantly opened door. The young man perused the letter, went away and returned with a file.

"We don't have Wang Qingming here, too bad. All the names are here."

"Please can we take a look?"

The girls stood by the table and searched the file. Suddenly Maomao pointed on the list and cried out "This is my baba!" and ran out. Yanzi started to follow but stopped at the door. 'I won't be able to come back again,' she thought. She carefully scanned the list but Baba's name wasn't there.

"Can I take a peep in the cowshed?" Yanzi asked.

"No."

"But please. I've got his pills, he will go crazy without them, and his glasses. I know he has to write confessions, he can't write with no glasses, right? If he can't write his confessions, your job isn't done, is it? You will have to stay and wait till he confesses? You won't be able to go home early to play with your younger sister …"

"Who told you I have a younger sister?"

"No one, I just know," said Yanzi, "I guess she is younger than me, right, and really cute? I imagine she has a lot of dolls and toys and her baba to play with her … I miss my baba, he's been missing for many weeks. Please help me. Let me take a look, if I find him you'd have one prisoner less to keep. Please … my mother is sick." Yanzi started sobbing louder and louder. The young man was getting irritated, so he pushed Yanzi out and locked the door.

Maomao was sitting on a bench waiting for her.

"Maomao, don't you want to see your baba?" Yanzi was pleased to find Maomao's father.

"No."

"Why? I would be dead pleased if I found my baba. What's the matter? Don't cry. I'm sorry."

"Mama reported Baba to the WPT, because Baba said he didn't like one person above everyone else, he didn't like how people were being made to hate each other, and he said it was wrong to make Chairman Mao like God. They argued and shouted at each other all night. Mama said he would get the whole family in trouble by holding that view." Maomao paused a little and said, "Would you report them if your family broke the law?"

"I wouldn't, never. Would you?"

"I don't know, but Mama was right too. She said it

177

will only be his crime if she reported it, and we'll still have a future. If not, the whole family is guilty, Mama said, something to do with our files. Yes, it'll be there for the rest of our lives. She said she had to draw a clear line between Baba and us. It's to protect us all."

"Like the Monkey King, drawing a circle for the Tang Monk?"

"Yes," Maomao smiled.

"You want to see him as much as I want to see my baba, don't you?"

Yanzi got back home, exhausted. Mama was asleep so she sat next to her bed, talking to herself.

"I wish I was the Monkey King who has diamond eyes that can see everything from above. I'll find you, Baba ..."

"Where are you, Baba?" Yanzi called in an echoing voice.

"I am here," a faint voice.

Baba was trapped in the coils of a giant snake in a dark and deep forest. Yanzi gripped a long sword in both hands, held out in front of her, as she advanced towards the serpent, aiming the point at its heart. The serpent slowly uncoiled from Baba, and glided towards her presenting its enormous vermilion mouth, big enough to fit her in whole, fangs dripping with poison ...

Yanzi sat up, eyes shut, and screamed in terror, then she cried, "No, no, go back ... I can save Baba, I can, please I want to go back ..."

Yanzi went to the office every day, as if she worked there. Maomao's mother had forbidden her to go with Yanzi after she had told her about the cowshed where her father was kept. Sometimes Yanzi helped out, fetching boiling water, sticking stamps on the envelopes, or passing messages between offices. She was sitting in the waiting room one day when Master Tan strode in, berating the two Red Guards hurrying after him.

"… doesn't need to come in! Does he think we are morons? Get Wei, Shu and Tang, and drag that little twat over here today! And don't spare the courtesies!"

His face softened as he caught sight of Yanzi, "What are you doing here?"

"Waiting for you when you are free."

"Go home, take care of your mama, Yanzi."

"Master Tan, you can help me, I know you can, can't you? I know you have a kind heart, you don't want me to be fatherless, do you? I am an abject wretch and I can't bear it. Do you ever feel wretched? Wouldn't your kids feel wretched if you went missing? Do I talk too much? I can keep my mouth shut if you want me to."

"Sit there quietly and wait for me to deal with this pile of paperwork, then we can take a trip to the personnel department," Master Tan said. Yanzi followed Master Tan back to his office and waited while he stamped through the paper in front of him.

With Yanzi on the back seat of Master Tan's bicycle, they soon arrived at their destination.

"Yes, some time ago now, there were two people from a factory asking for information on a Wang something, I cannot remember exactly. I just gave them the file. They didn't say much, but I wonder if it is related?" said a middle-aged lady staring at them through a thick pair of glasses, in the personnel department office.

"Do you remember who they were looking for?"

"No, but it was Wang, I think."

"Do you remember where they were from?"

"No," the lady said apologetically. "Wait a minute, I do have their letter of introduction somewhere."

She came back a few minutes later triumphantly waving a piece of paper in her hand. "I've got it, it's the Beijing Machine Factory."

"Thank you," Master Tan said to the lady. When they got out, he turned to Yanzi and smiled. "I have a contact there. I have work to finish here now, but we are going there tomorrow, OK?"

Yanzi was lost for words so she hugged Master Tan's waist.

*

After he had failed to escape the second time, Qingming's desire was extinguished for he knew he wouldn't be able to do it again and live. He couldn't move, his head was exploding and he had lost two teeth. It was stupid trying to escape like that, but he had become despondent after several attempts to send a message home had failed; he had even offered money to one guard, but they were drunk on principles and it had gained him nothing but a slap. After his attempted escape, while they were beating him up, Qingming had looked them in their eyes enquiringly, but this they had taken as contempt and only struck him harder. 'Who are these people? Students? Why so much hatred, to me, a total stranger?

I don't understand. I told them who I am, but they just beat me for it, and shout at me to confess,' Qingming thought. He was beginning to lose hope. He agonised over his wife and his daughter. Will Yanzi or his colleagues come to look for him? How long had he to endure physical torment and mental torture; how long had he to wait before he could go home? Through the window he stared at the big mulberry tree outside; wind had stripped its grace and thrashed the yellow leaves dancing in the air. The hour grew tired, so he closed his eyes. In his waking dream he heard Yanzi's voice. It sounded so real, he wanted to reach out, to touch her, hold her; a gentle calm suffused his aching body. Yanzi was talking to the guard, then her voice was joined by Master Tan's. Qingming snapped alert, gathered all his strength and shouted feebly: "Yanzi! Yanzi, I am here!" He pulled himself towards the window with his elbows, but several times he had to stop to ease his pain. When he arrived under the window, he took off his belt, threw it around the window catch and pulled himself up. He caught a glimpse of Yanzi from the back before they vanished into the work-yard. Again he called: "I am here," before collapsing to the floor, his face bleached with effort.

*

He was not there. Not there among the prisoners in the work-yard. Her hopes were crushed, a swallow brought to ground. She lay awake surrounded by grief. Her heart ached. "Where are you, Baba? Why can't I find you?" In the bleak darkness of that interminable night her imagination gave free rein to her innermost fears. She fell asleep silently weeping into the cold mound of earth that was her baba's unmarked grave.

The morning sunlight flooded in bringing renewed hope. Her baba was out there, somewhere. He needed her, so she could not, would not, despair. She continued to haunt Master Tan's office. The weeks stretched into winter. Under her care Mama's health gradually improved, and Yanzi would lie beside her, escaping into the stories she read.

A bitter wind had thrashed the posters into sodden pulp. Yanzi hurried through the doors of the facilities department. "Yanzi, you've come. Master Tan wanted to see you, he is in his office."

"Yanzi, I don't want you to get your hopes up, but my contact at Beijing Machine tells me they have a big struggle session coming up. That gives us a chance."

"Why?" Yanzi interrupted.

"Because all the accused will have to appear at the struggle session. I know we didn't find him last time, but it's worth a try. If you like, I'll take you there. Come and meet me here the day after tomorrow."

"Oh, thank you, Master Tan, thank you!"

*

A few days after his beating, Qingming was able to stand up. He was returned to the daily routine with the other prisoners. He knew he had no choice, but to admit to being Jingming. He struck a deal with the rebel authorities: he would confess if he could be allowed to visit his home after the struggle session. To assist him, Qingming was given the written evidence of the crimes Jingming had committed. From the file, Qingming learnt that Jingming had been a deputy party secretary for four years, until five years ago when he changed jobs. While at the factory he had promoted efficiency and productivity, and this had accorded him the crimes of 'Failing to grasp revolution' and 'Failing to promote class struggle', despite, or perhaps because of, the fact that production had tripled. It took him two days to summarise Jingming's crimes and create his confession.

Friday afternoon; the end of year struggle session was being held in the factory canteen hall. Qingming and a dozen others, their necks weighed down with placards bearing their names drawn in large black characters crossed out in red, were pushed onto the platform. The first of the accused was manhandled in front of the angry throng, head bowed, back bent, pinioned either side by a rebel rotating his arms behind his back and above the shoulders, as if in the strappado. Loudspeakers led the rally:

"Down with Yu Heng!"

The canteen was packed and spirits were high. Yanzi and Master Tan had arrived late. Yanzi couldn't see through the crowd of people, so she ducked down and eyed up her chances of advancing between the forest of legs, but Master Tan seized her collar, dragged her back, then lifted her up onto a nearby windowsill. She saw everything. In the limelight a man, forced to kneel at the front of the stage, was thrashed then dragged back. The next target was grabbed, head down, heaved forward, and the speaker shouted: "Down with Wang Jingming!"

"Down with Wang Jingming!" the crowd echoed.

In the brief silence that followed a voice from the crowd rang out, "He is not Wang Jingming!"

Qingming lifted his head up; long, messy hair veiled his eyes and a beard concealed his face.

"Baba?" Yanzi exclaimed, "It's Baba!" But no one heard her.

"Yes, he is not," someone else agreed, "Wang Jingming is much shorter than this man. Who is he?"

"He's right! Wang Jingming is much shorter. He doesn't look anything like him!" The crowd turned towards where the voice came. On the stage, it became slightly chaotic.

The leader of the rebel gang strode up to confront Qingming and slapped his face, "Why do you pretend to be Wang Jingming!"

"I have told you I'm not him, but you just beat me up," said Qingming, head bowed.

Yanzi slid off the windowsill and squeezed through the legs.

"That's right, this man is not Wang Jingming, you've got the wrong man."

"Let him go!" the crowd was shouting.

One of the rebels took off the placard.

Yanzi emerged from the front of the crowd, reaching

the stage, tripping up the stairs, and she launched herself into her baba's arms, hiding her face in his chest, shaking and speechless. The world around them had ceased to exist and the clamour disappeared into a vacuum.

The Helmsman

When He saw the dishes on the red sandalwood dining table, the red braised pork belly dish and fish head soup, He felt, at once, His mouth moisten and His appetite return urgently after one day's petulant refusal of food. He moved the sheaf of paper files to His left hand side and began His preprandial ritual: He picked up His very own silver chopsticks and dipped them into the food; while inspecting them, His hands began to shake and He dropped the chopsticks. An obsequious young man rushed in with replacements. He grunted His disapproval of the chopsticks that were too hard for Him to grip, so the young man fetched another pair, then tasted all the dishes and left. He paused for a while before diving into the food. The red braised pork was cooked exactly how He liked, free from soy sauce. He had always hated that from the time He had seen the layer of maggots floating on top of the fermented soy sauce His father made when He was a little boy.

The palatial dining room, in the part of the Forbidden City called Middle South Sea where the late emperor's family had lived, looked sparse with thick brick walls and tall ceilings. The room was lightly furnished; apart from the dining table, there were two modern display cabinets, some chests, a few armchairs and scattered

Chinese paintings depicting animals, cocks, shrimps or horses, by Qi Baishi and Xu Beihong. The room was a little dingy. Although one wall was made up of windows and doors, outside a veranda cut off much of the natural light. The dark scarlet, heavy, damask curtains gathered at the sides were never drawn closed. The original antiques had been cleared out before He moved in. He couldn't understand why those antique dealers were so obsessed by old things. He was adamant that old things should be destroyed to make way for the new, but of course, it should exclude Himself. He condemned Western decadence, espoused an austere lifestyle, and maintained that luxury would only soften the courage and harden the resentment.

It was in early autumn, a typical Autumn Tiger day at the peak of the Great Proletarian Cultural Revolution. The temperature had soared, but He didn't want the electric fan on while eating, as He believed the draught would carry His *Qi* away and make Him ill. He patted His forehead with His napkin but it stubbornly exuded globules of sweat. He was sweltering in His white cotton vest so He rolled it up to His armpits.

He was a big man of an inscrutable countenance, tall and handsome but with a rather feminine complexion, smooth and fair even in His seventies. He had a podgy face and the barest beginnings of a paunch around His middle. It was all perhaps because of His favourite dish, juicy, fatty red braised pork belly, over which He had lost His composure the last time they had argued. As she flounced out He had ranted on behind His wife's back: "That's right, I'm a bumpkin. I am a farmer's son and I have a farmer's habits, I don't like showers or baths, don't like leather shoes. I like to eat pig's fat, the red braised pork is good for my brain and it is the supplement for me, stupid woman. She is such a snoot that she can just bugger off. Bloody woman, look what she makes me do. From now on, she can just go away to have her own meals. I don't need her to boss me about. That's it!"

He put down the paper He was reading, He couldn't believe the plate was empty already. He tapped the plate with the chopsticks and the same young man came in and replaced it with another plateful of the red braised pork. He nodded at the boy with a broad smile.

He was reading a draft critique of Lu Xun, an esteemed scholar and writer, whom He adored and worshipped. He had once summarised Lu's philosophy into His famous phrase: 'To struggle with heaven is exquisite, to struggle with nature is exquisite, to struggle with people is exquisite.' He circled, in red ink, a paragraph, and added His scribble in the margin. As He read on He got more excited, and adrenaline started pumping into His bloodstream. He idolised Lu Xun like a saint, His kinsman and role model, and had learnt from Lu's tenacious, intolerant, austere, merciless approach to fighting his enemies. He had adopted many of Lu's maxims into a set of personal mottoes: 'Hold on to the arrows your enemy fires at you, and wait until the best opportunity arrives to fire them all back', 'Never forgive', 'Incessantly beat a drowning dog'. Lu's spirit, like a lucky charm, had helped Him to defeat so many of His enemies: Jiang Jieshi, the Japanese, and many of His own comrades. In His excitement He picked up a leaf fan to waft Himself with.

"Where was I?" He was annoyed at losing His train of thought. He fanned Himself irritatedly, before muttering; "That's it, Lu Xun." There had been an awkward moment recently when a journalist had asked Him what Lu Xun would be if he were alive today. He had paused some while for an answer, and then said indifferently: "He would either be writing confessions in jail, or just be sensible and keep quiet."

After the meal, He set off strolling along the colonnade into the garden in His *boocei*, a pair of cotton shoes with hand-stitched soles, as inseparable from Him as the cigarette dangling between His tawny fingers. Behind everybody's reverence and loyalty He sensed evil and malice; someone was there to get Him, and He had never before felt so tired and alone. As He was approaching the lily pond, He came to a halt, deviated from the covered walk and veered towards the Fu rockery, a man-made hill and the highest point within the Middle South Sea compound. He distrusted high-rise buildings, believed in only standing on solid ground, and the Fu rockery certainly satisfied His desire. With only intermittent shade from trees, He was drenched and out of breath by the time He reached the top, coming into the Grand Pavilion. He gazed thoughtfully towards the far end of the compound beyond the woods as if to ascertain that the high wall which He had ordered to be built was still there. He sat down into the cushions on the bench, puffed hard at His cigarette and narrowed His eyes, musing on the enclosure formed by the shabby grey temporary walls, starkly contrasted against the grand red background; like it was a trophy, a symbol of His success and His prize for winning the game.

He trembled at the thought of what would have happened if Liu Shaoqi, the Chinese president that He had hand-picked, had beaten Him. It would have been He who was the one locked up in that dog kennel. Only He Himself could fully appreciate how fortunate He was to have swiftly seized a tremendous victory out of a humiliating defeat only a few years earlier when He had been pushed aside and blamed, naturally by Liu, of being responsible for the thirty million deaths during the famine. He was politically weak then, so He had swallowed His pride and secluded himself away from the capital deep in southern China, like a turtle hiding in its shell. But He had no appetite for defeat, not even with the red braised pork belly, and His indomitable thoughts turned once again to long years of waiting and plotting. In the meantime, and much to His dismay, Liu Shaoqi had engineered a successful economic recovery. Liu was threatening His leadership and a fierce power struggle ensued, leading to a deplorable loss of control at the last Party convention just before the Cultural Revolution. He recalled with great chagrin the overt challenge from Liu, the expletives like "piss head", "shit brain" and "fart mouth" bandied between them. He took a hard drag on His cigarette then flung it away. "No one should beat me!" He exclaimed to Himself. "Even if I must turn the whole world upside down!" The odds had been against Him, though. To openly stir up a rebellion targeted at Liu had been a risky strategy, but worth the pay-off! He was rather proud of Himself, of the idea of the Great Proletarian Cultural Revolution, His gamble inspired by Chinese Go chess. He ran His finger over the Go chess board inscribed onto the stone table at the centre of the pavilion and contemplated.

'He thought he would win because he had bishops, knights and rooks and I only had pawns, but I didn't play his game, I gambled on Chinese Go chess, winning by numbers. Even though he had the whole Politburo on his side, I had seven hundred million people on mine. The Red Guards, rebels, the mob if you like; the disorder, the mayhem, the witch-hunts easily devoured him and wiped out the entire Politburo "with the tip of my little finger", just as I swore at the convention. Honestly, I'm surprised how easily he and his gang collapsed, like a sandcastle in the rising tide. Am I really a god?'

He chuckled loudly.

"Chairman," one of the guards came up, seeing Him in a good mood, "the doctor will be here soon, would you like to go back please?"

He beckoned both guards to come near, as He wanted to share His glory with someone.

"Do you know what is behind that wall?"

"Yes, the garden tool hut," said one of the guards.

"Was. What is it for now?"

"It's where Liu Shaoqi is locked up," said the other guard.

"Ah, you know. What else do you know?" He asked.

"They say no one wants to help him, they just leave his food and water by the door. They say Liu is too sick to get up to eat or wash himself, and he does his business in bed," said the guard, hanging his head as if he had done something wrong.

"Ha! Can you imagine your once mighty president, such an ostentatious figure, has such a sad fate? Do you know why we lock him up here rather than send him to prison? Because I want to remind everyone that the class enemy is all around us."

"Yes, Chairman," said the tall guard nodding effusively, but the other was totally confused.

Urgent footsteps, drubbing on the stone pathway, interrupted their conversation.

"Oh, it's you!" He said impassively.

"Chairman, how are you? I trust you enjoyed your dinner? Hunan cuisine, specially designed by ME and …" said Jiang Qing, His wife, a tall woman with an aged and harsh face. She paused as she detected the guards. "What are you doing here? Away." She cast them an exasperated look. They quickly retreated to a respectful distance.

Jiang searched His face for a reaction, which He refused to give, and continued heedfully, "I came earlier to avoid the traffic, but I waited, as I didn't want to disturb your meal."

There was still no response, but instead He was waving at a girl in uniform with an effusive bunch of flowers in her hand, walking towards His palace, on the path below.

"Who is she?" Jiang asked. He stopped her with the merest twitch of an eyebrow. Need He remind her that curiosity was inflammatory? She quickly changed the topic. "Has the Chairman heard the news? Liu has gone, moved to Henan yesterday. We don't want him to die here, do we?"

He stood up with His hand resting on His hip, looking content.

"It's funny, the plane was delayed because the stretcher-bearers refused to carry him on. They said it stank like a sewer. I made sure he received no medical treatment." Jiang paused as if for applause. "He is deadly sick, skinny and shrunk, won't last long. I'm his nemesis, you know. Fearsome President Liu's finally rotten and forgotten. Ha, Ha," Jiang chuckled, looking at her husband with veneration and waiting as if she was expecting a pat on the shoulder and a ruffle of her hair. Then Jiang casually presented her proof, a photo of an old man on a stretcher carried by four soldiers. The old man, buried in a blanket with noticeable holes, had an emaciated face, his long white hair strewn around his head, his eyes wide open as if just woken from a nightmare.

Jiang continued, "If the Chairman agrees, I'll get rid of those ugly high walls around the garden hut," and pointed at the enclosure joyfully.

He gave her a faint smile and an almost imperceptible nod. "I beat him. I won," He said coldly but triumphantly. "Who did he think he was? Just because he helped to purge a few of my enemies and eradicated the opposition earlier on, or even ended the famine; that rogue thought he could pee on my head? He does not know how to fight, how to play the game. He gave me no face, I'll give him no life! A brash, cocky and arrogant brat, he got what he deserved."

Jiang cautiously showed him the second photo, no doubt the one she really wanted him to see. It was Liu's wife, head hung and arms pinioned by two Red Guards, at a struggle rally. She was in the dress she had worn at her stunning debut as 'First Lady' when she had accompanied Liu Shaoqi, the Chinese President, for their international tour in the early 1960s. Matching high-heeled shoes along with a long necklace made out of ping-pong balls were hung over her neck. He harrumphed, and His face darkened reading His wife's thoughts: 'Look at your flirting tart, even you cannot save her now.'

"Chairman, it's hard to tell how much I revere and worship you. Like they say, one word of yours counts for ten thousand words," said Jiang, perhaps realising she had gone too far.

"Ten thousand words? What farting!" He scoffed contemptuously, "How could you not understand that flattery won't get you anywhere?" He was irritated by these slogans perpetually thrown at Him, 'eternity', 'live for ten thousand years'. It mocked His intelligence He felt, but oddly He encouraged His own personality cult among the people and demanded the status of a god from the public.

"Chairman, you mustn't let yourself fret." Jiang dusted

off the hair and dandruff from His shoulder. "Look at it, your vest is dirty and your hair, look at your hair. This girl, cannot find anyone good these days." She turned around and beckoned the guards, "Get me Xiao ..."

He growled with a scowl and sneer on His face.

Jiang tensed up and she looked baffled at what she might have done wrong now. "Is it a bad time? Shall I come back later?" she asked.

"What do you want?" He said, thinking: 'This useless wife of mine, makes everyone around her my enemy.' He hated her as much as everyone else but He couldn't denounce her, and let those bastards win the battle started nearly thirty years ago. And after all, she had her uses: To attack His enemies without getting His own hands dirty, like she had done so well to shit on Liu Shaoqi. In addition she was such a good barometer to test the loyalty of those around them.

"I've got a list, Chairman."

"Eh?"

"Yes, the list of those still plotting against you."

He looked at her inquiringly and saw her become exhilarated as if she was waiting for a reward. "Where did it come from?"

"What?"

"The list." He was irritated.

"Nowhere. I did it, oh, with a little help from Ye Qun ..." Jiang slowed down at the name as if to see whether she would be shouted at. "We stayed up the whole of last night," she finished in supplication.

"That atrocious witch, nothing good will come from

her. You stop associating with her. She is using you," He scolded.

"But, Chairman, please, you always teach me to make use of our enemies for our own advantage. It's a good opportunity, a one-time only opportunity, to completely clear out your enemies within." She sounded aggrieved.

He looked at His wife; something about her appearance was displeasing. Was it her army hat? Her hamster-like cheeks or her astringent manner? He couldn't put His finger on it. He had never doubted her loyalty, knowing she was the only person in the world He could really trust, and He was determined to give her what she wanted just to piss off those who had opposed their marriage thirty years ago. Unfortunately she was too much a bully on master's power. She barked at absolutely everyone she dealt with; everyone equally hated and feared her, even her own allies, if she ever had any. He resented having to clean up the mess His wife made, and that He had to show publicly that He was not pandering to her at the expense of Party principles. He had both protected and restrained her ever since He had had to accept their prenuptial agreement with the communist Politburo: that Jiang Qing could be His wife only on condition that she would never take up any political position. His wife was now in charge of the Cultural Revolution, and every single individual from that Politburo of thirty years ago who had opposed her marriage had been vanquished, destroyed, obliterated, or had died.

"Who is this?" He put His finger on the list.

"Just a librarian, at Peking University."

"Why?"

"The Chairman doesn't need to bother Himself with it," she replied.

"Do you want me to sign?"

"All right, she dug out some articles from an old newspaper and spread rumours about me. A diabolical act!" she grimaced.

"What about this one? Is this my brother-in-law? You put my brother-in-law on the blacklist as well?"

"Ex-brother-in-law," she corrected.

"Pen," He demanded, then scribbled on the paper.

"She hates you, she will sully your name, he is her accomplice!" Jiang screamed.

"She was my wife, you rotten egg!" He ripped the paper in half, flung it into a bush, dismissed His wife and walked down the hill. After a while He stopped by the fish pond, and the guard brought a basket. He watched, with ease and pleasure, the goldfish fighting each other fiercely for the breadcrumbs and wondered if He could come up with a ploy to make His enemies fight like that again. The guard had retrieved the paper He had thrown in the bush. He didn't want His wife to know that He agreed with her most of the time, as He needed to keep her firmly in her place. 'The bone is there to give not to demand,' He thought.

The heat of the hottest afternoon that autumn disconcerted him. He lit the fifth cigarette, but it couldn't cool him down. Then He remembered last night, the two dancers He had danced with, they were very cute, and He felt a frisson of excitement.

"Get me secretary Huang," He called at the guards. Shortly afterwards, Huang, a slim, tall young man in his early thirties, came over hastily with a notepad in his hand. He told Huang that He wanted to swim in fifteen minutes, and He wanted the two girls He had met last night to be there too.

"Chairman, what about the doctor's appointment?" said Huang.

"He can wait, change it to tomorrow."

"Chairman, I only know they are from the army dance troupe. What are their names?" Huang asked.

"Find out!" He retorted, irritated.

"Chairman, I need more time please?" Huang begged.

He dropped His eyes and after a long pause said, "How is your father's arm?"

Huang's face blanched a ghastly white, and he scuttled off. His father's hidden past had become a chain around his neck forever.

By the time the nurse had rubbed sun protection all over Him and got Him ready in His swim suit, the two girls, in their bright silky swimming costumes, were already bathing in the sun by the pool, like a pair of mermaids. He ensconced himself in a deckchair and watched them behind His sunglasses under the parasol. The sky was clear and the sun was fiercely unpleasant. He felt that drawing an analogy between Him and the sun was ridiculous, especially right now. One of the girls was pushed in the pool mischievously, sparking off a raucous splashing contest. They larked about in the water, laughing, splashing and screaming as if they were in paradise. When they spotted Him, the two girls sprayed water at Him in a frolicsome way to get Him in the pool. He reached out His hand, and when He caught a smooth, solid young thigh He could not resist any more. He whispered to the one with long silky hair and ordered Huang to reschedule the meeting with Zhou, His premier.

His office was like a library with walls of book shelves and mountains of paperwork on the desks. An overloaded porcelain brush pot, and a jade pencil case were side by side next to an inkwell. He stubbornly denied pens existed, using brushes and pencils only, but He loved His table lamps, green glass shades with golden brass bases. In His shiny leather club chair, He was shouting down the phone: "Do I play by the rules? No, I don't, I play by any means that win. Change the rules if I have to. Just do it!"

As He slammed the phone down, a young boy came in with a pile of files and set them down neatly on the desk.

"Haven't seen you before; how long have you been here?" He asked.

"Hi Chairman Mao, I have been here for nearly five months," the boy answered heedfully.

"Are you happy here?" He said, smiling.

"Yes, Chairman, very happy. People are very nice, helpful. It's the greatest honour to serve you here. I've learnt so much here, you are so amiable, approachable, so great, so–"

"Why are you happy? You shouldn't be. You are here to work, to work hard," He remonstrated capriciously. After a long pause He continued, "Listen to your glib talk, flattering, you are not telling the truth, are you? Are you a spy? Snooping on me? Guards!"

The boy looked completely nonplussed and began to stutter "P…please, I, I … I'm not, don't ss…send me back," while the guards escorted him out. He knew He did it for no reason. He did it because He could and because He was in a bad mood. What He didn't know was that the boy's life was shattered.

Back in the office, He had begun to rifle through the files; reports of industrial outputs, economic growth, unemployment, fraught with figures and numbers that really bored him. Then a hospital form caught His attention. It was a diagnostic report: 'Diagnosis: Early stage bowel cancer, Recommendation: Surgery to remove the tumour followed by chemotherapy.' He stood up and paced around; the electric fan was whirring. "I cannot allow him off work for three months, there is too much to do," He pondered. "He is the only one who can deal with the Red Guards and rebels. No, No, No." He stamped a red 'Top Secret' on the form and wrote: 'Absolutely no one should know this including himself' and signed. By now He felt exhausted, His hand was shaking, His sight blurring and His vigour fading. He knew His time was limited, but He wouldn't give up the fight. How could He give up His soul, His blood and His life? Even were He the last man standing, still He would continue fighting. Having no enemy was never a problem, He could always create more.

Zhou Enlai, His premier, arrived at eight o'clock sharp along with his personal secretary C who carried with him a heavy file case. Tea was brought in and Zhou sat in an armchair opposite.

"Hello Chairman, how are you?"

"Good if you want me to be," He replied as He handed over Jiang's torn list to C. "Copy the list, investigate each of them, give me the report tomorrow. And this pile, about the economy and development, I don't know why they sent me these nuisances. You sort it out, will you?"

"Yes, Chairman," Zhou said and handed the pile to C.

"You've been attacked last week, haven't you? You need to call a meeting, do a thorough self-criticism and make a sincere confession. Then you might be let off."

"Yes, Chairman, please advise me what I should confess," Zhou said with deference.

He looked at Zhou incredulously and said, "Are you challenging me? Confess what you said, what you did in the past, what about the declaration you made in February 1932?"

"But it is not true, Chairman. The Party investigated it and concluded it was a ploy made up by Jiang Jieshi," Zhou said.

"There's no smoke without fire. Yes?"

"Yes, Chairman, I'll call a meeting," Zhou acquiesced.

"That's better. What's the news?" He said, puffing at His cigarette, seemingly calm.

"Chairman, the Red Guards resist going back to

school and workers refuse to work in their factories. The Cultural Revolution is being treated as a long holiday. On the other hand the violence is extremely widespread as well."

"Do you enjoy making up bad news to upset me?"

"Oh no, Chairman, we need our greatest ever leader and your guidance," he said, fumbling his files.

"I want you to stop the Cultural Revolution, and return to normality now," He pronounced decisively.

"Chairman, that is great. But how? The situation is out of our control," said Zhou.

"I heard some nine hundred people were arrested from just one university. That's too bad. What do they do when locked up?"

"Sweep floors," Zhou replied.

"Release them."

"Does the Chairman know this morning that a mob of rebels were trying to force their way in here, as they wanted Liu Shaoqi for a struggle rally. It's frightening; if a mob really got in it would be difficult to stop them unless we used the army."

"Double the security."

"Yes, Chairman."

Zhou pulled out a sheaf of paper from a file and said, "I received this information on Wednesday; since the beginning of this year, four hundred thousand have died in violent clashes …"

"Don't make such a big deal about it. People do die, everyone will die. Thirty million died during the famine, so what? It's the cost of the communist future.

We didn't fall apart. Those leaders, senior officials, so called revolutionaries, even killed themselves after a little criticism. That was so pathetic." He gave Zhou an insouciant glance.

"What are we going to do with the Red Guards? Sixteen million youths, energetic adolescents who have nothing to do, no schools, no jobs, marauding around in the cities causing trouble," protested Zhou.

"Yes, they had their use, they were effective in getting rid of Liu but …" He mused.

"We could open more factories, build more roads, railways and other infrastructure. Have a second industrial revolution," Zhou suggested enthusiastically.

"So you want to hand over power to the rightists who criticised us as incapable of running the economy? You want the intellectuals, economists, capitalists and financiers to run China again?" He sneered at Zhou, and stared at Zhou's emaciated face, hollow-eyed, with sunken cheeks and thought, 'What an old woman he is sometimes, begging to save others, not even knowing about his own cancer.'

"The Red Guards, the youth, the rebels," He murmured to himself, and then declared to Zhou, "order the army to stamp down on unrest!"

"But our army is in chaos too. Many generals were purged," Zhou simpered. "Chairman, we have misgivings about the way the Red Guards are led and we need to reinstate our senior generals and bring back law and order."

"Nonsense! Class struggle always takes precedence

over any other matters. Class enemies are hiding among our people still!" He stopped suddenly, looked at Zhou slyly and said, "You might be one of them. Aren't you?"

Zhou was aghast but quickly regained his composure. "Oh no, I have been following you since the 1930s and have always supported you."

He did not respond, His silence announcing the grudge more deeply than any words, so quickly did the tension loom up.

With a wave of the hand He dismissed the meeting, as He had a real headache that night and wanted to retire early. The nurse wiped His body with warm towels, tucked Him into bed, pulled down the mosquito net, switched off the main lights and quietly closed the door behind her. He lay face up, still and straight like a sculpture on a sarcophagus. He didn't read like He normally would, He couldn't sleep either, His mind too active, rearranging His thoughts.

He felt He was losing vigour; His physical frailty had desiccated His passion for making enemies and winning. He had, throughout His time, always gambled with other people's lives, sometimes millions of them. He wanted to be remembered as a winner, but He knew that one day He would be cursed for so much death and destruction. He wanted the Cultural Revolution to stop, and He particularly didn't want the fire He had ignited to destroy Liu with, to come back and burn Himself. 'It isn't entirely impossible. What do I do if they break into the Middle South Sea? How can I get rid of sixteen million frenzied Red Guards?' He quivered at this thought.

It made him jump when He felt something glide onto His stomach underneath His vest, cool and soothing. He called the guards, only to find it was the dancer from the swimming pool. In the dimmed lights, He let the white, marble-like, smooth snake run all over His body, under His underwear, and He felt himself becoming aroused. The girl climbed up on him, riding His leg, bent down slowly, gently stroking His body then sucked on His lips. She murmured He was too tense, asking Him to relax and enjoy Himself. He grasped the breasts dangling at His face but He couldn't do it and He became frustrated and exasperated. As He thrust her off him He growled, "Damned Red Guards." The white snake quietly climbed up again, but this time she landed on the floor with a thump following a forceful kick.

He started thinking of His first wife, killed by Jiang Jieshi when she was nineteen. The memory took him back to a small village in Hu Nan province where He had joined the revolutionaries. He remembered how they emerged from non-existence by amassing very small numbers of people from each part of a vast countryside, flowing to the cities and in the end to power.

Suddenly He jumped out of the bed and exclaimed: "Yes, the reverse! From existence to non-existent." He rushed into His office next door. It was 2.30 in the morning. On a piece of paper He wrote in brush: 'It is absolutely necessary that the educated urban youth go to rural areas and be re-educated by poor peasants.' After fumbling in the drawer, He stamped on the paper

'Urgent!' in red and wrote at the bottom of the paper: 'Implement it nationwide immediately'.

Starting the next day sixteen million one-time Red Guards, now the re-educated youth, were sent to the most remote and desolate areas of China. Separated from their families they learned to struggle for their daily survival under atrocious living conditions. Sixteen million counters on two men's Go chess board were scattered and forgotten.

The Heavenly Earth

At the Beijing Central railway station, amid the urgent hooting of the snake-like trains gliding in and out, whistling steam swirled through the acrid air. Prolonged autumn rain had brought thick grey cloud and the lowering sky had descended. The platforms were bubbling though, and people were scurrying to and fro to the bombastic drumbeat of the bands, like ants on a hot pan. The red-banner slogans shouted out, 'Farewell city youth!', 'Go forth to the great countryside!', 'Be re-educated by peasants' and 'Answer Chairman Mao's call, make deep rural roots!', alongside ranks of red flags and troupes of propaganda performers. Avid teenagers crowded round the distribution tables, staffed by grown-ups, to collect their red flower and meal box.

"Which school?"

"Name?"

"Coach No. 3. Your hero flower and meal for the journey. Next!"

Family and relatives were milling around in all directions. The station had not been so lively since the end of the Great Free Travelling at the beginning of the Cultural Revolution in 1966, yet this time the youth were travelling out of the city rather than into it.

I stood by coach No. 7 of the train from Beijing to

Xian, with Mama and my thirteen-year-old, younger brother Jianjun, facing each other in silence. Mama clenched Jianjun's hand like a limpet, as if he would spring off if she let go. With her other hand she tidied my green army uniform and hooked the red flower onto my chest. Staring into Mama's haggard face I was wringing my hands as if I was trying to squeeze the right words out of them.

"Be good, become a paragon of the city youth, work hard to join the Communist Party, that will be best. I am so proud of you," said Mama.

I turned away and spotted Linna and her family, talking lovingly. I wanted to greet them but I thought I shouldn't intrude. I looked at the platform clock and said to Mama, "I've got to go." What I really wanted to say was: "I don't want to go and I don't know if I can ever come back." I turned to my brother and simply said, "You look after Mama for me." The first whistle sounded as I boarded the train, and as I was winding down the window, the platform started moving, along with Mama. I looked at her tearful face and couldn't stop my own tears welling up: "I'm sorry, Mama …", but I couldn't hear her reply before she faded away into the mist.

"Goodbye, Mama, goodbye Beijing," I said to myself, overwhelmed by the uncharted world ahead of me, feeling like I was walking forward towards complete darkness.

Inside the carriage it was a riot of excitement, like troops going to a war. Hats and flowers were thrown up in the air and the carriage was suffused with green and red. Someone started singing the People's Liberation Army's marching song eliciting a rowdy chorus:

Forward! Forward! Forward!
We march on our motherland to the sun,
Burdened with our nation's hopes, an invincible force
* all as one,*
We children of workers and peasants, so mightily armed,
Without fear or retreat we heroically battle for our cause
* so charmed*
Until the enemy is wiped out, hold up the fluttering
* banner of Chairman Mao!*
Hear our bugles ring out on the wind right now!
Hear our revolutionary songs ring out our inspiration!
Comrades, march on towards the battle of liberation!

Not all joined in, however. Despite the exuberant youths eager to stand out by showing their high political correctness, many were morose teenagers who had no choice but to go. They knew they were just sand swept up by this violent tempest, launched by a wave of the hand from the greatest leader Chairman Mao. I felt so alone and missed home terribly. I tried to recall what I had said last night, and was drowning in regret that I hadn't made it up with Mama before we parted.

"Why do I have to be the first to go? It's as if you don't want me here any more. Sending me thousands of kilometres away, for what? Glory? Or so you can boast to your comrades?" I had said bitterly.

"Because you are answering Chairman Mao's call,

because you are the revolutionary successor, because we don't want to be accused again. The Workers' Propaganda Team is knocking on the door every day. After all you don't have anything to do here, lingering around," said Mama in her commanding tone of voice.

"So what do you do every day? Study Chairman Mao's book? Write confessions? Or like Baba waiting for his exculpation, beg for forgiveness? I have lots to do in Beijing, I can ask Aunty Liu to give me violin lessons ..."

"How could you be so rude? Your father has devoted all his life to the people and country."

"I know, I've heard it a hundred times: he went through the long march and nearly got killed several times. If he is such a hero, why can't he save people from destructions by a dictator? Why do they let it happen again and again?"

"Shut up! Are you out of your mind to say such a thing?"

There was a long silence, then Mama said calmly, "People are human, they want to follow someone, or something; they need a leader to guide them, like sheep need a shepherd to rely on, so they created one. Your father's generation fought their whole lives to build a united country and they don't want it all to disintegrate back into civil war again."

"Just excuses."

"How could you talk to your mother this way! All I am doing is to protect you and the family!" said Mama. I retorted with a sullen pout and stomped back to my room. I was angry; there was so little control I could exert over my own life. With the list supplied by the Workers' Propaganda Team, Mama stayed up the whole night to pack my trunk, and I stayed up the whole night being depressed. I was such a headstrong girl that I lost my head.

The train quickly sped up as soon as it left the city. An expanse of nebulous sky with flecks of sunshine spread out over the flat, open countryside divided by roads with colonnades of birch trees, which flashed past us. I leaned my head on the window pane and stared outside: jagged mountains appeared on the horizon, like in the Chinese painting in our sitting room, moving imperceptibly towards me. My vision started blurring with the soporific motion of the train and, unknowingly, I drifted into sleep. I woke up to the drubbing sound of rain on the pane. The landscape was drab and grey, but the distant mountain ranges shrouded in mist looked rather attractive and mysterious. The carriage itself was now placid and tranquil, with only a couple of groups playing card games. I felt much better after my sleep but was still fraught with regret and shame. How could I be so mean to Mama, kicking up a fuss like that in my frustration, and treating her like my punchball. I didn't even bother to tell her that we really had no choice after all on the matter of signing up. We either jumped off the cliff voluntarily or were going to be pushed in the end. At least signing up early meant we could pick the nearest place to go, which in my case was just over one thousand kilometres away from home. That would have made Mama feel better.

The skinny girl sitting opposite was Fang, plain-looking and too young to be here, who spoke with a strong accent and was ashamed of it. Because she was clever she had jumped up a year and was in the first year of secondary school, while others of her age in primary school escaped being sent to the countryside. She was affable, humble and almost obsequious to the people around her. Fang handed around the flat, pan-fried *bing* bread her mama had made for the journey. It was delicious, but the two girls, Ping and Anning, sitting next to her gave her an outright refusal. This pair were glued to each other, supercilious and both from high-ranking army officer backgrounds, they took out their own shop-bought biscuits and chocolates. It appeared that they were here purely to be 'gold-plated', as they had no hesitation in boasting that they would be gone to the army within three months. I could only think the reason children of army officials got such favourable treatment was that Chairman Mao was worried about upsetting the army. Since the start of the Great Proletarian Cultural Revolution, 99% of civilian high officials had been proscribed, while only a handful of army officials were touched. Anning and Ping were the lucky ones.

Sitting next to me was Linna, with her head resting on my shoulder fast asleep. Linna and I had become good friends and like-minded company since the first day at middle school, before the Cultural Revolution, despite our contrasts – I was short and quick while Linna was tall and graceful. At school Linna attracted a lot of interest from the boys, and I became her guardian, shielding her from unwanted attention. Heaven only knows how she could be so beautiful. Even now I sometimes couldn't stop wondering why God had so favoured Linna, creating such a flawlessly attractive girl: a pair of limpid, large, dark brown, serene eyes, her silky long hair tucked behind her ears, tall and statuesque. We both liked music, literature and rice, which made it easy at lunch when one of us could queue for rice while the other queued for dishes. We were both Gao Gan Zi Di – Children of High Officials – who had started the Red Guard movement, and had fallen from grace after their parents were all condemned. Linna was a reticent and quiet girl, who would conceal her knowledge and opinions, or pretend she was just a pretty little fluff-head. It puzzled me at first, but then I concluded it was a camouflage tactic to protect herself, or put herself in a position where she could receive favours and help. On the other hand I doubted anyone on Earth would attack her, such a beauty, such a fragile figurine. I didn't know much about her family and background, but then again maybe I shouldn't know about it. She was a mystery to me yet I fully respected her privacy.

It was getting dark outside and inside the carriage there were only dimmed, flickering sidelights. I took out my atlas and started tracing the towns we were passing. We were still in Hebei Province.

"You aren't supposed to bring books," said Ping suddenly.

"It's not a book, it's just maps," I replied.

"What about that one?" Anning said.

"It's a dictionary." I began to get annoyed.

"Surely you cannot have any books. As you might know you are going to be re-educated by the peasants and trained by them physically, not intellectually. For your information, peasants own no books which means a repudiation of intellectual activities. They need to know no more than land, weather and crops," said Ping.

"A dictionary? Hardly intellectual. Are you being sarcastic?"

"It's up to you to decide." They both giggled.

The next day we arrived at Xian, the capital city of many dynasties of ancient China, in Shaanxi province, from where we boarded a local train to Tongchuan, a provincial town seventy kilometres to the north of Xian. From here a convoy of twenty open top trucks took us on an eight-hour journey into the endless arid hills. We were quickly immersed in the thick yellow dust which the region was famous for: yellow earth, barren and burnt-up on the high ground, with steep cut ravines abraded by rain and flood, sparse vegetation clinging to their sides. As we proceeded, the long journey disheartened me, and I became afraid that I might never be able to return home.

Eventually our truck stopped and unloaded us by the road. On the right-hand side I could see a narrow path snaking up a valley between the hills and boulders. We had been prepared that the last part of our journey would have to be on foot. I was intrigued and drawn in by the exclusivity, inaccessibility and mystery further along that path. A few locals and donkeys were there waiting for us. They told us this place was called Dog Tail Mouth, and about half a mile further down the road was a small marketplace with a post office, shops and a coach stop. I smirked at Linna and whispered into her ear, "Dog Tail Mouth? Are we going to be devoured and masticated in there?" This thought disconcerted her, her face turning marble white. Ten of us from the same school, five girls and five boys, were assigned to a village called Yellow Knoll. We were supposed to live and work together like a family unit. We had known of each other at school but the journey had brought us closer.

Jin, our leader, was quiet and thoughtful, a tall, gentle young man of seventeen, two years above us; Shan in contrast was a loud, flashy boy, quick to show a temper, and quick to form opinions very volubly on things about which he knew nothing. Sometimes he appeared to be a bully and, of course, sometimes a coward. Shuming, a kind, shy, hesitant boy who found it difficult to maintain any opinion of his own, was easily swayed, and usually adopted the view of the last person to whom he had spoken. Tan, a small, petty boy, was not very bright but was dogged, and always followed authority. Helin, on the other hand, was a strong, forceful young man, extremely opinionated, but humourless and intolerant, accustomed to forcing his wishes and views upon others.

Us girls were standing slightly apart from the boys: Anning and Ping were giggling to each other, totally ignoring the rest; Fan and I were helping Linna with her back-pack.

We set off following our local guide Dabao, a robust,

215

affable man in his mid-twenties. I couldn't help but stare at him, in his clean, black cotton clothes, thin ropes wrapped around his waist and at the bottom of his trousers, and his head swathed with a white cotton cloth. He looked just like the peasant in that massive poster on the East Changan Avenue next to Tian An Men Square; except for his shoes. I signalled at Linna to look at his shoes, a pair of hand-made, half-worn, cotton shoes in a woman's style. We found it hilarious and couldn't stop ourselves giggling. We began to like him when we found out that he was the only one who had volunteered to come and pick us up, as if the others were afraid we would eat them up. Despite the fact that he was terribly economical with his words, we didn't stop assailing him with questions, about everything from the local people and the schools, to the cleaning facilities and toilets. We did learn that Dabao didn't have a mother, as she had died when he was little; he lived with his father only, but he had many uncles, aunts, cousins and nephews, most of whom lived in a neighbouring village, only ten kilometres away but separated by a deep ravine. Something unusual about him intrigued me; he was thin, a little emaciated, yet he had broad shoulders and shiny big eyes. He wasn't as craggy as the other locals we had seen. His eyes kept returning to Linna and he blushed when they met mine.

The sky was sullenly grey and low, and the area was bare and dusty in the bitter winter wind. As our long and hard journey on foot progressed, our words faltered. All the girls' back-packs ended up on Dabao's shoulder.

Finally the path plateaued, and we reached the yellow highland where people had lived for thousands of years, yet now it was only an endless barren wilderness like the Gobi Desert. I stopped, gasped at the vast emptiness, and searched for the boundary where Heaven and Earth merged. Were we in Heaven or on Earth? Or both? I asked myself. I held up my arms to the sky and screamed at our convoy which had moved onwards, "LOOK!"

"What are we looking for?" Shan asked, alarmed.

"There is nothing here, except us," Tan said.

"Exactly, see this vast emptiness of space. We are the only beings, but we are so tiny, so insignificant," I said.

"This is no time to get philosophical. Come on, let's go. I just got into my rhythm," Jin retorted.

The troop continued. The donkeys carried our luggage in silence, and so did we, dragging our feet and hoping there would be no more hills to climb. I became too tired to look at the view, doggedly staring at the unchanging, dusty yellow earth in front of my feet. Just before dusk we descended into a valley to arrive at our new home: a couple of weird earth caves the like of which none of us had ever seen before. The entrances were set into the cliff of an earth bank, as if a vertical slice had been chopped out of the hill. They comprised a lattice door and wooden frames covered by translucent paper. After we had unloaded, the night fell upon us with impenetrable darkness, and someone shouted desperately: "Lights, where can I find the light switch?" It was Shan of course.

"Are you insane?"

"In Beijing!" was followed by a roar of laughter, but

not for long. Peace returned and became mingled with soothing, snoring sounds and murmured words from dreams as if we were all drugged.

When I got out the next morning, I was embraced by a fresh smell of wilderness. I took a close look at the canopy of barren hills; I was astounded that such a sombre, bare scene could be so impressive and beautiful.

We were given one day to settle into our new home, a five-metre-long earth cave on a man-made cliff. Inside there was a mud and brick-constructed fire-bed called a 'kang' that ran along one side of the cave. At the entrance end of the *kang* stood a large wok upon a stove, the chimney of which made its way through beneath the *kang*, like a hypocaust. On the other side of the cave stood our furniture: one handmade table, one spindly chair and some shelves. The walls were filthy, crying out for a coat of paint, and the ceiling arched low above our heads, but we were as excited as if we were a group of friends on a camping trip. We dubbed our home the Bear Hole, where rats would run around at night taking no notice of the new residents.

Although a few furtive faces popped up and down around us while we were out working or outside our caves – some of the bolder local kids scouting us out – we were only formally introduced to the villagers at the weekly evaluation meeting, following a whole week digging trenches for the irrigation systems. The moment we walked into the village hall, amid the clamour of the locals, the sound was immediately switched off. In the dim light of the oil lamps a couple of hundred eyes stared back at us like we were chimpanzees in a zoo. Then someone started clapping and the atmosphere warmed up. A middle-aged woman who was sewing a shoe sole came closer to us and touched my hair. It made me recoil. She looked so dirty, not just wrinkles and crevices, but as if lice would infect me through her touch. She said something that I couldn't understand in the local dialect, and it was followed with a peal of laughter. An old man, squatting on a wooden bench, coughed; the room went quiet. He wrung his brow into several vertical furrows, took a puff at his long wooden pipe, and said petulantly: "Ten more mouths to feed for the winter, but no work for them. What are they here for?" We stood silently under the tense scrutiny of unconvinced and distrustful eyes. At that moment a boy brought in a bundle of letters addressed to us, arousing much curiosity which almost immediately dispelled the icy air.

"What is this blue thing for? And wings?" a young man held up a letter and pointed at the airmail sticker.

"Airmail sticker, it means the letter was delivered by aeroplane. It goes fast," Shan said.

"Aeroplane?"

"Yes, those flying machines," said Shuming, flapping his arms up and down.

"Oh, yes, like those planes of the Japanese devils, throwing bombs or leaflets. Letters thrown like that?" said an old man.

"What this?" A young teenager was pointing at the electric torch that Jin brought out to read the letter. The room gasped, many young mouths dropped open, eyes enlarged and a ring formed around Jin. Jin was obliged to give some demonstration of how it was switched on and off.

"Quiet now," the chief interrupted, and kicked off the meeting.

At the meeting, every one of us was evaluated for the week's work we had done. Erliu, a scrawny and stunted young man who had a fox face and busy eyes, son of the village chief, read out from a piece of paper. For a day's work, our boys were given eight points, compared to a ten points a day average for the locals, and we girls got only six points a day rather than the eight points local average. We learnt that the food we received would be based on our accumulated points, and cash would be paid out at a rate of 0.2 yuan per ten points. I thought it wasn't fair and stared at Erliu closely. His narrow body was topped by a thin, dark face riven with lines from which a pointed chin protruded. His manner swung between formidable and smarmy.

"It's not fair we subsidise you girls," said Shan as soon as we got back to the Bear Hole.

"Why didn't you say so at the meeting? It wasn't fair we have such low points," said Ping.

"We can eat less if that makes you happy," said Fang.

"What about cooking, do you want to cook for yourself?" I was rather annoyed by the conversation; what had happened to all the promises about helping each other we made before we came? What about team spirit and camaraderie?

"Hold on, hold on!" Jin shouted, "stop arguing

between ourselves; we should be united in getting a fair deal."

At the next weekly meeting, we were given the same lower points even though we did as much as the villagers. Shan stood up, "Our greatest leader Chairman Mao taught us: 'Everyone should get equal pay for equal work.' Chairman Mao wants us to be equal, so all of us should get ten points each. Agreed?"

The chief squinted his eyes, irresolute and said, "Show me the quotation." Shan handed him a full volume of Chairman Mao's collected works.

"Where is it?"

"There! Can't you see?"

"You read it." The chief pushed the book back to Shan.

Shan read: "It is a serious problem to educate farmers. Communism is the whole ideology of the proletariat, but it is also a new social system. This ideology and social system is different from any other ideology or any other social system in the whole of human history; it is the most complete, the most progressive, the most revolutionary and the most reasonable. Equality is the fundamental communist principle and everyone should get equal pay for equal work."

The room went silent. The chief said, "What is the meaning?"

"It means we should get ten points each per day and our girls get eight points. It's simple."

"It's OK if that's what Chairman Mao wants," the Chief said happily.

We chattered triumphantly along the way back to our home.

"You made it up!"

"Of course I did."

From that day we all readily agreed to a division of labour. The boys promised that they would do the heavy work, like fetching water and chopping wood, if the girls did all the cooking.

The first winter came suddenly and struck us with the harsh reality of country life. For two months we were sent out each day to build a small reservoir and dam. The ground was frozen as hard as rock. One day Jin injured his leg when the pickaxe bounced back as it hit the ground. There was so much blood that Linna hid her face behind my back. The next day we were back to the building site again, pushing wheelbarrows and shifting rocks or earth. At night, we counted our wounds; the hands were always the worst, outside were chilblains and inside raw flesh exposed from blisters and cuts.

Unlike us city girls, who were out with the boys doing man's work, most of the local women would gather around their fire, making baskets from willow sticks, repairing tools, knitting or crafting for the market in spring. We were unremittingly cold and hungry. One rare fine day when the sun was shining and the air was clear of the perpetual haze, we took a break and went out exploring and foraging further down into the valley. As we walked past an earth cave, a woman came walking towards it carrying a bundle of straw. Ping stopped her at the door and asked loutishly: "Got any food to sell? Or you know where we can buy food?"

She smiled at us kindly and invited us in while putting more straw in the fire. The inside of the earth cave was filled with the warmth from the fire and three children were sitting on the *kang* muffled up in a filthy thin duvet. The woman told us that we wouldn't be able to find food in the direction we were going, and that we should walk in the opposite direction. She apologised that she hadn't had any food to sell us, but she brought out a jar of pickled turnips. Linna was talking to the children and asked the girl why they were in bed during the day.

"Cannot get out, it's too cold, our big sister is wearing the padded trousers."

"Out with our father to the market, to sell ropes we made," the older boy added proudly.

"Do you mean only one pair of trousers to share between the four of you?" said Linna. The children all nodded. Linna took out some paper money from her pocket and put it on the table. The woman picked up the money and the jar, shuffled them into Linna's hand and shook her head vigorously. We left with her pickle jar without paying for it, and felt like we had just robbed them. For the whole day, even Shan, who never stopped complaining about the lack of food, didn't grumble.

On days when there was no building work we had to go deeper into the hills to gather fuel, with a rope tied round our waists and an axe thrust down the back. Only a few miles out there were bushes, wild plants clinging onto the rocky hills where nothing else would grow. We chopped branches of dead wood, bundled them together, and carried them on our backs to our home. On a good day we could do two trips, then have a splurge of fire that would heat our Bear Hole for the whole night.

"I cannot fucking eat this every day," Shan said bitterly, "Not a drop of oil! Just sweet potato, nothing else."

"Don't eat then," said Tan.

"What's your problem?" said Shan angrily.

"You should consider yourself lucky to have sweet potato to eat. You should thank our girls, without them gleaning the fields after harvest and before the ground became frozen, we wouldn't have anything to eat now. You always have the choice of not eating by the way," said Jin.

Shan muttered something.

"You can go to town to buy some food, that will help," Fang suggested.

"Me? Walking a day each way, carrying a fifty kilogram weight on the way back? No chance," said Shan.

The next day Shan went out sulkily with Shuming. They returned in the afternoon, and as he tipped out his basket, Linna screamed in terror. Shan had brought back a dead dog.

"You killed a dog? How could you?"

"For all of us. Do you want to die? I'm hungry!" said Shan, "It's only a stray dog."

"How do you know? Maybe it has an owner?"

That was the first full-blown fight between us. But hunger had debased us, and in the end we cooked the dog. As Jin pointed out it was dead anyway, and there was no point in wasting it. Linna didn't touch it however, even though it was delicious.

One Chairman Mao's book study day, beautifully calm and sunny, we were all out in the yard bathing in the winter sun. Hua, a twelve-year-old local girl, was there with her little brother. She had brought a small basket of dried dates for us to boil in our porridge.

Hua sat with us watching me rinsing Linna's hair when I heard Tan's scolding bawl: "What the hell are you doing?"

"What a silly question, haven't you got eyes?" I said.

"You just wasted the water I collected from the well."

"You didn't collect this water, we saved it from washing vegetables," I retorted.

"Still a waste, we agreed not to wash …"

"I only used one cup, only one cup, why can't you let me be?" said Linna, almost in tears.

"Yes, Hua showed us this method that only needs one cup of water to wash hair. Do you want to try?" said Fang.

"Why are you so mean, little man?" said Ping. So the squabbling between girls and boys that had broken out went on. They couldn't understand why we girls had to be so clean; conversely we didn't understand how they could stand lice crawling over their heads. Linna was crying, Ping was shouting, while Fang held her head between her hands. Water was scarce, and hard to get, but the real problem was that it didn't come out of a tap. The initial excitement of camping had long gone and the prospect of spending the rest of our lives here plunged us all into deep despondency.

When spring arrived, the days became longer, and so did our working hours. From dawn to dusk we were in the fields, ploughing, planting, watering, weeding: endless work; even lunch, the only break in the day, was taken in the fields. Then the summer finally arrived with three continuous sunny days; the earth became too hot to touch. After a full day of hoeing, we were filthy and spewed out an acrid and pungent smell of sweat. We were all dying for a good wash, and five of us bunked off work early to head out for our 'Blissful Pool'. It was a small pond we had discovered, scoured out of the rocks by the water flow in the rainy season. It was now stagnant and muddy, and an hour's walk into the valley from around the back of our hill, but to us it was like being in Heaven. It lifted our spirits and imbued us with a bubbly mood.

"Come on Fang, it's late, we don't want to cook in the dark," Ping hurried Fang, who was the only one still in the water, faffing while we were all dressed and waiting.

"Wait a minute, just a little more." Sometimes Fang was a bit of a pain, almost hard to abide. She didn't realise we had gone until we were totally out of her sight. To her terror we had gone with her clothes, so Fang leapt out of the water and chased after us, barefoot in her dripping knickers and camisole. Anning brandished her clothes in the air which made us shriek with laughter.

"Please, don't be so mean," pleaded Fang. We continued to walk back. She was greatly distressed, squatting on the ground howling, burying her head between her knees with her arms around her head.

"Wait for her," I said.

"She'll catch up," said Ping.

"But she's not," said Linna.

"Oh, well, teach her a lesson then," said Ping.

"She has no clothes."

"No one will see her, it's getting dark."

"And we have to prepare food," said Anning.

Half an hour after we had got back home, Fang still hadn't turned up. I grabbed the oil lamp, Linna picked up a scythe by the door, and we went out to look for her. It was a dark night without any moon and I began to regret not asking one of the boys to come with us. Our fears suddenly abated as we heard familiar laughter from a distance. The voices were getting clearer and closer; it was obviously Fang and a man.

"Hey, Fang?" I shouted.

"Yes, where are you?" Fang appeared by the light of our oil lamp, dressed in an oversized woman's cotton blouse with a flowery print, accompanied by a good-looking and attentive young peasant.

"Where have you been? You scared the hell out of us," I said.

"I've been with Taiming. He's a shepherd, looking after the Yaodian orchard …" Fang said eagerly. But I was not in the mood for socializing, I needed to get Fang home, as supper would be ready.

"Come on, you're late. Everyone is waiting for you,"

"If you hadn't taken my clothes," said Fang sulkily.

Ping came out when we got back. "What have you been up to?"

"I went to ask for help and I met this guy. He was very nice."

"What did you do there, naked?" Ping snorted with derisive laughter. Fang blushed.

From then on Fang started behaving strangely, rather cheerful and talkative, quite unlike her normal self. She never stopped talking about Taiming: he was kind and intelligent, he had lost his wife two years ago and had a son living with him, and he sang *Xintianyou*, a type of folk song, marvellously. She often went to see Taiming, sometimes for hours, but she cheerfully did all the housework she could and no one complained about her absence. I apologised to Fang for the prank, but she said it wasn't my fault because it wasn't in my nature. I still felt bad about it because I hadn't stopped it, and because I had found it funny at the expense of her pain.

Two weeks later, Anning and Ping left Yellow Knoll to join the army; Ping was going to be a dancer in the entertainment troupe, while Anning was training to be an army nurse. Two boys, Tan and Helin, left a week later, also joining the army. That same week, four city youths in a nearby village were killed in a flash flood. They were so young and naive that when the flood came they ran down the valley to escape and were flushed away.

Only six of us were left: destitute teenagers, hapless rejects of Chairman Mao, trapped here to rot and die. On the day Tan and Helin left, Shuming, on his water duty, came back with only half-full buckets of water. Shan rebuked him. Shuming kicked the buckets, spilled all the water and broke down crying. I had never seen a grown man cry like that before and it made us all sad.

"Why are we here? Living like fucking animals. Bastards just bloody deceived us. We were told there would be rivers, forests and lakes, just like a big garden. We would have transportation to go to work and to come back home. Bullshit!" said Shan.

"Be quiet," said Jin.

"Do you know those high fucking idealistic activists, the censorious, arse-licking loyal ones, our Red Guard leaders, have dodged all this crap to stay in the city? Son of a bitch!" said Shan and turned to us. "Stop crying! For Heaven's sake."

For three months we had had a yearning hope of going home to Beijing for the 1969 Chinese New Year. When Linna and I received travel money to Beijing from our parents for the holiday, we were over the moon. Fang's mother hadn't sent her enough money for even half the journey. I felt uneasy that we had to leave her behind here, alone, and when I asked Fang if there was anything we could do to help her, she asked if we could possibly visit her mother in Beijing. Only now, after more than a year of our close confinement together, did Fang finally take us into her confidence. Her father, a high-ranking officer in Jiang Jieshi's army, had been executed after the liberation in 1949. As a dependent wife, her mother had no education, no skills and no money. She now worked in a soap factory as a menial labourer to raise her daughter and son. She encouraged Fang to work hard, to become well-educated and be independent, so that Fang would have a better life than herself. She had been devastated when the Cultural Revolution had shut down all the schools and universities; the only window to get her daughter out of total darkness had been shut in her face.

"I can never get back home to Beijing. Unlike you, my mother has no money, no connections." Fang paused. "I should accept Taiming's marriage proposal, he is so kind to me. Yes, I will. I am going to tell him tomorrow." I was speechless.

"We can never know our fate, can we? Did you have any idea that your prank would've had such a happy outcome for me?" Fang said thoughtfully, full of joy and bliss. It sounded so wrong, but I couldn't argue with her. Despite my misgivings, I was happy for her, and glad that I needn't feel a burden of guilt for abandoning her during the New Year holiday. She would have good company for the New Year and there would be a wedding soon. We parted merrily with the hope of seeing each other on our return. While in Beijing, I bought the wedding presents: an embroidered bedding set in light blue, and a box of sweets. Linna got Fang a pair of Thermos flasks. On the return journey, we were planning the wedding, thinking of us as her family and how we would be giving her away.

We rushed back to our Bear Hole to tell Fang how we had met her mother in Beijing. The Bear Hole was dark and dank, as if it had not been lived in for weeks.

Fang's clothes were scattered on her bed, the table was covered with paper, scissors, pieces of cloth and clutter, as if a family with no mother lived there. Linna said Fang must have already moved in with Taiming, but I was not convinced. We gave up unpacking and went out to look for her.

The news of Fang's death stunned us, it was too horrible to accept: Fang had committed suicide. She had hanged herself on a tree next to the Blissful Pool. I had no premonition of such devastation. The village had buried her in the valley, not far from the Blissful Pool. Her mother could not afford to come for the burial and it was too expensive to transport her body back to Beijing. We were told that after we had left for Beijing, an investigation team had come out of the blue and accused Fang of immoral conduct. Fang was under pressure to confess. One night she was caught in Taiming's home and humiliated at the village meeting the following day. After that she was treated like a criminal: isolated, excluded from normal human contact, and was sent to muck out the pig sties. She was let free when she received approval of her marriage application. No one could give a proper explanation as to why she had still done it, knowing she was going to marry Taiming. She was so young; how could she be so decisive and so final?

"It would be easy, never to have been born," I moaned.

"Do you think about death?" Linna said.

"No, I haven't figured out life yet."

"She was so young, only nineteen."

"Maybe life was too hard for her and the easiest option was to sleep forever."

"So morbid."

"Yes. Death is as weird as life," I said.

"Meaning?"

"There is no meaning of life if there is no hope in death," I said. "We are burdened with the consequences."

We blamed ourselves bitterly, but still could not understand why the investigation team had come. We were baffled as to who had reported Fang and betrayed us. It could only have been one of our small group.

Now there were only the five of us left from the original ten. We were still together as a family unit despite sporadic fights, squabbles and fallouts. The second year was tough, for the initial assistance from the government had stopped and we were supposed to feed ourselves completely from now on. We worked to our limit, doing everything we could, such as offering a clerical service for the village administration to augment our meagre income, but there was still not enough to eat, and we had to rely on our parents to send money. I missed the intellectual stimulation of school; learning mathematics, physics, chemistry and how things worked. Here books, except Chairman Mao's, were forbidden, and life was as dull as our smelly dishcloths. Clearly we lived like cavemen, scavenging for food to fill our stomachs and for fuel to keep us warm. All we had was a pair of hands, weather on top of our head and earth under our feet; like people who lived a thousand years ago. The acute sense of self-pity led to a deep depression among us that would surely one day break our spirits. Linna and I emotionally clung on to one another more than ever before. Together we could endure and keep our hopes for the future alive. I thought at the time we would be inseparable for the rest of our lives.

Harvest time came around, and the whole village focused on getting the precious crop in quickly. We had to work day and night to fill our daily quota. By the end of each day, my back gave up and I had to kneel down to cut the wheat with my scythe. I was so drained that I had no energy to cry. At the end of one long day digging out sorghum under a scorching sun, I came back exhausted and was surprised to find Linna wasn't at home. She had been sent to help Erliu with the accounts, but it was only a half-day job and she should have been at home preparing dinner. I had a quick cat wash and set off to find her.

"Hey, Linna, there you are." I saw Linna scuttling back across the yard towards our home.

"Eh," Linna avoided my eyes and continued to walk. So I followed her. She looked strange, as if she had seen a ghost and fear had blanched her face. Her hair was ruffled.

"Did you have a good day? Why are your eyes red?"

Again she did not answer but sped up her stride.

"What happened to your lip, it's bleeding?"

"I accidentally bit it. It's OK."

"It was that petty little man, he gave us the east slope again," I complained about the job bitterly. Linna remained silent for the rest of the evening. I took a close look at her and her eyes were puffed up like she had been crying. Something had disturbed her, but she would not tell what. Perhaps there was a good reason. I don't like prying. I am not one of those people who won't be your friend any more if you don't tell them your secrets. Of course the whole of Chinese society demands to know every detail of your intimate life, but I don't like to share my secrets, so I don't like to encroach on others' privacy. My guess was boy troubles.

It was no surprise that Linna had many admirers, and some were more chivalrous than others. Although I felt a duty to protect her, I had never interfered. Linna always kept a cool distance from them. She later told me how she had first let Dabao walk back with her on a day when I was away. The sun had gone down, a cool breeze brushed her hair, Linna stopped hoeing and looked around. There was no one in the cornfield any more, everybody had finished their quota and gone home, even our boys. She unwrapped the handkerchief on her hand and her palm was covered with blood from the crevices in her blisters. She wanted to cry and she let herself as no one was around. She screamed like a baby rabbit caught between the sharp teeth of a cat. She felt her head was expanding and as painful as if it were clamped at her temples. But she knew she was running out of time and she had to finish her quota. The world had vanished down to only the time and the sound of a hoe as she strove towards the point that marked her quota.

She became aware of an echo to her own hoe, but stronger and longer at each stroke. She thought she was going crazy, but the echo was getting louder and even when she stopped it continued. Dabao led her to the side, sat her down, and completed her task. Soon it started raining, he picked up her hoe and walked back by her side without a word. Darkness fell just as they got to the Bear Hole where thick smoke was spewing out of the door.

"Why didn't you cover it yesterday? The straw is too damp to start."

"Are we going to have food tonight?"

"What a stupid question."

"It's a simple question."

"Stop complaining, it's all your fault we can't cook."

"You didn't lay the fire yesterday."

The squabbling went on and the fire refused to start. Dabao went away and returned with a sack full of firewood. Linna was grateful for his rescue. On the following day, Dabao came again and brought us a bag of flour and we had noodles for supper. The boys were so thrilled and kept on shouting: "Long live noodles!"

Not long after my return, Linna fell ill. She couldn't eat anything, and kept on throwing up. We were determined to take her to see a doctor in town. "No, I'll be fine," Linna insisted. She had turned into a virtual recluse. She worked so hard that one day she lost consciousness in the field while digging. To stop me making further fuss, she confided in me that she was pregnant and she wanted to get rid of it. To me the word 'pregnant' sounded disgraceful and gross, but Linna was my friend: there must have been a reason why it had happened. Despite many attempts with natural remedies I collected from the locals, her body continued to grow and she couldn't conceal it any more. Rumour wafted around through mouths to ears; it was impossible to deny.

I lost my temper when we overheard our boys' conversation: "Looks like we'll have another mouth to feed," said Shan with a tincture of bitterness in his voice.

"What are you talking about?" said Shuming.

"Don't you see, she's going to have a baby? Heaven knows whose baby it is, just some bastard."

"Can you be quiet? They'll be back soon."

"Why should I? Just a way to avoid field work. Maybe I should try it."

"What?"

"Having a baby. Ha."

"Shut up, you son of a bitch!" I yelled at them. I was agitated, and had a premonition of something bad. That evening two authority-looking types appeared claiming to be our chaperones from the district council.

"You are Linna Chen?" said the man with a bald head and round face.

"Yes."

"Are you married?"

"No," Linna said quietly and started sobbing.

"That baby. Did Zhang Dabao force you to have, you know, that word?" Linna didn't respond.

"Did Zhang Dabao rape you?"

"No!"

"We are here to help you before it gets out of our reach. You are loyal followers of Chairman Mao and have rooted deeply into the countryside. You are our treasure," the bald man paused.

"Without you we would be out of our jobs," his companion helpfully added. I took a close look at his tobacco-stained brown teeth, thinking that they were just peasants like the villagers, but had weaselled themselves into a salaried paper-pushing job away from the land. I certainly had respect for the real peasants like Dabao, even the chief, but not people like them, who only had a little power but would surely use every bit of it.

"Think about yourself. Do you know how shameful it sounds? If you tell the truth, you won't be charged."

"I am telling the truth."

"Is this your attitude? No remorse?"

"She told you what you want to know, the rest of it is not your business, so just leave her alone," I said, her guardian.

"You… how dare you? You will take the consequences."

"What consequences? Expel us from the village? Ha, put us in prison? At least we'd get fed." I retorted angrily.

"OK, there will be a village meeting unless you repent, Zhang Dabao will be charged one way or another. The question is will you?" The interrogators left in a sour mood.

Linna ran off and I couldn't catch her so I panicked. I went to Dabao to ask for help, and four search groups set off in the dark. In the moonlight I saw a prostrate figure on what we called the 'Table', a massive rock on the east side of our hill. It was Linna, lying face down on the rock. She told me the Table would take her baby away, if she pressed hard enough. By the time I got her back she was delirious with fever, so I fed her ginger and some herbal remedies, and we locked the door in case she tried to sneak out again. For two days she refused to talk to anyone, until eventually she told me she had decided to accept Dabao's marriage proposal.

"What? How can you do that?" At once, I regretted what I said, disbelief at how I could be so judgemental, when this was what I most despised.

"I didn't do it. Dabao didn't want me to go to jail so he admitted to it. I couldn't let him go to jail for me," said Linna, tears streaming down her face.

"Don't you want to go home any more? You promised we would go back to Beijing together." Again I found myself talking to her in that remonstrative tone of voice, I couldn't help but interfere. Linna started to cry. "I'm sorry," I said and softened my voice: "Do you really want to do it?"

Linna didn't answer, she was avoiding eye contact, instead she was biting her lip as if she could not show her true feelings. I couldn't stand seeing the blood welling up from her lip and I shut up and just hugged her.

They didn't want a traditional wedding: one day's gruelling ceremony followed by two days feasting. Instead, they went to the registrar's office in town, and held a dinner at the weekend. I couldn't say I was happy for Linna. To me it was a precarious marriage, discharged under sufferance because she was not strong enough to endure her humiliation and exclusion. I also felt sorry for myself as I had just lost my friend.

The wedding dinner was held in the yard in front of Dabao's cave; a long trestle table was set up to seat about twenty people. The chief presented the wedding gift from the village: four volumes of Chairman Mao's collected works. The atmosphere was effervescent – the anticipation of a good meal would put a smile on anyone's face.

On the table there were tantalising dishes of fried peanuts, preserved eggs, and tofu snacks that I had not seen since our arrival at Yellow Knoll. My arm shot out almost involuntarily as I quickly snatched a tofu piece, while I looked elsewhere pretending nothing had happened. It was delicious. After a while, all the guests were seated, and a procession of hot food was brought out to great announcement: 'meatballs' made from millet, 'peacocks' fashioned out of green leaves and carved carrots, and within seconds, almost before the end of their announcement, 'chickens' – actual chicken and the only real meat – had become carcasses. Then hyena-like the diners chanted: "Fish", "Fish", "Fish", … It was a traditional way to bless or call for good fortune as 'fish' was a pun on a word meaning ample, a superfluous abundance of food or wealth. As the fish dishes were placed on the table, the crowd calmed down, but no one seemed to go for them in stark contrast to how the chicken was treated. The fish looked odd, perfectly fish-shaped, like a child's portrayal, covered with a dark brown glutinous sauce. I used my chopsticks to poke at one curiously, but it was hard and the table roared with laughter. I sat there blushing, nonplussed.

"It's wood, made of wood," someone shouted. Dabao called for a toast just in time, to save me from further embarrassment.

I was fascinated by the homemade rice wine, a smooth, milky-white luscious liquid, sweet yet not cloying, nothing like normal alcohol. I couldn't get enough. It tasted mythical, what celestial beings drank in Heaven, and had a supernatural effect on me; I felt happier and started to enjoy the moment. I became aware that a fight had suddenly broken out at the head of the table. I saw Dabao punch Erliu in the face before Erliu was dragged away by the guests. I remembered little of what happened after.

Without Linna to talk to at night, I often found myself lost in my thoughts; my memory and my mood swinging from one extreme to the other. The best memory was when Mama had taken me to visit her composer friend, whom I called Aunty Liu. She played piano for us. The sound was so majestic that the room dissolved into a tinkling stream under a cerulean sky, sweet meadow fragrances, the sound of bees bustling, then fading into melancholy songs, sad crying, and on into a thundery storm. Aunty Liu had put me on a stool next to her and showed me how to press a few keys, she said it was called an arpeggio. It was pure bliss and I had resolved to be a composer when I grew up. It would never happen now. I was plunged into despondence and started to worry about Linna. Is she happy? Does she love Dabao? And why? I remembered at the wedding dinner, Linna, her sad and impassive, yet elegant, countenance, sitting stiffly amid the locals, like a perfect lily stuck in a pile of pig crap. Why couldn't she just be patient, wait for better and going home? As they said: 'Marry a chicken go with the chickens, marry a dog go with the dogs'. What a waste, I thought.

Linna continued to come to the Bear Hole every day, helping whenever she could. Her belly had swollen up like a watermelon and she was forbidden to do any physical work, not even cooking. Life for us city youth was little improved, and we were facing another year of penury. So when the opportunity arose, I accepted a part-time teaching post at the neighbouring village with alacrity. Shuming was trained to be a part-time 'barefoot doctor'. Mama sent me a bicycle from Beijing so I could cycle to the school every day. The day my bike arrived at the village, I was stuck solid in a crowd. People, strangers, touched the bicycle cautiously, rang the bell, and argued about how it worked and begged me for a demonstration. They were amazed that I could go so fast on two wheels and not fall over.

More and more of the city youth had left for jobs in cities, and we grew increasingly despondent. Jin's father was a convicted rightist; three times Jin was referred by the village for a town job, but three times he was turned down. Nor was there any good news from either Linna's parents or from mine. Obviously our parents had been classified as Incorrigible. In fact, Linna's parents, along with her little brother, had been sent to a cadre's labour college. For a while Linna was happy, seemed to accept her fate and dedicated all her efforts to her baby son. One evening she came with her son and brought us a basket of apricots and two eggs, which cheered us all up. Even Shan offered to help with the cooking. I carefully cracked open the eggs, poking my finger in to scrape every drop of the egg white out. The meal was sumptuous and four of us sharing two eggs was an absolutely unexpected luxury. After the meal we sang together, from Peking Opera to Russian love songs, complemented by Jin's harmonica. Our mood was ambivalent though. After the boys had left, Linna and I sat down and talked. Linna fumbled in her pocket, took out an opened envelope and handed it to me. It was a letter from her mother: the good news was that her father had been exonerated from all accusations and returned to his ministerial post in Beijing. I was thrilled; I held her son, who was just over one year old, and threw him up in the air. "Yes, yes, I knew it!" I shouted. Linna said nothing though.

"They are going to get you back to Beijing, cheer up," I said and then turned to the boy, "You haven't told them about him, have you?" She shook her head.

"I couldn't do it when they were suffering. They would be so upset."

"You've got to tell them. Write a letter now."

There was no response from Linna's parents for nearly three months. Then eventually a telegraph arrived: "Come back with husband and child. Talk later."

"Father won't let Dabao go," responded Linna by telegraph.

"Come with child first immediately," the telegraph ordered.

Linna's parents sent her enough money for three

trips home. The decision wasn't easy; Linna and Dabao argued day and night but couldn't reach an agreement. Linna and her family wanted the three of them to go to Beijing, Dabao and his father wanted them all to stay in Yellow Knoll. In the end Linna told me she had decided to go back to Beijing with her son. On the day Dabao and I went to see Linna off, we left Yellow Knoll at dawn. We were surprised to find Dabao's father and five other men, uncles or cousins, waiting for us just outside the village.

"How could you let her go?" Dabao's father said.

"Because it'll make her happy."

"I told you before, son, don't do it. City people will always dump you. She can go if she wants, we cannot stop her, but I will not let my grandson go! He is the root of our life" The father pushed Dabao aside and advanced towards Linna, Dabao regained his balance and grasped both his father's hands. He bawled as if his heart was riven apart: "No!"

"What? You want to strike your old man, for what? For that bitch?"

"Don't you dare call her a bitch!" shouted Dabao and thrust his father back. Dabao's uncles and cousins moved forward and punches were exchanged.

"Yes, she is a city bitch, just like your mother." The old man got up and stood right in front of Dabao, "Yes, your mother never died, she left us when you were three to catch up with her army unit, but she never came back. Oh she sent money, many times after the liberation, but I didn't take it. Can't you see? At least I have you." The old man abandoned his son, who stood stupefied, and snatched the little boy from behind his mother's back. Linna screamed and chased after the old man like a tigress. All of a sudden she baulked, and stood still as a statue.

"He's not your grandson!"

Her anguished cry stopped the old man in his tracks. He slowly turned round, his gaze passing from her wretched face to Dabao. Dabao nodded slightly and said, "Let him go, father."

"How could that be?" the old man sighed, disappointment and incomprehension playing across his face.

Linna walked up to Dabao's father, wiping her face of her tears, she took her son's hand away and said, "I'm sorry." Dabao's father stood impassive for a few moments, then silently he waved at Linna to signal her to leave. Linna lifted the boy up, and wrapped her possessive arms around him.

I also parted with Linna there. She wanted to be seen off by Dabao alone. Although we promised each other we would be forever friends, and for a long time maintained a correspondence, I never saw her again.

Three months later, my father had returned to his position in the Party Central Committee administration. He was cleared of any wrongdoing, forgiven, something he had been waiting for a long time. Lessons had been taught and hands had been slapped by the greatest leader Chairman Mao, the father of the nation. Mama manoeuvred me into an editorial job in a publishing house in Beijing.

★

After the end of the Great Proletarian Cultural Revolution, when the higher education system in China returned to normal in 1977, I passed the entrance exam and gained a place at Peking University studying philosophy. Jin left the village one year after me and also got into a university to study history that same year. I ran into Jin once in Beijing. He told me it was Ping who had reported Fang in a letter she wrote to the town council after she left Yellow Knoll.

Apart from Fang resting in the cold, yellow dust, the only one left in Yellow Knoll was Shuming who had married a local girl and went to a medical school at the same time as us, to become a real doctor. Linna was remarried to an engineering graduate in Beijing, and they moved to America in 1981. She sent me a letter before she left for her new life. She told me the father of her boy was Erliu. She didn't tell anyone because she was ashamed and she didn't want Erliu to have any claim to her son. After he had raped her, Erliu threatened Linna that if she told anyone, he would make sure that no one believed her and he would make her a whore. He said, provided Linna kept the secret, he would help her get a job when the recruitment quotas came.

Could I have done more to help Linna if I had known? Probably not. Perhaps I had always known but chosen not to see … The wail of a horn pierced my reverie and I gazed around me from the middle of the platform at the Beijing Central railway station. Thick

245

grey cloud scudded across the sky, threatening rain. I felt overwhelmed by the noise, and colourful hustle and bustle on the platform. Not far from me stood a beautiful girl, tall and statuesque with long, silky hair and limpid brown eyes. She was talking and laughing with a young boy and a woman, clearly her mother. The girl hopped on the train gleefully and reappeared at the window, waving goodbye to her family as the train started forward on its journey. I waved at her subconsciously, smiling.

Big Sister

Yesterday I saw her, my big sister, the one I used to have, in the middle of the town centre: the sister I have never told anyone about, not even my mother and my brother. In the beginning I was afraid of their reproaches, and in the end I just couldn't any more. It seems a long time ago.

*

"Come on Lanlan, can we come to your home? Please?" I drawled. Several of us surrounded Lanlan half-intimidating and half-entreating. She was ten, two years younger than me and lived downstairs from us. She walked out of the building and we followed like flies. She stopped at the flower beds, and pressed her lips together, cogitating.

When the Cultural Revolution began our school closed, and my mother, along with all the grown-ups in our compound, was detained at her work unit, the North-Western Bureau of the Chinese Communist Party, an enormous place about fifteen minutes walk away. Our home comprised two ex-office rooms in a five-floor, ex-office building in one of the Bureau's residential compounds. Hosting over three hundred families, the compound was surrounded by a high wall. Our parents all worked in the Bureau, which was the Party's headquarters for the five provinces in the north west of China, and the children all went to the same boarding school, so everybody knew everybody, even down to the very details of each other's eating habits. When our parents became absent, we were left to our own devices. Without teachers or parents supervising us, we were in heaven. We got up to all the things girls were not supposed to do: climbing trees, sitting on walls, rolling on the ground and worse. We had soon invited ourselves to raid each other's homes, and my gang had been everywhere in the building except Lanlan's flat.

It seemed there was more to do at other kids' homes than at ours. I discovered that every home was different, with its own attractions. My home was one of the first to be invaded. Compared to others it was stark: Mama had nothing but a wall of books – even our furniture was rented from her work unit – and soon after the kids had played with Mama's enormous Russian radio, they lost interest. To me, everyone else's home was fascinating. Lin's had nice pots and vases with a smell of spices; Hui's had pretty boxes and a lingering ink smell; Bao's was full of beautiful figurines and statuettes, with whiffs of a sweet musky smell. My favourite was Anning's home; it smelled like a museum and it was full of models: cars, ships, bicycles and quaint houses. It took us a week to lose interest in it. As we had now exhausted our options, Lanlan's home had become our prey, and more so after rumours started circulating that her father was descended from the last Qing imperial family, filling us with the hope of finding her family jade seal or a gold chalice or even a long plait.

"Hey, Lanlan said yes, just the three of us, you, me and Anning, don't tell anyone else," said Hui with concealed excitement at our lunch in the canteen. I was thrilled, congratulating myself for following one of Mama's favourite adages: "With time and effort, a metal bar can be ground to a needle."

Lanlan's father's office was dark and humid, with lots of books in the wall of glass-fronted display cases. The dark-red, wooden desk was huge, standing on two columns of drawers and looking grand. The top three drawers, which I assumed stored the treasures, were locked. We didn't find a gold chalice or Qing costumes, only jade animals and stationery pieces to fiddle with. I stared at an old photo hanging on the wall, of a middle-aged woman in peculiar clothes, who had a stern face and sullen eyes. "Who was this?" I asked.

"Don't know."

"Must be Cixi," Anning teased.

"She looks scary."

"Lanlan, what is this?" Hui pointed at a turquoise box on a stand in the corner.

"It's a record player," Lanlan said reluctantly.

"Can you play it?"

We crowded over it, gazing with amazement as the platter went around and around; then the music began, instantaneously filling up the room. We were astonished by the sound of the violin, and the music resonated through me.

"Meimei, someone's looking for you." The door was opened, the head of a little girl popped in followed by Wendi.

"Here you are. Look at you, you little minx," Wendi said and gave me her usual wry smile.

I don't remember how we became friends, but it was sometime at the beginning of the Cultural Revolution. It was rather a strange period, so weird things like that did happen. Wendi was a Red Guard, eighteen years old. Older students were all Red Guards, but younger children, in the absence of adult supervision, had all become like street urchins. I don't think she was a very keen Red Guard, unlike some of her staunch comrades. She fiddle-faddled around at home all the time, unlike my brother Ming who was taking part in the revolution at school, only coming home occasionally when he had collected a massive amount of dirty laundry.

I dithered, undecided between playing in Lanlan's home and going with Wendi, but the allure of Lanlan's house couldn't compete. As Wendi and I walked along the avenue of the compound, in the shade of the trees, past rows of bungalows on both sides of the avenue, the heat rippled the air and I could smell burning. I looked up at her from below her shoulder height, adored her, and admired her short silky hair and thick glasses in their clear transparent frames. Her eyes were kind and her lips were smirking. When she smiled, she gathered her lips as if she didn't want her mouth to appear too big, or that it was improper to show her teeth. The cicadas were a thrilling accompaniment, the sunlight slanted above the roofs and the wind brought refreshing air. Housewives were gossiping in the shade, and a few members of the residents' association were sitting outside their houses, fanning themselves lazily while keeping critical eyes on the children, ready to exercise their self-awarded power. A group of girls were playing, screaming either for excitement or in some sort of disagreement, while a shout of boys were spraying water from an outside tap at each other. Others seemed drawn apart, dispersed into small islands of twos or threes. Suddenly a boy was pushed into the group of girls and the culprits started chanting, "Ding loves Lian, Ding loves Lian, …" Ding, red-faced, sprang towards the scattering boys in a rage, while the girl, Lian, burst into tears. They stopped playing as we walked past and I could feel their gaze following me. I straightened my shoulders and lifted up my chin, flaunting my big friend whom I had to skip to catch up with, full of rising hope and excitement.

"Hey, where are you going, Meimei?" one shouted behind. I waved my arm indifferently, gesticulating that I would tell them later.

"Warm day, isn't it?" Wendi said.

I nodded and said: "We were sleeping on the roof of the building last night. It was great fun."

"Was it?" She smiled at me.

"Yes, we played 24."

"What's that?"

"Well, it's a card game played by four people, each –"

"Has your brother come home lately?" she said. I felt a pang of disappointment that she was more interested in Ming, but I forgave her instantly and said no.

"Can you be my sister? Please," I said timidly.

She laughed, "We have to share the same parents."

"What about blood sister."

"Let's not get into any blood, I have a blood phobia."

"Can we play sisters, pretend to be sisters?"

"Wait a minute," she said, and overtook an old woman with a walking stick in her right hand and a blue bag in the other.

"Nainai, I'll carry this for you," Wendi said. The old woman smiled at Wendi and nodded.

"Wait for me at my home, I won't be long, just to drop her bag," Wendi said and strode away.

There was no one at her home when I arrived. It was tidy and clean, with a large glass bowl on the table filled with fresh fruits. It made her home pleasant and welcoming. She came in and gestured, offering me a banana, and I declined with courtesy as was expected. I knew they weren't for eating but a decoration. Her own room was very small and bare, a single bed behind the door and a little desk under the window. I was surprised to find a mirror on her desk. Wasn't that a bit petit bourgeois? I glanced at her. Unlike her two younger sisters, she had a rather coarse complexion and a big mouth. She showed me her sketches: buildings, streets, flowers and a peculiar foreign man.

"Who was that?" I asked.

"His name is Darwin, an English man."

"Are you a xenophile?" I teased. She laughed.

"Have you heard of evolution?"

"No."

"It's about how we were made from monkeys." Then she explained it.

"What were monkeys made of?"

"Fish."

"Fish made of?"

"Something else."

"It's weird."

She told me so much stuff I had never heard of. I listened, admired and wished I could grow up immediately so I would know as much as she did.

I asked her about the music we heard at Lanlan's home and she said it was called Liang Shanbo and Zhu Yingtai, a violin concerto. I asked why I had never heard anything so beautiful before. She smiled and said it's because it wasn't revolutionary. Revolution and beauty, like water and fire, can never coexist.

Later that day, she told me a story about her Grandma Wei. She grew up in a little town in Anhui province and was a stunning beauty at sixteen. A local wealthy businessman of fifty admired her statuesque grace and proposed to her parents for marriage. She accepted the marriage proposal but with conditions. After she married as his third wife, she set up the first school for girls in the town, and a fabric shop with only female shop assistants. The town was aghast at this unconventional conduct, but her husband supported her and the school was a success.

He died of heart disease at the age of sixty-five, leaving her vulnerable to his first two wives. The two jealous wives threw her out of the house. In desperation, she remarried, to an army officer of the Guomindang, and she had two children with him. Unfortunately her new husband was an alcoholic and womaniser. She was left alone to look after her two children till the new China was born. Her husband was executed in 1950 during the land reform movement. Wendi's mother was one of his two children she brought up successfully.

Wendi was the first born and had two brothers and two sisters. Both of her sisters were younger than me but her brothers were older. One of them was Ming's friend, and Mama was a friend of her parents. However, it was still a mystery as to why she spent time with me; I was six years younger than her and knew nothing of the world. She said she was proud of me, but she had never explained why. One time she took a photo of us together. I was in my blue trousers with two patches on the knees that I had stitched roughly by myself. She had given me her usual wry smile, but I couldn't work out if she had liked it or was just mocking me. At the time I didn't care, it was just an act of defiance, of yearning for new clothes. She made a copy for me, the two patches looking like two big eyes staring at me from the photo.

She took me with her to her school once.

"This is Meimei, my sister," she introduced. "I found her under a tree, digging cicadas with a bunch of dirty girls, so I adopted her."

I was terribly shy, and sat there quietly listening to their conversation. It was fascinating though. They sounded so sophisticated and clever. I wondered if one day I could talk like them. They were so passionate, talking about 'philosophy', 'dialectics', 'social science', 'economics' and more which didn't make any sense to me. I told Wendi I wanted to be a Red Guard like them, wearing a Red Guard armband, shouting at bad people like a hero. She gave me her wry smile and said how lucky I was. When I got back home, I found a dictionary on Mama's bookshelves and began to absorb it, page by page.

I went with her to a Red Guards' rally at the Transportation University one day. "Treat it as a day out," she said. I couldn't believe my eyes when we got there; the flags, banners, loudspeakers, drums and a brass band, tens of thousands of people, like a wild festival. There was no reason for me to be excited as I had absolutely no clue about what was going on, but I was exhilarated. I stared at the stage from behind the crowd, a beach of black pebbles which roared and shuddered with each wave of propaganda. When the band stopped, a man on the stage delivered a tirade into a microphone. I wanted to ask Wendi why he was so bad-tempered but decided to keep quiet as she and her mates didn't seem to be bothered with the rally at all. We sat down on the grass in a circle far away from the stage. Wendi emptied her bag, food was placed in the centre, *baozi*, *bing* bread with marinated tofu, followed by grapes and apples. This must have cost her at least two food coupons, I thought.

"Is that all?"

"What happened to the peanut sweets?"

"And the biscuits?"

"Sorry, I …" Wendi blushed. She proffered me a *baozi* and said to her friends, "Do you remember Meimei?"

"Of course, your adopted sister."

The girls began to introduce themselves to me, but I was too shy to remember all those names. Everyone dived into the food. The girl sitting opposite dropped a piece of marinated tofu; she squealed, and quickly picked up the tofu from where it had fallen onto a piece of dried banana skin, shovelling it into her mouth at once as if she was afraid of losing it again. My jaw dropped. I looked away in disgust. When it was finished they settled back and started cracking sunflower seeds while chatting, an almost ritual ceremony.

"Li Juan hasn't turned up since yesterday. Anyone noticed?" said Ting, the girl sitting next to me.

"She's supposed to be sick."

"She's always ill when things happen. Skiving, I suppose."

"I don't blame her. I would do the same if I could," said Wendi.

The conversation drifted, strangely, to eyes and noses. Some said bigger eyes with double lid lines were prettier and some disagreed.

"I think it really doesn't matter about the size of the eyes, the important thing is if they are bright, if you can see the soul in them. The eyes are the windows of the soul. That is what matters," Ting said.

Taking no notice of the incendiary harangue broadcast from the stage, they began to talk about boys.

When a name was brought up, one of the girls would blush and turned defensive. The rest of them would giggle, imitate or jeer. Wendi listened with her mouth slightly open, nodding, always in a hurry to agree, but she was the only girl there who never became the focus of their attention. I was relieved.

"I kind of miss school classes," Wendi said pensively.

"Why? School classes means exams and being told off by teachers. You never had good marks, did you?"

"Just bored with all this; rushing about, achieving nothing …"

"Shut up, don't you know enough to keep your opinion to yourself?"

"Yes, we've been left alone so far, just go with the flow, treat it like a holiday."

"Exactly! Who knows what is going to happen next."

I sat there and listened indolently. I was amenable, but wished they would talk about something more mysterious, especially something I wasn't supposed to know about. My attention wandered to our closest neighbours: a group of young people, slightly older than Wendi's friends. I guessed they were university students. Like Wendi's friends, they paid little heed to the speakers and the rally, and sat on the grass in a circle; unlike Wendi's group, they were all in pairs. Some couples sprang up to chase each other around the circle and screamed with laughter. When they had settled down, a boy turned towards his girl and rotated her knees towards him. They stared at each other in a strange way, then the boy dropped his head between the girl's thighs.

I was horrified and turned away. Looking around, no one had taken any notice of it. How could that be? I had never seen girls and boys so much as touch, let alone such inappropriate public behaviour. I looked again, but not a wisp of a reaction from their circle of people. It puzzled me.

"Do you know, she's read Dream of the Red Chamber?" said Wendi. Before I realised what they were talking about, they were all beaming at me intensively.

"I …"

"Wow, that's so clever."

"How old are you, ten?"

"Twelve? Still, it's amazing."

"But I …"

"Unbelievable. I have never read it myself, have …"

"Did you understand?" Ting asked.

"No," I said, slightly abashed.

"Why did you read it if you didn't understand?" said another girl.

"I'll understand when I'm older, right?"

Everyone laughed. I was astonished by the fuss it had caused.

On our way back home, Wendi told me she had been the leader of the Red Guards for her class in the beginning, but there had been too much gratuitous violence which she didn't like.

"What does 'gratuitous' mean?" I was impressed by the big word.

"Unnecessary. Like if a problem can be resolved by talking, there's no need to use fists." She looked unhappy. She moved her eyes away from me as if she were talking to herself: "She writhed in agony on the ground, her glasses were smashed. Her legs twitched before she stopped moving. What if it was me?"

"Who was she?"

"Our Chinese teacher."

"I don't like my Chinese teacher," I said.

"But does she deserve to die?"

I hung my head, and was silent.

I had often dreamed about having an older sister instead of Ming. My brother Ming was a handsome fifteen-year-old with deep, refulgent eyes. His uptight decorousness and utmost propriety were put on for praise and admiration, like he was in a show. Everyone liked him, and he won the acclaim of all. Mama was extremely proud of Ming, but I saw that behind his masquerade, he was self-doubting and insecure. When he was unsure, Ming would tell me off, throw an offhand comment at me, or sometimes just totally ignore me, as if to put me in my place by letting me know I was an insignificance. I was proud to have an older brother who was famously clever, for that I gained respect from my peer group. But what I really longed for was that he would care for me, like Hui's brother, Anning's brother and Dingding's brother. But it seemed he was gloomy whenever I was present. Worse, if I talked to his friends, he would either frown at me or simply walk away; except, that is, when he wanted something for his stamp collection. "Did you say Lanlan has Mei Lanfang stamps?" he might say.

"Yes."

"What does she want to exchange for them?"

Or he would say: "I need those trousers cleaned."

"But the weather has not been good," I would defend myself.

Sometimes I felt he blamed me for apparently holding him back, keeping him from what he wanted to do, depriving him of his glory and admiration. When I was little, I had saved my sweets, biscuits, anything nice for him, which he had taken for granted. When I grew bigger, I did his bidding, cleaned his clothes, fetched meals for him, collected stamps and badges: anything he liked, just wishing he would stop avoiding me like the plague. Now I would give away ten Mings in exchange for Wendi as my big sister.

There is no such thing as an endless dinner party, Mama often said. My luck seemed to have run out. Two years into the Cultural Revolution, Mao decreed that all teenagers must go to the remote rural countryside to reform their thoughts. Ming was scheduled to leave in two weeks' time. I felt apprehensive as I had not heard anything from Wendi for a while. I hunted through my belongings and settled on a butterfly notebook that Mama had given me for the new school term that had never started. I made my way to Wendi's home. The sky was low and heavy, the wind had stripped the trees bare and flurries of leaves eddied along the road. The compound looked deserted and children were nowhere to be seen. I started to run, out of breath.

"She left yesterday," her sister told me apologetically.

"Oh, really, I must have messed up the date," I

pretended. Then I asked quietly, "Has she left anything for me?"

"Don't know. I'll go and ask Mama," her sister said.

"Don't bother, she'll write," I said, knowing it wouldn't happen.

It took me many months to get over her, my ephemeral big sister. I felt I had been abandoned once again. Life in the compound, without teenage brothers and sisters, became tediously boring. The novelty of the outlaw excitement paled. The same games were played again and again, three meals a day again and again, the scolding pelted out from the residents' association women again and again.

"Keep your voice down!"

"Stop running around! Go away."

"You rascals, my clothes, for heaven's sake!"

The battle with the residents' association was impossible to win, as we would always give in when they threatened to report us to our parents. The last thing we wanted was to add to our parents' burden of misery. We extended our activities beyond the compound walls, queuing at shops, prowling markets and shopping centres or just hanging out on the streets. It was fun for a while, before the excitement petered out. A year drifted away unnoticed. The winter came so suddenly that suitable protections were overlooked. I suffered from chilblains on my hands and feet. It was on one of those mornings, that the bad news came.

"Seized! Seized a lot of the bureau's youths," the kids were telling each other around the compound in great panic.

"Where?"

"Baoji, where my brother was sent."

That was where Ming had gone too, I recalled.

Mama came home and told me we were moving home, to a cadre's re-education camp in Yan An.

"I've got Yan An badges," I said.

Mama smiled and replied, "It's the sacred place."

I didn't care at all where we were going, I was gleeful simply to be going to a new place, as long as I had other children to play with; I was at the age that is incurious about the future.

After three consecutive days of snowstorms and disruptions to transportation, Ming turned up on a dark, cold night when I was already in bed. I was excited to see him, but a little scared as they urged me to keep my voice down. His eyes had lost their shine and were sunken in. His cheeks were hollow, his hair long and dishevelled. He was in a pair of trousers he had borrowed from a friend, and his boots were bemired and covered with thick ice.

"Mama, I'm in trouble," he said. Tears circled in his eyes, but he didn't cry. Mama sent me back to bed because he wanted to be alone with her. I listened of course.

"Two weeks ago the local police embarked on a manhunt. Two hundred and fifty city youths have been arrested already. Two of our team members were taken away last week. Dashan, the tall guy you met at the station, remember? A group of police raided our earth cave, breaking open our door. The police beat Dashan up before he could put his clothes on and he wet his pants. He was taken away. Now they are after me."

"I've warned you not to get involved!"

"I didn't do anything! I don't know who informed on me."

"What's the charge?"

"No one knows. The police said they were looking for the members of an underground counter-revolutionary organisation called the Flying Tiger Team. I've never heard of such a thing. What do I do Mama?"

"Not much you can do. Stay at home, they might forget about you and things will calm down."

"But how long do I have to hide? I'm so scared."

"Come with us to Yan An for two months then go back to your village. By then the dust will have settled, you might be vindicated. If not, at least things will be clearer. You can tell them you were helping me to move home." There was a pause in which I heard sobbing and moaning.

"Do you know Uncle Li's eldest daughter?" Ming said suddenly.

"Wendi?" Mama said.

I shivered when I heard Wendi's name.

"Yes, she was arrested first. She was accused of convening secret meetings and running a secret counter-revolutionary society."

"Surely that's not true. She's such a nice girl, polite and sensible. Although there was something disconcerting about her," Mama said.

"Nobody knows how she got herself into trouble in

the first place, but rumour has it she turned into a police informer and gave them a list of names, and claimed they were her accomplices. She made it all up to save her own skin. Absurd. Most people on the list have never even met her. I don't know if she betrayed me or someone else who was arrested later did."

"That's dreadful!" Mama said.

"Someone said she was locked in a room without sleep for three days. Now everyone hates her and they call her a traitor, grass, bitch. Some have sworn to break her legs. There is such panic and everyone turns on each other."

"Thank heaven and earth you are here," Mama said, "I wouldn't know how to cope otherwise."

I listened, quietly, with my fists clutched tightly, disbelieving. They talked for so long that my eyes kept on closing. When I woke up again, the lights were still on. I overheard Mama explaining to Ming that my father was a convicted rightist, and had been taken away to a labour camp ten years ago. Mama had only narrowly escaped the calamity with help from her friends, and was camouflaged in the North-Western Bureau. So that was what had happened to my father, I thought. Mama had never told me why I didn't have a father like other children.

The next day, I couldn't get Wendi out of my head. It couldn't be true. How could she? Betray so many people, some were her friends and some she didn't even know? Why? But behind the condemnation I felt there was a reason that I might forgive her, because she was my big sister and my best friend. I liked her and I felt easy and comfortable being with her, although I still didn't understand why. It might have been that she didn't judge me and accepted me for whatever I was. I didn't dare to ask Ming, even though I was dying to.

Wendi's parents had been exiled to a village not far from the re-education camp and her two little sisters were with them. At the New Year's holiday, I went to visit them. Eventually I broached the subject that I had been avoiding. The two sisters exchanged looks and said they didn't know what had happened. For some reason I felt I was responsible for Ming's misfortunes, because I preferred Wendi to Ming. After a few weeks, Ming went back to his village. He soon wrote to say he was all right, as the grass, which was not Wendi, had reneged. Although I felt relieved I was still troubled by not knowing what Wendi had done, since so many versions of the chain of the events were circulating around. I wanted to know so that I could defend her reputation whenever possible. There must be some extenuating circumstances I thought.

After two years' tough life in the countryside, I had discovered all I wanted to know about rural indigence and suffering from starvation. At long last Mama's exculpation allowed us to move back to the city and she was reinstated in her job. However, there was nothing for me to do. I was fifteen, back in the city but with no friends, eager to learn and to live independently, but denied any opportunity. I became grumpy and frustrated.

At a bus stop one day, a young lady approached me. "Hey, are you Meimei?"

"Yes, you are …?" I was rather embarrassed.

"Ting, remember me? The rally at the Transportation University? My goodness, you have grown," she said.

"How are you?" I said politely.

"Oh, you know, worked two years as a peasant, now good to be back in the city. I'm working in a water turbine factory on Dong Hua Road. At least it's a job."

I told her how frustrated I was, after nearly a year doing nothing but looking for a job. We talked and talked like long lost friends. Two buses had come and gone, and still we sat there and talked. Then I asked her about Wendi. She sighed.

Like all educated city youths, Wendi had been sent to the rural countryside, where she had continued to be aimless, uninterested in politics and lackadaisical. Instead of working in the fields she loved going around different villages, visiting other exiled city youths. After the autumn harvest, winter had come quickly, and with little farm work to do, several groups of city youths had gathered at a neighbouring village to have a party. When Wendi and Ting had arrived the hosts were busy cooking donkey meat in a massive pot. The poor donkey had fallen off a cliff, and had been too old for the villagers to eat, so the city youths had acquired this unexpected luxury. Everyone was elated by the alcohol and abundant meat. But Wendi had just sat in a corner quietly, looking lost in the cacophonous crowd. Suddenly she had stood up, walked into the centre of attention and announced: "I don't know if I should tell you this. I have a secret reading group."

"What's that all about?" two boys showed some interest.

"I'll tell you if you can keep it to yourself."

"Yeah, OK."

"We meet up secretly and read banned books, such as *Dream of the Red Chamber*, *Three Kingdoms* and so on."

"They are not banned books."

"What about *War and Peace*? And we read French books too, you know Hugo's *Ninety-Three*, *The Hunchback of Notre-Dame*? Dickens' books? Have you heard of any of them?"

"Yeah, yeah." The crowd's attention had dissipated through lack of interest but a few gathered to talk about the books they had read.

Ting went on: "There was a snowstorm that whole night, and when we left the party the next morning the plateau was brilliant white – everything else was invisible. We got completely lost and had to stop at a farmer's house to ask for drinking water. Even though he was so poor he gave us both bread with the water and directions. By the time we got to the bus stop we were covered with ice crystals on our hair and eyebrows, and while we were waiting there the locals circled around us as if we were zoo animals."

Three weeks later, the local police raided Wendi's village at night and arrested her while she was in bed asleep. They tied her wrists with a straw rope that made her scream with pain, and pushed her onto an open top truck. She didn't resist the arrest but was utterly frightened and confused. The villagers took fright and couldn't figure out how this quiet and hardly noticeable girl had become so infamous over night. The official line was that she had organised a secret society and was plotting to overthrow the Cultural Revolutionary Committee. No one took it seriously as they knew full well that she couldn't even organise her own trip back home. It must have been some kind of prank or a simple mistake. But she didn't come back; instead there were more arrests of city youths. The local police were brutal. Many of the accused youths turned on others and confessed to crimes they didn't commit, giving the police any names they could think of.

"What about the Flying Tiger Team?" I asked.

"Oh, that's funny. It was an extinct rebel group, active three years before, but there was a leftover poster on the wall in a side street. The police used it to frame the youths." She paused.

"I went to the county jail to see Wendi and to bring her a change of clothes and other daily necessities. It was a frightening experience and I couldn't imagine how Wendi had coped. I was stopped by a burly man, who searched through me and my belongings. I couldn't stop myself from shaking as he stared at me, for fear I would be kept there for good. I can still remember him now, as clear as day. He had these dark brown, stained teeth that stuck out from his square face and his eyes were triangles. Wendi sat in the corner on the floor. The cell was tiny, dark and dank, and there were five other inmates. She stared at the floor blankly and didn't even look at me. Her clothes were torn and filthy. I put my arms around her shoulders and stroked her matted hair. She began to sob in convulsions. That was the last time I saw her. There was nothing we could do. Legality was never a thing that the police should be worried about. It was like wartime and people disappeared without trace," she said.

Gradually suspicions had surfaced and percolated that it had been Wendi who had given out names to the local police. Hundreds of names, perhaps any names she could remember, or that were suggested to her, which had led to so many arrests. The witch-hunt lasted nearly a year and some five hundred people had been incriminated. The local police had always hated the city youths, some locals resented having to feed these city mouths, and couldn't have been happier to have had an excuse for punishing them. It was revenge. Without a shred of evidence, simply names, you could end up in jail and be tortured. The arrests had cast a pall of terror over the region. City youths ran away and hid. There was an outcry afterwards, Wendi was reviled and some of those who had suffered planned to beat her up. When it was all over, and the arrested finally released, she had had to hide, but now she was simply ignored and forgotten. No one was close to her any more. It was as if she were infectious; even her family had turned their backs on her.

"Where is she now?" I asked.

"I heard she is back in Xian, but no one knows where. She is hiding, I think. Why do you ask?"

"Just want to know," I said.

She went quiet then she said: "It's just everybody

hates her. My little brother was arrested and beaten up because of her. How could I ever forgive her? How? ... Will you?"

"I'm sorry."

"Oh, forget it. One day I might forgive. Who knows?"

I found the photo of Wendi and me in my drawer after I got back home. I was so skinny and short, in that pair of trousers with each knee patched deliberately. Now I couldn't see the point. I was leaning slightly on Wendi's chest, blissfully content. Wendi, short straight-cut hair, like the heroines in the films, was posing, one hand propped against her waist, dressed neatly in her Red Guard uniform. She was smiling, her usual wry smile. Because of her, I read books I wasn't supposed to, I grew confident and I had plucked up the courage to use big words I had learnt from dictionaries. I had been so happy. I couldn't condemn her, she was once my sister.

On a perfect Sunday afternoon in August, the leaves just turning a reddish gold colour, the sky was high and pleasing, and I was wandering down the street to kill time. The Cultural Revolution was in its eighth year. The street was much tidier than before, most of the scruffy posters were gone, the shop windows were clean and the pavement litter-free. I sat on a balustrade next to the Bell Tower, and watched the passers-by, imagining their lives. A little girl hung on a young couple's hands swinging and skipping along the payment. Would she be lucky enough to go to school when she was older? A figure just coming out of the department store, walking with a familiar gait, caught my eye. She was in a faded blue blouse and black trousers. Her glasses frames were darker and her eyes more sunken. She walked quickly past but didn't see me. In fact, she only looked straight ahead as if she were in a hurry and nothing else existed except her destination. I scrambled after her, dodged the other pedestrians and jumped in front of her, "Wendi, it's me, Meimei." She startled, then looked at me with her once bright eyes. She was thinner and prettier than I remembered and she had lost her smirk of a smile. Flecks of light caught in her bleary eyes, but then died out like a shooting star. She made her way around me and moved forward.

"It's me, your sister, don't you remember me?" I insisted.

She didn't answer, but reached out her arm to prevent me getting close to her, as she moved off. "I believe you! It's not your fault!" I shouted behind her, but she lengthened her stride and quickly vanished into the crowd in the crepuscular light.

Perdition

Vice Chairman Lin Biao, wrapped up in a thick towelling robe in spite of the hot September day, silently sat alone in his carmine armchair in the corner of his palatial office deep inside Maojiawan. There he had sat for an alarming six hours. With all the windows and curtains shut, the room was stuffy and dingy like a clammy cave. Light squeezed in through the chinks between the silk velvet curtains. There was an oversized globe in the corner and next to it was an old music box, the only entertainment in the room; it had been confiscated from the Qing royal family after the liberation. The walls were bare and bereft of colour, complementing his complexion. The only other decor was a banner of his own calligraphy opposite his imported French desk, '天马行空，独来独往' – 'Pegasus roams the heavens; sovereign, alone.'

Maojiawan, his secret residential complex, sat on five acres of ground right in the centre of Beijing, not far from Middle South Sea compound where the top Chinese Party leaders lived and worked, including Mao himself. Maojiawan comprised a range of grey brick buildings with red windows and doors, and stood behind four-metre-high grey walls. Inside the compound, passages, colonnades and alleys twisted and turned around the buildings, rooms within rooms, halls within halls, in a labyrinth where mystery waited around every corner. Outside the walls it was an enigma to the good citizens of Beijing. According to hearsay, it was a former residence of a Ming scholar, but at present it was actually a modern residential complex equipped with a heated swimming pool at a constant 23 degrees centigrade, a cinema with the very latest sound system, photographic studios, private massage parlours, and a small conference hall. Security was formidable: the seven gates offering access to the compound were guarded twenty-four hours by military security personnel, but secrecy was paramount. People who worked in the complex, the secretaries, service corps, chefs, nurses, officers etcetera, whatever they did, had one thing in common: their work was kept strictly secret from their friends, family and even spouses, therefore no one knew what they did behind those grey walls. In that place, curiosity was strictly forbidden.

He heaved himself out of the chair hesitantly and, dragging his short thin desiccated body, paced over the golden patterns in the cherry-red carpet from one corner of the room to the other, ruing that decision to back Chen at the plenum. He was just a small, frail old man with a mien of malaise; pallid face, shrivelled small eyes set in deep eye sockets; his black bushy eyebrows the only feature to reflect his glorious past. However, his name appeared in every newspaper, every single little red book, in slogans on the streets and in buildings; wherever Chairman Mao was visible, his name was pronounced; in radios, films, orations and announcements. Alongside

'Long live Chairman Mao!', his forever good health was chanted at ceremonies, rallies and marches everywhere in China. If Mao were a god, he was a demi-god.

He gasped suddenly as if his throat was being constricted. He had been hiding to parry the intense oppression from his supposed best friend, all appointments cancelled and his telephone lines disconnected. His acute despondency had led to a deep depression, and he had not touched food since the day before. Now he felt weak and his headache had come back. A poignant sense of regret pervaded his thoughts and as he sank back into his armchair with his eyes half closed, he saw hundreds of eyes, ears and mouths whirring around him, and fingers and arms all pointing at him. The noise grew louder and louder, excruciated screaming, frustrated shouting, a grating sound as if it were made by running a bow along the strings while fists hammered on the keyboard; it was a frenzied, bloody and chaotic fight. He tried to swing his arm frantically in an attempt to scare them off but he couldn't move. He began to sweat and his hands were shaking. He opened his eyes, the room was still and empty, yet impregnated with menace. He was confused. He closed his eyes again, the struggle returned and the noise was more dissonant and rasping. He felt he was disintegrating. Before he opened his eyes again, he heard a knock on the door. His body tensed up and leaned slightly forward. Are they coming to arrest me? No, it cannot be, they wouldn't knock, surely. He relaxed a little and sank back into his chair. His wife came in, holding a white china bowl, and softly closed the door behind her.

"The cook made turtle porridge for you specially, come and have some before it gets cold," she sang, smiling tensely but concealing her emotion, standing an arm's length away. To her surprise, Lin looked rather relieved as if he had just been saved from drowning. His head shifted in an imperceptible nod. She sat next to him, watching him masticating slowly, then she moved forward with mouth opened as if she wanted to say something. He frowned at her and put the spoon down.

"Have a bit more to make you stronger. Everyone wants you to get better soon," she implored.

"Do they?"

She understood his accusation, so she quickly changed the subject.

"Do you want to resume your briefing sessions today? Dongfeng has some news for you."

He didn't answer. He looked sadly at his wife, whom he had never been able to keep close or treat like a friend, to whom he could never confide those deepest thoughts. He dismissed her with an indifferent head gesture. The nurse came in with a tray of medicine, put it on the 'big enough to sleep on' desk, then left. He was alone again.

He had never been interested in the post of vice chairman, the second to Mao, as no one could ever find acting with ultra fidelity and devotion to Mao an easy task. He had protested the nomination vehemently, as though the Vice Chairmanship were a death trap. Who would want to be so close to a tyrant? All those who had been close to Mao were either imprisoned or dead. However, Lin Biao, to whom pursuing personal pleasure was more amenable than taking on responsibilities, had discovered his honorary high status could serve his hedonistic lifestyle well, as his political duties were largely delegated or generally neglected by way of excuse through his poor health. Especially when the pressure was high, or the situation became complicated or fuzzy, he could quickly sink into his own inanition, claiming illness. The strategy did not necessarily reflect a lack of ambition, or the absence of blood on his hands. A brilliant general during the civil war, a good soldier, adroit at staging battles, winning many for the Communist Party before 1949, he thoroughly believed he deserved all the power he could grab.

"Let your wife come to meetings if you are ill," Mao had dictated.

"But I'm always ill."

"So let your wife represent you," Mao had decided.

Lin Biao had had no choice but to accept the post, yet real power wasn't accorded to him. By any measure, he was a perfect second in-line to Mao: sickly, fragile, vulnerable, passive and easy to manipulate. Written into the Party constitution, Lin became the officially anointed heir to Mao. He was well aware he was treading on thin ice. No one knew where one stood without a written law. The law was in Mao's capricious head, and reading Mao's mind had proved to be highly challenging, so Lin Biao slipped into the position of chief apostle in a Mao personality cult. He did extremely well, fawning over Mao to further his own best interests. At Mao's prompting, Lin originated the little red book that ran a billion copies, distributed as a bible and used as amulets. He concocted many of those outrageous phrases that had such an irresistible and penetrating effect on the human heart: 'the genius', 'the greatest', 'the helmsman', 'the saviour', 'the uppermost correctness', 'the zenith of Marxism and Leninism'. It was so easy, it came so naturally as if he had been born to suck up. He had a great many other inventions to his credit as well. Mao was delighted, happily sitting on the altar that Lin helped to build, with a halo on top, a god; yet inadvertently Lin's popularity was dragged sky high in the wake. This was not what Mao had envisaged, and a profound fissure opened up between them, exacerbated by Mao's jealousy and Lin's stubbornness, or perhaps Lin just grew tired of abasing himself all the time. He would never have dared to stand up against Mao, never dreamed of anything other than a life of servitude, not in a million years, but he misread Mao's mind, or perhaps it was a simple lack of discernment. Although loyalty had never crossed his mind, self-interest and deception was always at the top of his agenda, one fatal move that even the great many brownie points he had accumulated wouldn't save him from, Lin reflected gloomily.

Lin felt he was being kept on a short and tight leash and was immensely vulnerable to the unpredictable moods of Mao. What he was most afraid of though, was to die like Liu Shaoqi, one time Vice President of the People's Republic of China, who had lain in his own waste in a dog kennel, died alone and was buried in an unmarked earth hole somewhere remote. He remembered Liu Shaoqi's speech at the Party Committee conference that had ended the Great Leap Forward, the movement responsible for thirty million deaths in the famine. Liu's speech had received a ten-minute standing ovation, while Mao was humiliated. Mao had bided his time, but, pitiless, unrelenting, had staged the Cultural Revolution to annihilate Liu and others. It was a bizarre coup, led by the uppermost leader, to topple everyone else below him in authority, with the help of the mob, and the army led by Lin. Lin was now in purgatory. He was truly contrite, not because he felt remorse for the comrades he had destroyed in the past, but because he had got himself into a situation he failed to foresee. He couldn't prevent his mind roiling, and a procession of monologues ran through his head. "Serves you right!" a hissing voice whispered in the dark corner. He had no compunction about purging those generals or giving up those officers to the Red Guard to torment. They were obstacles in his rise to power. However, among those who were destroyed by Mao with his support, there were close colleagues, friends or even his relatives. Some memories were physically painful, they made his head spin.

"Oh Heaven!" Lin cried silently, "How crassly stupid I was; I stood up at those conferences and spoke out supporting Mao when he was under attack and weak. I exalted him and now he has turned around to destroy me. Am I that stupid farmer who saved a frozen snake? Why didn't he just die, he is so old and I'm young. I could have had it all if only he had died. I've shot myself in the foot, haven't I? Why am I still sitting here? I cannot even remember what happened yesterday. Did I sleep last night? I cannot remember waking up. That is it, I was sitting in this chair, I came out with that brilliant idea, the little red book of his quotations. I followed him everywhere he went, clutching a copy of the 'little red book'. It worked superbly, the whole nation copied me…"

He sighed and continued: "He accuses me of hyperbole! How ironic! He encouraged me when he needed it. He knows how to torment, poking his finger right into your wound. Am I already in prison? Why is it so dark? Have they brought my special chair to my cell? So thoughtful. He just resents the public's applause and adulation of me. They called me 'beloved Vice Chairman Lin'. My reputation is as high as his is, overshadowing him. He would be mindlessly stupid if he were not worried. What do I do? I have watched him destroying his opponents one by one and said nothing! Is it my turn? I cannot face his taunts any longer. What is this dictatorship of the proletariat nonsense? It is his one man dictatorship surely! What does he want from me now? Confession and apology for sure, but I cannot write a confession; I cannot put a noose around my own neck; I cannot face the humiliation of millions of Party members reading my confession and excoriating me. I would become a nobody, might as well be dead. A crass playground bully tactic."

"Why do I feel like a drowning dog?" He trembled.

"No sign, no warning, just like that with his one

word, in the middle of the Standing Committee conference, he had Chen handcuffed and dragged out in front of over two hundred delegates; it didn't matter that Chen was such a prominent and senior Politburo member. Dead silence, as if the hall was our tomb and we were merely the effigies of two hundred high rank officials. And after five minutes pause, those who had advocated Chen slithered behind others' backs, or made themselves as small as possible, their fear turning into a tirade of condemnation of Chen. I did it with the rest. It was impossible to do otherwise, no matter whether I wanted it or not. Haven't we all done that before? I was the hangman for many of his political enemies and several of my own opponents. I had to do it. To get rid of those above me, I had to do his bidding. Why are my hands red? How could this blood be on my hands? Oh, no, they are coming back to haunt me. Denouncing Chen and denying any involvement with him didn't grant me a way out. How can I make him forgive me? He refused to see me even when I was waiting outside his door, begging like a dog. What outcome would it have been if I had done what Madam Mao and her gang did? Kneeling on the floor, holding his legs, crying. They begged him to back them up. How could I? I had the majority of the Politburo members' support, as everyone wanted this greatest disaster to come to an end. Excoriating Chen was just his well-used trick: killing the chicken to frighten the monkey, he is coming after me with his terrier-like grip." He started speaking out loud: "You've had your fun, got what you want. It's over now.

Everyone wanted a swift solution to end the Cultural Revolution crisis but you started purging again. I'm in serious trouble now!"

Tormented by his regrets and the pressure, Lin languished in his dark room, though despite this he still held himself ramrod straight. His self-abasement had left him feeling sweaty and dizzy, so he pressed the button. The nurse came first and checked his pulse and blood pressure, then Madam Lin flurried in.

"It's the heat, isn't it? I've told you we need to go. The seaside will do you good. I know you want to see Chairman Mao, but isn't it obvious he doesn't want to see you? The car is ready, it's all packed. Can you get up?"

Lin Biao made no reply, looking into empty space with a straight stare, then he stood up and moved towards the door in silence.

In his private limousine terminal hall, specially built to prevent any chance of Lin Biao catching a cold, the Red Flag was ready and packed. Lin Biao climbed into the limousine, and set off to his private seaside retreat.

★

One month later in Maojiawan

His eyes popped open with a shock of terror. Hu Dongfeng, a young military clerk, woke up suddenly, as if from a nightmare, to muffled footsteps. Someone was on the roof. He could hardly move, not even to wipe his

281

wet forehead. It was pitch dark, the wind was moaning and leaves were rapping the window panes. The decrepit hands of the alarm clock next to his bed sat at 2:44am. Should he get up or not? He held himself very still for a moment till he realised he was not at home but on duty at Maojiawan. What could he do that a company of armed guards could not? It might just be some builders making a noise. He calmed himself down and went back to sleep.

Four years before, Dongfeng had been transferred to Maojiawan to work for Marshal Lin Biao, the prominent revolutionary hero, Vice Chairman of both the Party and Central Military Commission and the closest comrade-in-arms of, and anointed successor to, Chairman Mao. Dongfeng was chosen from a military unit in the north by Madam Lin, for he was neither too tall, nor too short, neither too handsome, nor too unpleasant looking, neither too red, nor too black, and most importantly, he was discreet and obedient. It was undoubtedly an honoured promotion for Dongfeng to join the team of six personal secretaries in Lin's office at the zenith of Lin's glory. Dongfeng's family, friends and whole village shared in his good fortune; he was proud, privileged and worshipped. It was not just the status that pleased Dongfeng; it also gave him great security against political risk in an arbitrary and unpredictable climate. His job was simple: reading files, newspaper articles, internal memos and documents, and summarising them into a twenty-minute daily brief for Lin, who was accordingly so well-informed that no one would have believed he had not read any books, newspapers or magazines, with the occasional exception of a medical book or some nutrition guides, since the Cultural Revolution had started.

At 06:30 hours Dongfeng's alarm clock went off, he got up, made his bed and folded his duvet as neatly as a piece of perfectly cut tofu. He was proud of it, a product of his ten years' military training. He had a quick cat wash, combed his hair, and put on his army uniform and hat. At 06:55 hours he straightened his hat in front of a mirror, before opening the door. To his exasperation he found himself blocked by two armed soldiers, neither of whom he recognised.

"Comrades, out of my way, I've got work to do," Dongfeng said peremptorily.

"Stay inside," replied one of the soldiers sternly.

"I order you to step aside, are you deaf? Who is your commanding officer? Do you know who I work for? Vice Chairman Lin!"

Yet the soldiers looked at him blankly, with no sign of letting him out. Dongfeng was stunned.

"You will be charged with obstructing my important work for Vice Chairman Lin …" Dongfeng's voice waned as he became conscious of the swarm of armed soldiers; scuttling around the houses, crouching on the roofs, in quickstep along the path. He recoiled and threw himself into his chair, a premonitory tremor chilled through his body at this apparent anomaly. Despite the fact that since the Cultural Revolution had begun, anything could happen, absolutely anyone could be kicked out of the

Party, dragged into the street and beaten up by mobs, it was simply not possible that his boss, Vice Chairman Lin, the closest friend of Chairman Mao, supremo to all except one, could ever fall from grace. Beset with questions, he looked through the windows for answers. Soldiers were scurrying around, carrying boxes, like ants moving home. The houses opposite were searched, locked and sealed, and cooks and housemaids were led away. Although it was just the servants' quarters, Vice Chairman Lin would never have let this happen, it was sheer desecration. He riffled through his memory for clues and flipped anxiously through recent newspapers for portents.

At 09:45 hours Dongfeng, curtly ordered to follow a young officer, was taken to the hall where Lin Biao often received official visitors or foreign delegates. The hall was opulently furnished with deep red armchairs, sofas and a stunning long conference table installed on the ruby-red carpet. Three army officers Dongfeng did not recognise sat at the end of the table. About twenty armed soldiers stood on either side of it. Behind them on each wall, a poster with enormous ink characters declared at him: 'Leniency to those who confess', 'Severity to those who resist'. He could smell the gunpowder and sense the terror. Dongfeng clicked his shoes and saluted the officers, although he couldn't see their faces clearly in the glare of the spotlights.

"Name and occupation?"

"Hu Dongfeng, personal secretary to Vice Chairman Lin." One of the officers' pens ran along a piece of paper then made a tick.

"Date of birth?"

"1943 June 6th."

"How long have you worked for Lin Biao?"

"Four years."

"Are you his loyal follower?"

Dongfeng hesitated, wondering why he asked.

"Are you?" the officer pressed.

"Yes … it's my job."

The three officers exchanged glances and nodded. One of them plucked up a piece of paper, scribbled on it and handed it to a soldier who then pulled Dongfeng's cap off and tore the red star from it. Dongfeng was flanked by two more soldiers who pinioned his arms while a sack was harshly shoved onto his head. He was handcuffed and thrust away.

"Where are you taking me? Am I under arrest? On what charge? You cannot do this to me, I'm personal secretary to Vice Chairman Lin," Dongfeng shouted and struggled. His voice was devoured in the silence like a pebble dropped in the ocean.

Handcuffs and hood removed, he found himself propelled into a small room, comprising three walls with no window and a wire-mesh wall to a corridor, like in a zoo. He sat down on a bamboo mat on the floor, next to four volumes of Mao's selected essays, a little red book, a sheaf of paper and a pen brush. What was that for? A suicide note with a Chairman Mao quotation? He inspected his surroundings and cringed as his hand touched the clammy wall. He knew he was still inside Maojiawan, though somewhere he had never been, most likely a storage unit. He ardently wished that he would be lucky enough to see some familiar faces. The food, brought in by a mute soldier, was just some cold bread and leftovers, so it looked as if the chefs were absent. A bucket was sent in later, obviously a substitute toilet. He tried to make some sense of the sudden change of fortune. What had Lin done? And what had he done to deserve this harsh treatment, like a criminal? He reflected on his past, but only corroborated the fact that he had been loyal to Chairman Mao, had done his utmost in his job and had totally eradicated a selfish solipsism. The pent-up frustration exhausted him, his mind went blank, he could not think straight.

★

As he calmed down, memories leaked back into his consciousness. He was back in the limousine hall a month before, helping one of the chauffeurs, Xiao Li, to pack the Red Flag ready for Marshal Lin's departure for the seaside. He had just explained to Xiao Li how he had not been able to fulfil his duties because Lin was refusing his twenty minutes daily briefings. They had also both had to put up with Madam Lin's intensified ill temper.

"She threw a saucepan at the chef because the marshal refused to eat, then she shouted at us," Xiao Li gossiped, before relating the engagement saga of Lin's daughter, where Madam Lin had conducted a fourteen-month nationwide search in the army and had found her daughter a fiancé, only to be spurned. Madam Lin had sworn at and cursed her daughter Doudou, and flatly rejected Doudou's choice of boyfriend, an army doctor. In her tantrum she had slapped Doudou, which made Lin Biao so angry he had threatened to divorce her.

"I heard Doudou had some mental problems; isn't she a bit mad?" Dongfeng asked.

"That was just Madam Lin's propaganda."

"Really? Mother and daughter, what a family."

"Ah ... rumour says she was adopted."

"Blimey!" They were silent for a few moments, then Dongfeng observed: "You know, I don't think the marshal will get any better by visiting the seaside. He suffers from hydrophobia."

"Hydrophobia – what's that?"

"It's a fear of water."

"Water? You are kidding!"

"No, it's very weird. He can't touch, or see or even hear water flow. It gives him diarrhoea. All the paintings of rivers or lakes were taken down. On top of it, he can't cope with draughts, too much light, maybe even air. Do you know I sit three metres away from him when I brief him?"

"Why?"

"For fear I might generate a draught when I turn my papers. Absurd, but that's what it is. Apparently it is a result of his injuries in the Liberation War."

"The marshal is pretty sick as far as I can see; is that why Madam Lin is so jumpy and nervous? Never know what mood she is in at any particular time."

"It's not that, it was her blunder that meant the marshal upset Madam Mao, and that annoyed Chairman Mao. Haven't you noticed that since the Lushan plenum last September, even though Madam Lin is often in a mood, she isn't as bitter and cutting as before; although she did get rid of half of the staff. Lin's music box has been silent since the Lushan plenum; he's been languishing, more reclusive, seldom opens his mouth, and his daily routine has completely changed. No one knows what he does in his room and what he is thinking."

"Is he mad?" Xiao Li enquired.

"Shh … it's hard to imagine, isn't it?"

"I overheard her phone call," Xiao Li mimicked Madam Lin's squeaking voice: "'Comrade Lin is not well, he is in poor humour and cannot sleep … double dose of sleeping pills, … but history will be on his side, …, he advocated him, stood up for him, exalted him, but now he is tormenting and bullying comrade Lin …'"

Dongfeng laughed aloud and said, "The May Day celebration was another incident that was out of the ordinary. I was on duty that day. We received the order for the marshal to join Chairman Mao on the Tian An Men Gate. The marshal absolutely refused to go, lingering like a boy not wanting to go to boarding school. I answered Premier Zhou's call. He said: 'Has he left? Tell him to hurry, Chairman Mao is on his way'. When I told the marshal, he had no reaction. Usually he arrives at a venue before Chairman Mao. Madam Lin nagged him like crazy as if he was going to commit suicide. Zhou called again and said Chairman Mao was already there. In the end he stood up and let the assistant put on his coat, but he came back in half an hour. The next day the *People's Daily* front page ran the news of the May Day fireworks celebration and I saw they had used the photo of Chairman Mao and the marshal taken together from last year. A photo without the marshal would have suggested trouble."

★

Dongfeng had almost drifted off in his reverie, when the door clanked open. Two heavy set soldiers entered.

"Get up! Hands behind your back," one of the soldiers barked, then shoved Dongfeng out of the door abruptly before he could heave himself up. They entered a small dark room in the same building, where a long-faced officer sat behind a desk with a paper pad in his hand.

"Your name and occupation?"

"Hu Dongfeng, personal secretary to Lin Biao." The officer checked the answers.

"Date of birth?"

"You have it already."

"Date of birth!"

"1943 June 6th, of course."

"Strip."

"What?"

"Take your clothes off."

"Why?"

The officer waited for a moment in icy silence and said: "If you don't, they will do it for you."

With a bashful expression, Dongfeng took off his uniform.

"All of it."

"What?"

"You heard me." The long-faced officer dropped his face further and waited.

Dongfeng trembled with rage and embarrassment, yet he took his shoes and socks off.

"All of it!"

With his quavered hands he removed his white underpants and quickly covered his private parts. By then his whole body convulsed.

"Turn around!"

"Quickly!"

"OK, sit down."

They left the room and the door was locked. Before he could calm down, the lock was rattled. A group of soldiers entered, led by a man in a long white coat. The man pushed Dongfeng's head down and started to cut his hair. Dongfeng struggled, so two soldiers clamped his shoulders till the man had finished.

They left too.

Dongfeng waited in the chilling silence. Someone came finally, and threw in a set of grey-coloured civilian clothes. With the clothes on, Dongfeng felt human again. Another wait, then he was taken to a room where, seated in a solitary chair, he was so blinded by the spotlights that he couldn't see the faces in the shadows behind.

"Hu Dongfeng, on behalf of the Party and the Chinese people, I indict you for treason, for conspiring to overthrow the Party and for taking part in a military coup to assassinate Chairman Mao. I command you to confess your crime," a voice read curtly.

"What coup? Assassinate? How?" Dongfeng felt a hefty thwack on the head.

"You stinking stubborn liar!" another voice roared, and a round face with pea-shaped eyes moved forward and became visible, "Don't think you can trick your way out!"

"I don't know of any coup or assassination. I am always a loyal adherent of the Party and I love Chairman Mao, He gave me life. You can check my file. Please … you've got it all wrong!"

"Nonsense! Are you testing our patience, you reeking little shit?" The round-faced interrogator gave Dongfeng a hateful stare and nodded.

Two young soldiers stepped forward and tipped the chair, and Dongfeng fell on the ground. They punched and kicked him till he pleaded for them to stop.

"Are you ready to tell?"

"What do you want me to tell?" Dongfeng was struggling to get up.

"Information! Everything about Lin Biao's coup and his other crimes."

"Lin Biao? Oh, are you sure? You aren't tricking me, are you?"

"Only if you are Lin Biao's sworn follower."

"I really don't know anything about a coup. What happened to Vice Chairman Lin?" Dongfeng immediately regretted the question, but it was too late

291

to take his words back. He clenched his teeth in fear of further assaults, yet he still hoped this was just a test.

"Vice Chairman eh?" a voice derided, "Thinking of him coming to rescue you? I wouldn't count on it if I were you." Suddenly the interrogator hit the table and shouted: "Watch your attitude!"

Dongfeng bit his lip and said, "I remember when we received the report of the Chongqing massacre, Lin said the Cultural Revolution is more like the Slaughter Revolution."

"Down with the traitor!"

"Smash down the enemy should they not yield!" the soldiers shouted.

"Lin Biao said the Cultural Revolution was a great big mess, absolute nonsense?" Dongfeng added.

"More!"

"Three … no, four weeks ago, Lin and his wife went to their seaside villa, along with secretary Xi Wen," Dongfeng said.

"Yes, come on, names, more names! Lin's cronies, his followers."

"Chauffeur Xiao Li, ah, nurse Ying and no more. They have a chef and servants at the villa. I helped pack for them, it didn't look like it was for a coup. Ow, don't hit me!"

"You think it's funny? Idiot! Pig head! Sign this paper, we'll finish today." The round face fell back into the shadows again.

Two guards each grabbed his shoulders and tossed Dongfeng back into the chair. Dongfeng perused the paper through the narrow slits of his red and inflated eyes and said quietly, "I cannot sign this. I haven't done anything like it says."

"Bullshit!" The table jumped with a thump and a tall figure emerged from the shadows.

"I cannot do it."

Suddenly an iron claw seized Dongfeng, dragged him out of the chair and pressed him up against the wall, "You fucking traitor!" Dongfeng felt chilling cold metal pressed against his forehead and trembled uncontrollably, his eyes shut.

"I'll blow your fucking brains out if you don't."

"No, please! I ... I'm just ... confused ..." The claw released its grip, Dongfeng slid down the wall, convulsed and writhed on the floor.

"Sign the paper! What different will it make? Everybody confesses one way or another in the end. Do you know anyone who did not confess and was still alive and well? Think it over."

The logic was so simple that no one, however eloquent, could possibly disagree.

"But I ... I have not done anything."

"Lin Biao is now No. 1 arch-enemy of Chairman Mao."

No. 1 friend the last time I saw him, Dongfeng thought.

"He committed high treason against the Party and country. You work for him, so you are the enemy of the country through association, if you refuse to collaborate."

Dongfeng relapsed into silence, as he was good at

taking twisted or exaggerated propaganda with a pinch of salt. He tried to comprehend the interrogator's logic, but he was mainly aggrieved by his sudden turn of misfortune.

"Your silence is further evidence of your treachery!" the round face stood up and shouted at Dongfeng's ear, "Do you know what the punishment for treason is?"

The next time he found himself in the interrogation room, Dongfeng was in a state of hallucination after two sleepless, floodlit days and nights, watched in turn by two guards in case he fell asleep. It was supposed to have given him time to think it through. He did not even remember at what point in the interrogation he signed the paper that he had refused before, yet he was relieved to extricate himself from serious criminal charges. He knew that eventually he would have capitulated to any demand they made. They were right, what difference would it make to confess or not to confess?

He had never felt so great about sleep before, and after a whole day of it, he felt reborn. So he was horrified to find himself in the interrogation room once again. Dongfeng watched, through his bleary eyes, the two officers sitting behind the table, though the round face was not there. His eyes focused on a bowl of hot noodles, and he suddenly remembered he was hungry.

"I hope you had a good sleep and the guards treated you well." An officer, a tall, scrawny, grey-haired man, looked at Dongfeng with a frigid smile. Dongfeng didn't answer but took this statement as permission to grab the bowl of noodles and shovel them up. He felt replenished, so he nodded, although he could still feel a throbbing pain in his head and back.

"We need your help to piece together Lin Biao's traitorous plan of his coup and to gather evidence of his treachery. We can start with what was the last contact you had with Lin Biao."

Dongfeng clasped his hands on his knees, and tried to take everything in.

"This is what I can remember. It was about a month ago, a very normal day, very hot. We did the packing for Lin's summer holiday. About three o'clock in the afternoon, the Red Flag drove out of Maojiawan and headed towards Beidaihe, their seaside retreat. It was Lin, his wife, secretary Li and Lin's bodyguard on board. Lin had been moody and quiet, I think because Chairman Mao refused to see him. I had tried for a month to get an appointment for him without success. Lin became even more morose after he found out Chairman Mao was travelling around in the south meeting the army generals. In the end he gave in to Madam Lin's nagging. I was at Maojiawan on office duty. The next day Madam Lin called from the seaside and asked me to find their daughter and urge her to join them."

"How did she sound?"

"She was pleasant and talkative, saying something like they were going to celebrate their daughter's engagement and so on. Nothing has happened since."

"Really? I think you will agree pain is undesirable for you, isn't it?"

Dongfeng reflected silently and said: "Madam Lin did call again a couple of days later. She sounded rather nervous and agitated. She wanted a Russian dictionary and some maps from her office. I packed them for her. I know she has been uneasy since the day she told us she would lose her position on the Politburo Standing Committee. Lin Doudou, Lin's daughter, also called and wanted to speak to Premier Zhou. She said it was urgent so I connected her to Premier Zhou's secretary."

"What about Lin Liguo?"

"Do you mean Lin's son? There are a lot of rumours about him. It was said Chairman Mao thinks highly of him. Uh … Last year Madam Lin instigated a nationwide search for a beautiful girl in the army to be their daughter-in-law. Everybody talks about …"

"Enough of that!" the other interrogator quelled him. "Did Lin Liguo act suspiciously?"

"Yes, now you mention it, Lin Liguo came here last week, and he was a little jumpy. He didn't stay the night, but he took some files and the things I packed for Madam Lin."

"Did Lin Liguo tell you anything?"

"No."

"Now we need you to think hard," the officer sitting next to the grey-haired one said coldly, looking Dongfeng straight in the eyes, a thin smile on his lips. "You see, we don't want to send the wrong person to prison, to a small cell that has no night."

Dongfeng's uneasiness grew stronger, and he stuttered, "H … he asked me if Chairman Mao had returned to Beijing. I … I said I didn't know and … I thought He was touring the south."

"What else?"

"He was shouting at a telephone for hours. Then I had to call our duty car to take him to the military base in the middle of the night."

"Who did he talk to?"

"I don't know, he had the radio on and he used the private line."

"Who did he talk to?" the voice pulsated.

"I really don't know."

"You will give me names, plus the names of Lin Biao's other cronies by the end of today!"

"Tell us about Lin's Trident now," the grey-haired officer interjected.

"Trident? Lin's private jet? … I have only been on it twice. It's massive, an amazing machine, one of only three imported from England. Madam Lin uses it like a taxi though. They fly with it everywhere that has a suitable airport. When they wanted to go to places, she would instruct me to ring up for it, sometimes just an hour beforehand."

"Did you book the Trident for September 13th?"

"No, why? For whom? Lin was at the seaside and no airport can land the Trident nearby."

"When did you last book it?"

"I need to check my log, but it was around the middle of August."

"Did you know why Lin's private jet forced a take-off on the 13th?"

"No, why?"

"So who ordered the plane?"

"No one can do it except Madam Lin, not even Lin Biao himself. Where did the Trident go?"

"It flew north and crossed the Mongolian border towards the Soviet Union."

"Why? The trip was not scheduled, I'm sure. And what for? I wasn't told. Who was on the plane?"

"You tell me, you are Lin's personal secretary. You should know everything."

"They are not coming back, are they?"

"So you did know! Tell me why they escaped."

"Not return? It's not possible ..."

"Of course it's possible. It's absolutely bloody certain that they will not return. The Trident crashed in the Mongolian desert. Everyone on board was burned to ashes. You see, if anyone rises up against our greatest leader Chairman Mao, they are doomed to be hacked into a thousand pieces and go to Hell after that. This is a traitor's destiny ..."

Dongfeng was dumbfounded as he listened in stupefaction. The interrogators, though apparently satisfied they had now broken him, quickly lost patience with his silence and left the room.

He was taken back to the cell again. After the tramp of boots had faded away, he heard some clanking noises travelling further along the corridor that ran outside of his cell, so he jumped up, dashed to the mesh door and screamed: "Who is there? Who is there, please? I'm Hu Dongfeng, what's your name?"

There was no answer except the echoes.

"Please someone, someone's there I know, what is happening? Please help me ... I don't want to be alone," he sobbed and hammered on the cage with his fist. No one came, not even the guards. He missed his previously comfortable and privileged life that flickered through his head like a film. As a dignitary he had enjoyed opulent comforts when travelling, visiting places or attending conferences. He could jump onto any train or plane without a ticket; he could order or exert influence; he could demand the hospitality of any restaurant or hotel; and he received anything he and his family needed every day as gifts, from a pair of socks to a dining table for his three bedroom, two reception room flat. Now his confident spirit had crumbled, his life had shattered, and his mind was lost in total darkness.

He lay on the hard bamboo mat in his cell motionlessly, his eyes fixed on the ceiling where the plaster had fallen off and water dripped through. He forgot to wind his watch, so without daylight he lost the sense of time entirely. He hated being alone. He'd rather be shouted at than be left alone. Eventually he settled himself down and began to digest the information that had been hurled at him in today's interrogation.

It had been just before 1:00am on 13th September when Lin Biao was dragged out of his bed, heavily under the influence of sleeping pills, and hustled by his wife and their son Lin Liguo into the black Red Flag. Lin's daughter had not only refused to go with them, she had also reported their flight to Premier Zhou, and accused her mother and brother of kidnapping Lin Biao. The order had even been given to fire at Lin's Red Flag as it fled the scene, driving at top speed towards the airport.

The airport had been pitch black, quiet as a tomb, as no one had been in the control tower to switch on the runway lights. Lin Biao had been lifted onto the plane by rope, and the Trident had executed an emergency take-off in the dark without a co-pilot while still attached to the fuelling pipe. Strangely, despite the fact that the army was at the airport and had received Premier Zhou's order, no one had tried to stop the plane. The Trident first flew west before veering to the north, where it crossed the Mongolian border and disappeared from radar. On the morning of the 13th of September, the Mongolian government made a formal complaint that a Chinese plane had entered Mongolian airspace without authorisation and had crashed on its territory. Nine bodies were found at the crash scene.

Was this true? But why? Dongfeng thought. If Premier Zhou knew Lin's plan, why didn't he seize him at the airport; not a fly could have got out. It was like he was goading Lin to run. It couldn't have been a well-planned action, as Lin was so intoxicated and ill that he couldn't even decide when to eat or sleep. There were so many unanswered questions that Dongfeng could not find a cogent explanation, his confusion aggravated by his shock at the fact that the second most important and loved person in China could become a traitor overnight. He delved into every corner of his memory to make some sense of it. His shoulders heaved for fear of saying or doing anything fatal, for fear of his and his family's lives. He sat on the floor, staring at the brush and inkwell bitterly. He knew he had to write something. He dipped the brush in the ink and wrote clumsily on the paper:

13th September 1971
Maojiawan seized by troops and Lin Biao is dead …

He hastily stripped the sheet off the pad and scrunched it into a ball. The situation impelled him to more desperate measures, so he wrote:

My Confession
I am a despicable person, I have committed heinous
crimes. I have committed unforgivable serious sins by
working for Lin Biao, therefore letting Chairman
Mao down. I am truly contrite, repentant, remorseful
and full of regret for my actions …

Dongfeng was next taken to the interrogation room a few days later. There were more soldiers, more furniture, and equipment was present that boded ill. The smell of urine and vomit, and the bloodstained floor distressed him greatly. One of the interrogators was reading a page in the folder that Dongfeng had submitted.

"Is this your handiwork?"

Dongfeng nodded cautiously.

"This is bloody nonsense! A pile of shit! You dirty dog, listen to this: 'Lin Biao adores Chairman Mao, he said no one would ever question Chairman Mao's authority and we are united under His hegemony.'"

"That was what he said," Dongfeng murmured.

"Bollocks! You son of a bitch! You've done this on purpose. Are you bloody mocking us?" The interrogator thwacked the table, so as to give the impression of strength he did not possess, and continued: "Does your dog-headed brain know how serious this is? Lin Biao attempted to assassinate Chairman Mao by sabotaging his private train in Hangzhou. When it failed, he ordered a fire to be set at a fuel storage station in the hope the blaze would spread to Chairman Mao's train next to it. But they chickened out. Then they planned to shoot the train from the air …"

In complete astonishment Dongfeng uttered, "Is Chairman Mao safe and well?"

"Of course, you pig! Our greatest leader Chairman Mao is a genius, no one can harm Him, not even a single hair! Traitor Lin Biao's evil plan stood no chance of escaping from Chairman Mao's omniscient intelligence," he said proudly, as if he believed in the occult.

"It's hard to believe that you know nothing. You know it is treason if you are concealing information or covering Lin's evil tracks."

"I really know nothing about a coup."

"Think hard! You don't want them to help you, do you?"

Dongfeng glanced at the two big men standing to one side of him, no uniform but with big black boots, who twitched a little. He said, "Lin is very ill, he is not capable of doing anything."

"I haven't got time to listen to your nonsense! Give us some names, who Lin associated with, who are Lin's sworn followers, any anti-Chairman Mao talk? Information to prove Lin's hideous crime. Come on!"

He hasn't got any sworn followers, he was Chairman Mao's sworn follower, Dongfeng said in his head.

Suddenly Dongfeng recognised the speaker, a square-faced young officer with a nasty reputation of being ruthless in his ambition. It gave him an idea.

"I do remember one evening in July, an officer came to visit Lin in his office, unscheduled. I was sent away as it was supposed to be a secret meeting. All the curtains were drawn, all staff were dismissed. He was there for over four hours. It's unusual for a meeting to have no secretary to take notes. Very mysterious. I wouldn't know what the meeting was about."

All three interrogators eyes were flashing with curiosity, the middle one asked pressingly, "Who was he? Do you know his name?"

"Yes, I do in fact. He was the air force commander General Tu. You know him well. Did he promote-"

"That will be all for today!" the square-faced interrogator stopped Dongfeng abruptly. Dongfeng gazed at his troubled face changing from nervous, to calm, to pensive; then a faint smile framed his closed mouth in cold resolution.

"Actually, let's continue. What else? Did he look suspicious?"

Dongfeng did not answer.

"We will set up a special investigation team to deal

with General Tu. Yes, he did promote me. However, for the people, for the country and for our greatest leader Chairman Mao, we must sever the close relationships with those who are the enemy, especially if they were our patrons, benefactors, friends, family or promoters." He turned towards Dongfeng and commanded: "You must report on anyone who is plotting against Chairman Mao. Hurry up, confess!"

Dongfeng's face turned white under the interrogator's scrutiny.

"After the Lushan plenum, I noticed Lin Biao became more reclusive – he was sullen and withdrawn. I was at Lushan with him and knew what happened when Chen was denounced and arrested," Dongfeng said.

He paused a moment to reflect on what had happened at Lushan. The delegates had rallied around Lin Biao and Chen, criticising Madam Mao and her gang. Chairman Mao didn't care much at first but had suddenly changed His mind when He saw Lin Biao gaining popularity. Mao had been furious and had decided to teach Lin a lesson. He had Chen arrested and launched a diatribe of denunciation, directed at Chen but clearly targeted at Lin. Mao had tried to coerce Lin Biao into confessing and apologising to the Standing Committee. Lin had refused. How could he? There were only two people in China who never apologised. For him to confess and apologise implied the end of his life.

"And?" the interrogator prompted.

"Oh, they argued and argued continuously, whilst mainly Madam Lin was trying to persuade Lin Biao to apologise, especially after she heard Chairman Mao was preparing to strip her of her Politburo seat. Madam Lin pushed Lin Biao hard to pay obeisance to Madam Mao, Jiang Qing, to beg her to speak for them. When she failed she took the four generals who were Lin Biao's subordinates to Jiang Qing herself," Dongfeng said.

He failed to add that the generals were furious when they had returned, cursing Jiang Qing for deliberately making them wait for hours, and then appearing in her pyjamas. One of them had mimicked Jiang's voice: 'You see, now you are in trouble because you didn't listen to me …' They were hopping mad and had sworn at 'that sordid fucking actress!' and said they had never been so insulted.

"The following day, I was ordered to write a self-criticism statement for Lin Biao using words dictated to me by Madam Lin. But Lin Biao has never used it. He refused to apologise to the Politburo Standing Committee. He said to me, 'I'm a soldier, I don't do confessions'," Dongfeng continued.

"Bollocks. Everyone confesses, so should he."

Dongfeng said nothing, though the irreverent thought crossed his mind that he had never heard of Mao apologising.

In this way, Dongfeng was in and out of the interrogation room several times that week. Under such vociferous pressure, he gradually gave out names, starting with the people he disliked, then adding Lin Liguo's sidekicks, then a few officers in the air force, secretaries, office managers, and even members of the Politburo Standing Committee and high-ranking army officers. He had few scruples about it. Ever since 1949 all political movements were kicked off by reporting colleagues, friends, even family members, as the more you reported the more likely you were to survive the purges. The reporting of others and fabrication of facts of wrongdoing were proven survival techniques. However, beyond mere survival, many people enjoyed seeing others' discomfort or suffering, especially if they had been victims of previous movements themselves. He recalled that Madam Lin had reported her nemesis to the Red Guards, and even went to his struggle rally in disguise, to secretly revel in his distress.

"Confess about project 571," an interrogator said one day.

"Project 571?"

"Yes, don't pretend you've never heard of it before. What is the meaning of 5?"

Dongfeng was completely nonplussed.

"Come on, you must know. It's code for 'armed', right?"

Dongfeng gave a faint nod, realising the sound of 5 could also be the character for armed.

"Now 71, what is it?"

"Armed, insurrection?"

"So you do know!" exclaimed the interrogator triumphantly: "Project 571 was Lin's plot to overthrow the Party, take control of the country and usurp the position of Chairman Mao."

"You know everything already, why are you asking me?"

"Hey, you've got gall. If you play up, you'll go straight back to the cell with those two to remind you of what position you are in," he nodded to the two guards who had brought Dongfeng in.

Dongfeng went silent.

"Let me make it easy for you. We need proof, but the only thing we could find is this little notebook belonging to Lin Liguo."

"I don't know anything. If I make something up, that will be different from what you know already."

"Stop interrupting! You must draft a dossier of project 571 as evidence to placate the public."

Dongfeng stared at the interrogator. "But I wasn't involved in anything, I didn't do anything wrong," he managed to say, lamely.

"Whether or not you have done anything wrong is not the point. The point is where you stand at this moment in time: revolutionary or counter-revolutionary. When you decide where you stand, what you write and what you say will become a lot easier. Just make something up, so we can finish our job here and be done with it. Unless of course you are one of Lin's staunch followers. That would be treason, and deserving of the death sentence. I hope we will have your collaboration on this matter."

Dongfeng opened and closed his mouth a few times, but no words could form in the maelstrom within his head.

"Do you love Chairman Mao?"

This was something he could hang on to. "Of course, I love Him deeply. Without Chairman Mao, I would have died, not to mention a decent job, a wife, two children and a house," Dongfeng said passionately.

"So Chairman Mao asks you to provide evidence … Do you want to go against Him?"

He capitulated.

Dongfeng's situation improved significantly after that. He even dreamed about going home soon. He was moved from the dank cell back to his ransacked office, from where he was expected to complete his new commission. He was to concoct a dossier of Project 571, that would reveal in assiduous detail Lin's crimes: conspiracy to split the Party, violation of Chairman Mao's thought, the staging of a military coup and planned assassination of Chairman Mao. Dongfeng was well aware he needed to exercise his imagination to the full.

He gained access to the *People's Daily*, was allowed to listen to the radio, and got permission to talk to others.

Dongfeng started writing industriously. Like any good fiction, the characters, the scenes and the time-lines all had to fit together well. On several occasions, while he was searching through the newspapers for the right phrases, he found himself thinking: 'It would be so helpful if there were a propaganda dictionary.' For weeks, he was not interrupted, no interrogations or questions. Finally, he sent word that he had completed the first draft of the dossier. He was proud of his work, the pages of his creation reflecting his imagination and talent.

After a series of consecutive storms, the leaves had

all blown off, eddied from one quarter to another, but were not collected up as they had been before. The temperature had dropped sharply too. He needed more winter clothes, looked forward to being reunited with his wife and children by the New Year, and expected he would now be permitted to keep his three bedroom, two reception room flat in the centre of Beijing.

At dusk, he was summoned again. A panel of six officers sat around the table.

"Are you Hu Dongfeng?"

"Yes, comrades."

"Did you write this dossier?"

"Yes, comrade," Dongfeng said quietly.

"What are you playing at?"

Dongfeng kept quiet.

"Listen to this," one of the officers in the middle read: "In fact, he has become a contemporary of the Qin Shi Emperor! He is not a true Marxist-Leninist, but in a line-up with Confucius and Menscus, masquerading in the skin of Marxism-Leninism, the worst feudal tyrant and dictator since Qin Shi …"

Under the acute scrutiny, Dongfeng had the horrified realisation that he may have gone too far, but gradually he regained colour in his face, and said cautiously: "I wrote in this way to make it sound genuine; it will be more convincing, therefore the public will find it easy to understand Lin Biao's treachery."

Two weeks later, the dossier of 'Project 571' was distributed and discussed in Party meetings nationwide. Lin Biao was excoriated on the radio and in newspapers, with the first public announcements of his disappearance and death nearly three months after the event. The whole nation was thrown into bewildered shock. Dongfeng, however, couldn't wait any longer to go home and see his family, to have decent food, clothes and sleep. He demanded an immediate release. In response, he was taken in front of a court martial, where he was summarily convicted of conspiracy to treason, and sentenced to four years in military prison. The dossier of Project 571 was the only proof presented.

"Why? Why are you doing this to me? What about the immunity!" Dongfeng fulminated with rage when the verdict was announced. "The dossier is all lies, it was me who made it up. Yes, it's all lies, many lies!"

"But the lies must become the truth, mustn't they?" said one of the prosecutors.

Dongfeng screamed and shouted but the guards just pinned him down on the ground, and he found it was as much as he could do to keep breathing. He writhed suppressed fury, the acrid blood roiled inside him …

As he trudged through the fresh snow in the line of prisoners towards the grey van, he looked up at the snowflakes flurrying freely in the dense mist. He hardly noticed the cold, absorbed in his world of anguish, and he missed his wife and children dreadfully. Suddenly something caught his eye: a red object flapping outside of the gate. It was his daughter's red hat that he had bought in Shanghai last year. The girl was waving frantically, and crying next to her mother and brother. Gazing at her from his hollow-eyed face, devoid of emotion, Dongfeng wanted to tell his wife that he was sorry, but she was too far away.

He stumbled onto the van, but as the door was slammed shut he pushed his way to the back and stared out. With his face squashed between the iron bars the tears began to flow. Catching the last sight of them before they faded into the bitter mist, Dongfeng could think of nothing but finding his way back to them.

Hat

Jun always wore a hat: different colours, different styles or different materials; a hat was on his head all the time, no matter the weather – cold, hot, wet or dry. Hats suited him, not only as a fashion accessory, but they also accorded him more authority, shrouded him in a little more mystery.

He was rather pleased with himself right now. Last year when he had heard that universities were reopening for the first time in the seven years since the Cultural Revolution had started, and were accepting only workers, peasants or soldiers who had worked for at least three years, he was tantalised by the prospect of living and working in the city. However, when he had found out there would be an entrance exam, he had chickened out. His education had never gone beyond primary school, and he had no wish to make a fool of himself. He had castigated himself for not going to secondary school; a few weeks later, he had nearly slit his own throat when it became known that the successful candidates were those with the worst exam scores! This surprising turnabout had been precipitated by an ex-Red Guard and farmer called Zhang Tie-Sheng. Like Jun, Zhang had had an inadequate education; however in his entrance exam, instead of answering the questions, he had written a letter of complaint. Zhang protested that he had been diligently taking part in the Cultural Revolution and so didn't have any time to study, and bemoaned it wasn't fair that people who had shirked their revolutionary duties to swot up, would be rewarded with a university place. This missive had found its way right up to the Politburo Standing Committee, where it, and the exemplary young man who had written it, were eagerly seized upon and used to counter-attack the revisionist clique who happened to support an exam system based on academic, rather than revolutionary, rigour.

Jun wholeheartedly agreed with Chairman Mao: "Do not test – what is it for? Isn't it best to test nothing! Abolish all exams, be absolute. Who will test Marx, Engels, Lenin, Stalin? Who will test me?" Luckily, this year Jun hadn't needed to do any exams at all. He and most of his forty-five classmates at his 'Workers, Peasants and Soldiers University', had been selected via quotas, their transfers rubber-stamped by their factories, villages or army units. This enlightened process was perfect for Jun as his father, the village leader, was the rubber stamp.

Recently arrived on campus, Jun was taking a while to recover from the initial shock: gigantic buildings with many floors, each with massive windows taller than a tree; palatial classrooms so spacious that his entire house, a manor house to his village, could have fitted in, and these classrooms so bright, at all times of day, regardless of whether the sun was up or down. The glamorous university campus, with its tree-lined avenue, stone-paved paths, and extensive flower beds and shrubberies, was situated on the outskirts of the city, and looked like an extension of the neighbouring public park. He could not imagine how anyone could have let this palace be left to ruin for seven years. He was even more surprised to find that he was given more money for food per month by the university than he earned per year in his rural home. Even before he had plucked up enough courage to explore the city, he had made up his mind that he would do anything not to go back to the impoverished countryside of his birth.

Jun, an effeminate-looking, yet rather weathered, young farmer in his middle twenties, felt he cut an important figure among his classmates. One of only two members of the Communist Party of China in his class, being gloriously poor, he was surely destined to be a leader in the re-education of the millions of city-educated students. He made sure that even his class prefects would have to consult him on everything: from the Chairman Mao's Thought Study materials, to the allocated seating plans at meetings. During the initial three-month induction period he became extraordinarily busy, demonstrating his leadership skills: guiding the teachers, chairing meetings, making sure the class studied Chairman Mao's book every day, and steering off any thought that deviated from Chairman Mao's theory, a task not made any easier as it was somewhat self-contradictory. Most of all he made it clear to everyone: "If you want a good job you need to join the Party, and if you want to join the Party you need to fawn over me."

As the term progressed into the lecture season,

however, his significance seemed to be petering out, and Jun had hardly anything to say regarding their studies. One sunny morning on his way to a lecture, he was pondering to himself: "I'm not stupid, I just don't like the equations; those symbols are so rubbish that they can be any number. It's absurd. If I ever start a revolution again, I will scrap Western letters and replace them with Chinese characters in equations."

So he spoke out in his mathematics lecture, squinting with his pea-shaped eyes: "Why do you teach us this useless stuff?"

The maths teacher turned around, leaving the half-written equation on the board and stuttered slightly: "W-what do you think you should learn?"

"To learn Marxism, Leninism and Chairman Mao's thought; politics, history or Chinese something," said Jun boastfully.

"So why did you come here – the Institute of Mechanical Engineering?" the maths teacher asked, truly perplexed.

"I don't know why I came here. There wasn't any choice, was there? A quota came and I wanted a job in the city," said Jun. This sparked a noisy discussion in the classroom.

"Me too, I come from a rural village. I don't want to go back, but I don't like maths."

"I find maths is interesting to learn, useful too," said Yan, a petite and vivacious girl with short-cropped hair.

Jun cast her a dark glance as if to say: 'I'll never allow you to join the Party.'

"What use is it? You can't grow crops with it."

"Don't you need to repair your farm machinery?" said Mei, the girl sitting next to Yan.

"We only have hands. We can use those to count up to ten, that's all we need. Ha."

"But you will use machinery in the future, I'm certain of it."

"You city people don't know nothing; that's why Chairman Mao sent you school kids to us."

"You use maths to fool us, humiliate us. I know it."

"Maths is stupid, we should have nothing to do with it," said Jun decisively.

"Why is that?"

"Maths is stupid because I don't understand it!" said Jun irritatedly.

"That's right. We don't need maths to understand Chairman Mao's book."

"Surely, if you don't understand it, you are stupid?" Yan whispered to Mei.

"What did you say? I have the Red Sun in my heart and I am not stupid!" Jun shouted, "Our greatest leader, Chairman Mao, taught us: 'To revolutionise education, proletarian politics must be in command'. Do you want to be a White Professional?"

Instantly the classroom went silent. The teacher stood there nonplussed, knowing he was not in a position to have any opinion, not after the long, hard experience of the Cultural Revolution, and with the universities just recently, cautiously reopened. No one knew what would happen next, so it was wise to be circumspect.

Jun didn't leave it there. He went straight to the university head offices to complain. He was passionately upset and couldn't stop himself thinking aloud. "This should not be how the university is run!" he exclaimed, as he ran into a young man in a Mao suit who looked lost.

"Sorry, hey – is something wrong?" asked the young man.

"It's nothing to do with you," retorted Jun as he started off on his way again.

The young man hurried after him. "I'm Chen Xidong. I'm a journalist from *City Daily*. I've come to investigate how your university is doing. It seems you're not happy with something, so would you like to share it with me?"

"A journalist you say? Follow me," Jun replied without stopping, and to himself again: "This isn't right!" He led Xidong along a corridor and slammed open a door.

"Have you got an appointment?" The secretary behind the desk tried to stop them.

"I'm proletarian class. I don't need an appointment." Jun barged through the reception and went straight into the room marked with a 'President's Office' plaque.

The president stood up and greeted him. "Hello, you are …"

"Our greatest leader, gracious Chairman Mao, taught us: 'Education urgently needs reform', 'Study hard and be a red expert'. We are moulded by the thoughts of Chairman Mao and we must follow His message. It is impossible to rightly govern the university without Chairman Mao's guidance. Education is the foundation for a proletarian China and is responsible for the moral and social development of the people. Only education grounded in Chairman Mao's Thought is the correct education for us. We must keep faith ..." Jun ranted on for half an hour without stopping, about his proletarian class, and duty to educate the rest. And while he spoke Xidong scribbled away on his notepad, and the president nodded continuously for the same half hour.

The following day an emergency curriculum meeting was called. All mathematics lectures were cancelled across all departments, and more hours were added to Marxist Dialectic. Two days later, a front page article appeared in *City Daily*: 'The Vanguard of University Education Reform Chairs Curriculum Committee'. Jun's name littered the article, and he became an instant celebrity at the university and beyond. He was invited to give talks on defending Chairman Mao's university reforms, and denouncing White Professionalism. Jun's success generated much gossip among his classmates.

One day at lunchtime the atmosphere in the canteen was exuberant: the inviting aroma of hot stir-fry, the clattering of plates and chopsticks, shouting between friends in the snake-like queues. Jun arrived late. He frowned and quickly surveyed the queues before jostling through the crowd, without stopping or even hesitating at the bitter complaints trailing in his wake.

"Yan, look at him, jumping the queue again," said Hua, a skinny girl with ponytails.

"Well, there are plenty of sycophantic followers in

the world," responded Yan, rising up on tiptoes to look at the beginning of the queue.

"That's not fair, we won't get the spare ribs, again! Especially as he'll grab double," said Mei.

"Come back, Mei," Hua exhorted, "you don't want to kick up a fuss when no one else does; remember the jobs he promised?"

"He doesn't have any jobs, for heaven's sake. Don't be fooled," Yan retorted.

"What do you make of him?"

"Jun? Not much."

"He's weird. Why does he hate maths so much? Now we can't learn it because of him. I don't understand why maths should be white, why it corrupts us? Maybe we should just learn it by ourselves."

"I guess it's too hard for him."

"But he doesn't need to learn it. I really enjoyed it, why do we all have to do what he wants?"

"Because he is RED? He loves Chairman Mao more than us?"

"I think he is afraid of being shown up."

"So do you think that's why Chairman Mao dislikes science and technology?"

"Woo … stop it. How many heads do you have?"

"Do you notice Jun never takes his hat off?"

"Really? That is weird."

"And he never eats vegetables, and he makes funny noises when he eats."

"Oh, that's because that was all he could eat in his home village: no bread, no rice, no meat."

"What, that's why he makes funny noises?"

"No, all the grain and meat were shipped to cities, and the farmers only had vegetables left to eat."

"That's not fair!"

"When did you start thinking of fairness?"

"They say he gets up at dawn and goes to bed at sunset."

"Still?"

"I don't like him though. The way he accused San and Lanlan of being too close – that stinks."

"Who?"

"San, that tall guy who sits at the back combing his hair all the time, and Lanlan, that girl from class B singing the duet last night."

"I wonder if he's jealous."

"Only one way to find out. I've got an idea …"

"Too risky, what if we got found out?"

Jun's dormitory was on the first floor of a grey brick student accommodation block, five minutes walk across campus from the canteen and lecture buildings. He had the best room, of course, south facing on the east end, cool in the summer and warm in the winter. His desk, by the window, was almost empty apart from four volumes of Chairman Mao's essays, and a Chairman Mao portrait was on the wall above his bed. With four beds, desks and chairs, the room was still spacious, though spartan. Coming back from lectures that day, Jun had found a pink envelope addressed to him pushed underneath the door. The evening found him sitting on his bed morosely contemplating its contents, in the room which he shared with three other students from his class. At ten o'clock, he jumped up and left without a word. It was dark and wet outside. Wind eddies swirled the rain around him, while he stood outside a campus side gate waiting patiently. By the time he returned, Jun was drenched and distraught.

The next day he didn't turn up at his Chairman Mao's Thought Study session. Rumour was that he had caught a cold last night in the rain. The girls smirked at each other, and congratulated themselves, while Jun was utterly annoyed, and couldn't decide if it should be declared a counter-revolutionary act or just let it go as a prank. He felt enemies were grouping and plotting around him.

The rest of the one-month lecture season passed pleasantly: no revision, no homework and, of course, no tests. This gruelling study period was ephemeral, and the class was soon despatched to an army base for a three-month military training programme, followed by three months of factory work experience, where Jun famously thrived; absolutely in charge, as he was, of the whole class. The factory made fibreboard from waste wood. The factory manager, concerned about the girls' health, said they should not work in No. 3 workshop. Women had never worked there, because the work was too heavy, the workshop too hot, dusty and suffused with chemicals. Jun dismissed these concerns and explained that the city girls needed to be tempered into true revolutionaries. For the next three months he spent his time touring around different parts of the factory, checking up on his fellow students, and never touched a single product or machine.

After their triumphal return, half of the class applied to join the Communist Party and naturally declared themselves Jun's disciples. With his increasing power Jun sat on all the important university committees, deciding the curriculum, staff hiring, the premises, student affairs and, the most important of all, job allocation for the graduates. At the end of the year, Jun was elected Most Outstanding Student for being the most loyal and devoted follower of the greatest leader Chairman Mao, and the Workers' Propaganda Team, the ultimate moral authority in the university, presented him with a trophy; a Chairman Mao bust in porcelain.

Jun didn't care if he was unpopular; he felt no need to be liked by his fellow students because he knew that Chairman Mao was on his side, and therefore he was invincible. However, he did care about having undivided and full attention when he spoke, like the respect he received back at his home village.

"Why so many absentees today?" Jun sat on the dais and looked around the half-empty classroom at the University Reform discussion meeting he chaired.

The remaining half-class looked at each other and said nothing. "This is an overt sign of the restoration of White Professionals," Jun uttered, so he called the register. The list of missing names, arraigned to a self-criticism meeting, was then posted, with a warning that job prospects entirely relied on behaviour. These discussion sessions were never popular, but absentees were only ever excused by direct permission, for a headache, diarrhoea, grandmother just died etcetera. Jun easily gave out favours, just so long as they paid homage. In this manner the course of life at the university went on.

That day came without warning.

Jun was showing some new students around this campus that he had taken possession of, when he heard the funeral music and sombre announcement blaring from the campus loudspeakers. He stood there frozen, as if hit on the head.

The news of Chairman Mao's death sent shock waves across China, and in an atmosphere pregnant with tension, rumours roiled the air in a vortex of emotion. What is going to happen? Who would be in charge? Was there going to be a coup? Who knows? The people of China had all lost a common parent. Some bawled in the street as if they were on stage, some quietly made wreaths at home. Some people cried because they couldn't understand why he had died so soon. They had been shouting all their lives for Chairman Mao to live for ten thousand years, so the least he could do was to live for a hundred. Some were sad for losing their dependency and being granted their freedom. They didn't know what to do. All day long radio stations played nothing but tributes, reports and obsequious commentaries on Chairman Mao's death.

The campus went hysterical, all lectures were stopped, all students were called back, gathering on the sports ground where black armbands and white paper flowers were distributed. Some girls huddled together crying as if the sky was falling, echoing the earthquake in Tang Shan a month before. It felt like the end of the world as some howled, "Jiang Jieshi is coming back!" while one shouted: "Long live Chairman Mao!" But most people slunk past each other quietly with their heads lowered to avoid eye contact and potentially serious trouble. It was not the time to bicker. It was not the time to speculate. It was not the time to show true feelings that could be an offence leading to arrest.

Jun rather struggled to regain his composure. He was upset: why did He have to die at this moment? "Before I settle myself into a good job? I am doing so well right now, what is going to happen?" He set off working in all directions, running himself off his feet. A series of memorial services were announced and prepared on campus. The assembly hall was cleared, and dressed with black festoons and white curtains. Only wreaths, embellished with colourful paper flowers made by the students, stood all the way around the hall.

After the departmental memorial service, while Jun was making his way back to his room along the corridor, he heard peals of laughter. He looked around, and identifying the source of it, strode up to the door and pushed hard, but found it locked.

"Who is it?"

"Anyone laughing here?" Jun shouted.

The door catch clicked, the door sprang open and Yan stood right in front of him.

"Oh, Jun it's you, to what do we owe the honour?" she asked.

"Why do you lock the door? You never used to," Jun said coolly.

"I was changing my clothes," Hua shouted from behind the door.

"Was anyone laughing?" He scanned the girls with his critical, quizzing eyes.

"No sir! Just them crying so hard, it sounded like laughter. Look at their eyes, full of tears."

"This is no laughing matter, it's important to show where you stand." Jun left, irritatedly.

Mei closed the door and gasped, "Phew, we do need to be careful."

"Sorry, I couldn't help it," said Yan and continued her mimicry.

"Did you notice, Jun didn't take his hat off?" said Mei.

"Of course he didn't, he wasn't chatting me up," replied Yan.

"I mean at the service, even in the one-minute silence. Didn't you see?"

"No, we were at the front, remember? But why should we care?"

"The Workers' Propaganda Team cared. Someone reported Jun and there will be a struggle meeting. Looks like he doesn't know it yet."

"Isn't that disrespectful to Chairman Mao? At the memorial service!"

"Yep, especially as he was such a henchman of Chairman Mao."

"Hypocritical I should say."

"Still, I don't think it should be made a big deal of. It's harmless."

"But consider the big deal he made when we were just a little bit late. Remember Lee was suspended?"

"That was harsh, but evil for evil? I don't know."

"Shouldn't we find out why?"

"Yes, we should. I'm intrigued."

The canteen was mute at lunchtime, and no one jumped the queues. The girls went up to Jun, who was sullen and haggard as if he had lost his soul. He responded that he didn't want to talk about it and told them to piss off.

But he wasn't left alone. At the afternoon struggle meeting called by the Workers' Propaganda Team, the classroom was filled up for the first time in weeks. Jun's usual bombastic manner had evaporated: he stood passively on the edge of the dais, head down, facing the audience seated at their desks, which were set out as if for a lecture. The representative from the Workers' Propaganda Team circled around Jun, alternately berating him, or playing to the room, haranguing so fervently his spittle reached the girls in the front row. He announced the unanimous decision of the university's Chairman Mao Memorial Organisation Committee: to issue a warning of expulsion of Jun from the Party. One by one, his classmates stood up to assail Jun with questions.

"You said that you had the red sun in your heart, and you would defend Chairman Mao till the last drop of your blood. You accused us of disrespecting Chairman Mao for being late to a meeting, but this is far more serious. This is clearly an important issue of where you stand on the class struggle, revolutionary or counter-revolutionary. Why can't you just take your hat off to show some respect, like everybody else?"

Jun lifted his head up, responding with his eyes silently: *You are going to pay for this!*

"You said you loved Chairman Mao, didn't you?"

"Yes, I do. Chairman Mao is like my father," said Jun.

"Why couldn't you take your hat off at the service?"

Jun made no answer.

"Is this your true desire? To disrespect our dearest leader Chairman Mao?"

"You are just a hypocrite. You often brought serious charges against others for more trivial things."

"You don't behave like a member of the Communist Party."

"Yes, you should explain."

"Yes, why?"

"Explain!"

"Look, it is this simple: take your hat off for the one minute's silence, then you can put it back on. Only one minute. Why can't you fucking do it!" The chief of the Workers' Propaganda Team was on the brink of punching him in the face.

"Speak up! Spit it out!" the others shouted.

"Why do you oppose Chairman Mao?"

"No! I don't, never!" Jun became belligerent, lifting up his head to glare at the questioner, then his focused eyes circled around as if to find a way out.

"So why don't you take your hat off?"

Suddenly, his self-possession crumpled, Jun gripped his head in his hands, and sank down squatting on the dais, sobbing.

"That's too much," Yan whispered into Mei's ear.

"I thought you didn't like him," Mei responded.

"I don't, but to taunt him like that."

"Repay him for taunting others?"

"It's funny, if you hurt others, it will always come back to haunt you," Hua added.

"I just want to know why? Why is it so bad to take his hat off?"

"I really don't see why it's so bad not to take the hat off. We are not forced to take our clothes off, are we?" Yan said.

"That's different."

"Not much different."

"I don't care, he seems to deserve it."

"It's probably something to do with the symbolism. Like swear words, if not taken as bad it's not bad."

"Yes, like burning flags."

"If no one said wearing a hat is disrespectful, it wouldn't be."

For two weeks the whole class talked about nothing but the hat, and Jun was under tremendous pressure to comply. He couldn't eat, could hardly sleep, all his past glories were stripped away. As the national funeral was now imminent, the committee had to crack this hard nut. Every day Jun was made to attend some help session, where through persuasion, threats and entreaty, in the end, Jun uttered in tears: "I want to show respect."

"That's better, show you do love Chairman Mao. You could be a pillar of the country and the Party. Show your true grit." The chief smiled and patted him on the shoulder.

On the day of the state funeral, with the students and staff gathering on the sports ground and almost ready to go, it started raining heavily. Jun was glad to hear that umbrellas were not permitted but hats were allowed. They all, most on sufferance, marched six kilometres to their allocated position in the town centre. The street was free from vehicles except a single open-top truck whistling back and forth giving orders through a loudspeaker. The university had a pavement patch, facing the People's Department Store, a five-floored Western style building. It was a prime location, with a wide pavement and row of grand street lamps, and one of the most prominent buildings in town. Behind them was a large book store, although shut, that had some books of interest. People from schools, factories, government offices and work units occupied every space, standing in orderly lines facing to the east like a terracotta army.

The loudspeakers started to broadcast the state funeral being held on Tian An Men Square. The tributes were read, the speeches made, then came the three minutes bow and silence. Suddenly there was a noisy disturbance from the neighbouring work unit, and the formation was spoiled, as someone shouted:

"He didn't take off his bloody hat!"

Three burly men, some kind of factory workers,

ploughed through the university troop. One of them grabbed Jun's shirt, another one waved his clenched fist in Jun's face while the third one seized his black hat shouting: "You, capitalist running dog, don't take your hat off eh? You got nerve!" Jun gave a piercing scream. Everyone stared. Jun was unrecognisable.

He had no hair.

Epilogue

When did the Cultural Revolution end? Was it with Mao's death, or when the Central Cultural Revolution Group, dubbed the Gang of Four, were arrested and put on trial? Some sense of normality was creeping back even before, while for many it took years to return from their internal exile. For some, it was never over, but most buried their pain and forged ahead with their lives. For me, looking back at this wasted decade of my life, the turning point was the unveiling of Jun's secret at the memorial service of his god, and his hilarious hypocrisy. Only a few years before, such obsessive vanity over something so trivial would have been given the power to destroy the lives of many people. But now the poison was drawn. Some sense of normality in people's behaviour, if that adjective could ever really apply, had returned.